D1336370

MR DARCY'S DIARY

Ever wondered what Mr Darcy was really thinking? Find out his secrets in this captivating novel of love, pride, passionand, of course, prejudice.

This intimate diary tells us of his entanglements with women, his dangerous friendship with Byron, his daily life in Georgian London, his mercurial mood swings calmed only by fisticuffs at Jackson's—and, most importantly, his vain struggles to conquer his longing for Elizabeth.

For the first time we discover what really happened between his sister and the dastardly Wickham. How did he distract his friend Bingley from pining for his beloved Jane? Why did he propose to another young woman? Only to his diary does he tell the full story. At last we see Darcy as he really is; and, beneath his polite façade, we find a sensitive, private and passionate man.

MR DARCY'S DIARY

Maya Slater

WINDSOR

PARAGON

First published 2007
by
Phoenix
This Large Print edition published 2008
by
BBC Audiobooks Ltd by arrangement with
Orion

Hardcover ISBN: 978 1 405 68600 6
Softcover   ISBN: 978 1 405 68601 3

British Library Cataloguing in Publication Data available

Printed and bound in Great Britain by
Antony Rowe Ltd., Chippenham, Wiltshire

For Nicky, with love.

Part I

NETHERFIELD

October 12th

All day I had G's letter on my mind, yet could not bring myself to dwell on it. It rained heavily; in the forenoon I had them saddle Caesar & out for a gallop in the rain, which failed to clear my thoughts. Later joined in the Library by Miss Caroline, shewing me the slippers she is embroidering for me, & urging me to admire them. Red *gros point* with green lovers' knots! When I protested that I never wear slippers, she informed me that now was the time to start.

Charles rambled on incessantly about tonight's ball. He had heard that numbers of charming young ladies live in the neighbourhood, & mentioned one family with five or six daughters, all said to be lovely—but I could think of nothing but G's letter. I have reread it three or four times, but still can find no solution to her predicament. All I wished for was the leisure to reflect on this: when we foregathered for the cold meats, I said that I would prefer to stay at home. Charles would not hear of this: 'Pooh, Fitz! You can't be such a killjoy. Come to the ball! They say the Assembly Rooms at Meryton are delightful. A couple of *boulangers* or a Dashing White Sergeant will cheer you up in a trice. I won't hear of you languishing here, whilst we all enjoy ourselves. Why, you'd miss the prettiest girls for miles around!'

Miss Caroline, I think, dislikes such allusions to petticoats. She retired to compose her evening's *toilette* with her maid. Her Brother continued to exhort me: 'You want some powders for your blue devils. I'll send for Nicholls, & get her to prepare

3

you one of her fortifying draughts. You'll see.'

Normally I would take pleasure in attending a ball full of pretty young women—but not today. However, I decided that it would be simpler to acquiesce. If only I were my own master, not a guest in Charles's house! Repaired upstairs & called for Peebles. He had already laid out my dress clothes; but tho' he packed at least three portmanteaux full of useless apparel, he has brought only a skin-tight pair of breeches. There was nothing for it but to squeeze myself into them.

At the ball, things were no better. To my disenchanted eye the ballroom seemed a hall of mean proportions, embellished with stucco pillars & a tinkling chandelier; a quartet of fiddlers scraped their way through the evening; a superfluity of raw young women, uncomfortable in long gloves, eager for dancing-partners, occupied the chairs. No matter: in the offending breeches I could scarcely sit down. Whenever I did approach a chair, all the matrons in the neighbourhood converged on me, seeking my opinion on Netherfield. As for dancing . . . I performed the minimum of courtesies with Miss Caroline & Mrs Louisa, since after all they are my hostesses; nothing would have induced me to take part in any further gambolling. Charles attempted to persuade me, crying: 'Come, Darcy! I must have you dance. I hate to see you standing about by yourself in this stupid manner. You had much better dance.' I did observe that there was one prettyish girl in the room, but she smiled too much; & besides, Charles monopolized her for the whole evening. He would have foisted one of her Sisters on me. I resisted. She seemed tolerable, but not handsome enough

4

to tempt *me*.

On the way home, in the carriage, listening distractedly to Charles vaunting the charms of his dancing partner, *'an angel'*, I became aware of Miss Caroline's knee, pressed against mine. When the carriage jolted it felt quite uncomfortable. She is not to blame—we want for room in the carriage. Edward Hurst snored throughout the journey.

I retired immediately, intending to reflect further on G's letter; but when I reached my chamber, I decided to write my Diary instead. Peebles has kept me from my bed for the last half-hour, complaining about a splash of candle-wax on the back of my coat. It must have been that confounded chandelier.

October 13th
At breakfast this morning, Charles reiterated his admiration for his last night's dancing partner. Her name is Miss Bennet. He accused me of being *distrait*. With an effort, I brought my attention back to my companions, noticing that on three separate occasions Edward Hurst refreshed his coffee from his hip-flask, despite Mrs Louisa's attempts to restrain him. As usual, he made no reply to her exhortations.

Miss Caroline is quite vexed with me: she asked me how I liked her striped silk morning gown. It is red & green; the colours do not suit her reddish hair. I regret that I was less than civil—I merely said, 'I am not fond of stripes.' Miss Caroline flounced out of the breakfast parlour, catching her sleeve on the door-latch.

After church, Miss Caroline challenged me to a game of piquet; but I had already agreed to take a walk with Charles, so she played with her Sister instead. We gentlemen had our punishment, however. The rain came down in sheets. I did not mind it, but my new beaver was much the worse for it. Poor Peebles will be heartbroken—he spent an age brushing it, he told me only this morning.

October 14th
I have resolved to go up to Town to purchase a pianoforte for G. I shall set off tomorrow, & take advantage of my stay there to enjoy a bout of sparring at Jackson's. It will do me good.

This morning Miss Caroline and Mrs Louisa received a visit. I was looking out of the Library window when I saw a carriage draw up before the front door, & a bevy of bonnets alight—six or seven in all. Realising that we were about to endure a courtesy call, I warned Charles & Edward Hurst, & we decided to make ourselves scarce. We rode off down the lane to Meryton. In the Lending Library, Edward found an absurd romance by Mrs Radcliffe, & read us extracts on the way home, at which the two of them grew very merry. We arrived just in time for a nuncheon; the visitors had long since departed. It transpired that they were the Bennet ladies. When Miss Caroline informed Charles, he grew quite peevish: 'You might have sent word to me who it was. I should have been happy to renew my acquaintance with the Misses Bennet.'

'You mean, with the eldest Miss Bennet,' retorted Miss Caroline; Mrs Louisa laughed, & Edward poked Charles in the ribs, & murmured something about an *'inamorata'*. I must say, Charles took it all in good part.

Later, I found myself alone in the drawing room with Mrs Louisa. She called me over to the window. The vista was bleak—the gravel drive, the windswept hills, a few lime trees with withered leaves clinging to their black branches—& the tall figure of Miss Caroline, striding energetically up & down, clutching at her bonnet, which constantly threatened to blow away.

'Do not you think that my Sister walks well?' enquired Mrs Louisa. But altho' Miss Caroline possesses an elegant figure, this was not the day to admire her through the window. I replied shortly that in a howling gale no body walked well.

I sat by the fire with Byron's new book—a cruel satire: I hope he will not seek my good opinion of it. After reading a page or two, I preferred to stare into the fire. It was at least half an hour later when Miss Caroline entered the Library, her hair ruffled, her face still ruddy from the wind. Had she been strolling in the shrubbery all that time? 'Was not you tempted by the fresh air to join me?' she enquired. I vouchsafed no reply—it was not clear whether the question had been put to me, or to Edward Hurst, dozing on the sofa.

Later we three gentlemen went out shooting— far too late in the day, but we all felt the need to walk. Bagged three brace of pheasants with Charles. Lurcher put up two more, but I missed them. Charles taunted me on my poor form. Edward resorted to his hip-flask every few minutes—but shot more birds than the two of us put together.

October 15th
Drove up to town, accompanied only by Peebles.

7

Miss Caroline & Mrs Louisa had intended to avail themselves of my carriage to make a short visit there also; but I discouraged them, preferring to travel alone. Charles has planned a day's cub-hunting with the local meet, so he will scarce miss me. Edward I saw making for the green baize door. I suspect that he has an interest below stairs, & had been hoping to take advantage of his Wife's absence from the house to indulge himself—tho' Mrs Louisa is a handsome woman, her hair a darker red than Miss Caroline's, with the same white skin but with fewer freckles.

Arrived in town before dark, with one change of horses. The house feels chill & empty: I could almost wish that Papa had exchanged the Grosvenor Square mansion for a less ostentatious dwelling. I may take just such a step myself—perhaps next year. Peebles complains that the damp will get to my small-clothes & make them musty. He insists that they build a fire in my bedchamber, altho' it is mild weather—he always will pamper me. I am spending the evening alone in the Library, reading in the newspaper about the Duke's victory at Almeida. The French losses blamed on misjudgment by Masséna.

October 16th
To Jackson's first thing for a mill. The sport has somewhat improved my spirits. Thence to Great Pulteney Street, Golden Square, to bespeak a pianoforte from Johannes Broadwood. The instruments very fine, of a beautiful tawny colour. An assistant played them for me, as I have not the skill. Chose a superior instrument, & ordered them to build it a marquetry case. Mr Broadwood

assures me that I will readily find a tuner capable of doing it justice in Derbyshire. The only difficulty will be the jolting of the cart during transport to Pemberley; but with careful packing of the mechanism, this should be easy to solve. Unfortunately, the instrument will not be ready for some months—he explains that making it will involve much labour.

I have changed my mind about returning to Hertfordshire immediately, & have sent word to the Bingleys that I will be unable to be with them for a few more days. I am awaiting Pargeter's arrival in Town, bringing with him the Pemberley estate ledgers. I am fortunate in Pargeter: he has proved an excellent steward, comparable in merit to old Wickham before him. It is high time I attended more closely to my affairs, tho' I am persuaded that Pargeter is keeping a good eye on the estate in my absence, as his frequent letters have proved. Several letters were awaiting me from him, concerning Tugley Wood. Do we coppice after twenty years, or after forty? And should we plant other species amongst the hornbeams? We will discuss these matters when he arrives. Most important of all, he will have seen G, & can give me news of her. I have not yet replied to her letter.

October 17th
This morning, after fencing at Angelo's, I felt that the time had come to write my reply to G; but no sooner did I sit down at my writing-table, than Bolton announced a gentleman caller. I had no time to think whether I wished to see Byron or no: his Lordship immediately entered the room, elbowing Bolton aside.

'How do, Fitz!' cried he. 'I am happy to find you in town. Last time I called, your door-knocker was removed & you away somewhere in deepest Hertfordshire.'

'Yes, on an extended visit . . . What can you want with me, George?' Byron's ulterior motive for paying me a call is never clear to me.

'Always so abrupt,' he murmured; then he called over his shoulder, 'Bring me a brandy. A good one, mind!'

Bolton bowed & hastened to obey.

Byron limped over to the chair opposite me, & made himself comfortable. He has transformed his gait from the dot-&-carry-one of his schooldays to a curious shuffling glide, which resembles a peculiarity rather than a disability. He looks paler & thinner than formerly. I believe he has improved since we came down from Cambridge, where he was somewhat fat. I teazed him on his romantic looks, which pleased him, I think. Apparently he sups off little more than vinegar, except when indulging in a drunken orgy. Recalling his excesses at Cambridge, I doubt me not that such occasions arise only too frequently. He bade me admire his white sharkskin pantaloons. He wears them once only, then discards them. He tells me he has purchased eighty pairs. His valet must be in funds, selling the used ones to less fastidious gentlemen. Apparently Byron is not; in his lordly way, he has condescended to relieve me of 50 guineas, to save him a visit to his Banker's. I do not expect to see my money again.

'What's up with you, Fitz? You look wretched,' said he. 'With your advantages of fortune & looks you should be more frolicsome.'

I muttered some evasive remark. Why cannot Byron be more like Charles, who, whatever my mood, is bracing but never prying?

'Still vegetating in Hertfordshire with Bingley, eh? I have half a mind to join you there. Are there any pretty girls? Have those Sisters of Bingley's improved at all?' continued he.

'Miss Louisa is now married to a Mr Hurst; Miss Caroline is much the same as ever,' I replied repressively. Byron & Charles's Sisters—it will not do. If he has not mended his ways since Cambridge, he is scarcely a suitable companion for any lady.

'Forget them for a few days,' said Byron carelessly, helping himself to more brandy. 'Come with me to the fleshpots: you could do with a little sport.'

'I regret that I am not at leisure to attend you,' said I—tho' I admit that part of me was tempted. He then left for an engagement with a *society lady*, saying, with a grin, 'I shall not reveal her name. 'Twill be all over London, soon enough.'

I have promised to meet him at Brooks's in a day or two.

It was by then too late to write to G.

October 18th

LETTER

My dearest Sister,

~~I was greatly saddened by your letter.~~ I infer from the tenor of your recent letter that Derbyshire is sadly lacking in diversion! ~~If only you would permit me to succour you!~~ At this distance I am at a loss what to suggest. Do you still consider a visit to London impossible? Now that we are satisfied that your new

11

companion, Mrs Annesley, is ~~trustworthy~~ *suitable, you might achieve it with impunity. It would perhaps be indiscreet for you to brave the metropolis; but there must be some pursuits available to you, &, moreover, I should be at leisure myself to attend you. Think on it, dear Sister.* ~~For a week or two only — surely you could come to no harm!~~

Poor G! I picture her, in the breakfast parlour at Pemberley, gazing out at the leafless trees in the park . . . How will she contrive, on a melancholy autumn eve? Her pianoforte, & her singing, & her sketching—of what use are they? If only this new woman, Mrs Annesley, could keep her chearfully occupied! Can any body help her now?

My dear Georgiana, I am aware how lonely Pemberley can seem in the autumn. The house must feel very big & empty to one young lady & her chaperone. I am preparing a fine surprize for you, which I hope will please you. Dearest Georgiana, if I can do aught to assist you, pray ask . . .

G is too young, too young . . . She needs a brother's comfort. If she would only permit me to travel down to Pemberley! Why must I be marooned here, so far from my beloved home, my poor Sister?

Should I instead abandon the Bingleys & Netherfield & remain in London? But what would be the use? Besides, at present I derive much benefit from Charles's chearful presence. Let me return to Hertfordshire, for just a little longer.

*   *   *

When I came to copy out my letter, I found it inadequate. I shall not send it.

October 19th
Sparring at Jackson's. I defeated Edwardes again—he claims that my height gives me an unfair advantage; Jackson himself avers that I have superior strategic powers, which pleases me.

Pargeter has arrived from Pemberley. There the apple harvest continues apace; Mrs Reynolds has enjoined him to keep me informed about the stillroom—I now have every detail of the pears & plums which she has bottled. She is to try preserving medlars—I cannot imagine how.

Apparently old Mountmain is anxious to purchase Tugg's Dell, which marches with his land, & would immeasurably improve his shoot. I am not prepared to part with a substantial acreage of prime land for a mere pecuniary return, & have written proposing that his Lordship exchange it for Puddelcombe Meadow, which conveniently borders my trout stream.

[Omitted: more information about land transactions, yields and receipts for home farm, redecoration of Miss Georgiana's private parlour, and estimates for repairs to three cottages in Pemberley village].

Miss Georgiana seems a little dull & out of sorts, says Pargeter; she mopes around the house for much of the day. The weather has been so bad that her morning walks have had to take place in the Picture Gallery. Poor G!

That evening I dashed off another letter to her, gave it to Bolton to post before I could change my mind, then went to Brooks's to meet Byron as arranged. Byron in an outlandish black cloak which he said had come from France. How do these fripperies continue to cross the Channel, war or no war! He called it a *rocolo* or some such name. It would not do for Peebles to catch sight of it—he is for ever wishing me to emulate his Lordship's sartorial excesses. Tom Bullivant was there. He tells me there is much disquiet about Perceval's retaining the position of Chancellor as well as Prime Minister. I agree—it is more than any man can handle. Byron was at the gaming tables, & I distinctly saw him hand over my money in exchange for counters. I recognized the purse. He lost heavily, then appeared to bethink himself, borrowed a large sum from the Bank, handed me back my 50*l*., ordered a fine supper for the three of us, and, having gorged on pickled salmon & brandy, repaired once more to the tables. I felt no inclination to play, but went & sat in the smoking room with Tom. I took much Port Wine, & raised no objection when Byron came to find us & carried us off to meet some *'charming women'* of his acquaintance. I remember little of the evening after that. My bit of muslin was fair & curvaceous, with a loud laugh. She had fine paps to her. Her name, I believe, is Clarabelle.

I am not sure who brought me home.

October 20th
Peebles exuded disapproval as he brought in my shaving water. Took myself to church in the forenoon—All Souls, Langham Place. Cold meats,

then a quiet session with the Pemberley accounts. Dinner alone. No Port Wine. To bed early. Wrote yesterday's & today's Diary.

The time has come for me to forward the first instalment of moneys to that blackguard Wickham. I will arrange it with Pargeter tomorrow before leaving Town.

October 21st
Trafalgar Day! Much celebrating & flag-waving in the street. No body seems to remember that this was also the day the Admiral died. Out & about in Town all day.

October 22nd
Yesterday evening Byron came & persuaded me to accompany him to Brooks's again for a Trafalgar Day celebration. I a trifle reluctant to let myself in for more debauchery, but allowed him to prevail without much difficulty. The fellows in festive mood. Cracked several bottles of clairet with Colebrooke, Fitchett, & some other old schoolfellows. Byron drank no wine, saying indignantly: 'I never touch liquor!' I cannot fathom him.

They are all talking about His Majesty's violent grief at Her Royal Highness the Princess Amelia's illness. They say she is very poorly indeed. His Majesty is beside Himself, & Colebrooke whispered that he has it on good report that the King acts most strangely, & looks like to lose His reason once more.

Afterwards we all visited the *bordello* together. My charmer is called Esmeralda—I was mistaken as to her name. She has told me artlessly that her

15

ambition is to perform circus tricks like Madame Scacchi, & that she is acting the courtesan to pay for lessons in circus craft. At present she is learning to stand on a horse's back. She showed me the calluses on the inside of her thighs from riding astride, wearing only spangled stockings.

The distractions of this & the previous days have been lively, but I cannot shake off my anxieties. I have decided that London is too hectic for me in my present mood, & have resolved to return to Hertfordshire & Charles. Am writing this as they harness the horses.

*   *   *

Arrived at Netherfield, to find a dinner-party planned: The Lucas family, a Mrs Long, & the Bennet ladies invited. I am sitting in the Library, writing this. Miss Caroline has just come in from the garden, bearing armfuls of chrysanthemums & berries to dress the table. She has trodden some fallen petals into the carpet, russet & gold. Peebles is upstairs laying out cravats for me to tie an Oriental—wretchedly uncomfortable, & a deal too formal for a country evening's entertainment, but I am loath to disappoint him.

*   *   *

At dinner, Miss Caroline & Mrs Louisa placed me between them: the former whispered that this was to protect me from the local *riff-raff*. Charles insisted on being seated next to Miss Bennet. She is handsome, & Charles has not been laggardly in furthering the acquaintance: I noted that they

16

greeted each other like long-lost friends. Charles appears to be considerably *épris*—but then he is always falling in love. There is little danger of her fixing his affections: she has but a paltry fortune, I understand. Miss Caroline told me that they have already spent three evenings together—an agreeable rural interlude for Charles—& pointed out the Mother to me. The latter matron directed loud remarks at the person opposite for most of the repast, ignoring her neighbours on both sides: she is indeed a strident lady. She leant forward so far that I began to fear for her ribbons in the soup. Then Miss Caroline indicated another young lady: 'You remember her, surely.'

I replied that I had never had the pleasure of meeting her.

'But she was at the ball the other day,' she protested.

'I have no recollection of it. Who is she?'

'Miss Elizabeth Bennet, younger Sister to Charles's Miss Bennet,' she whispered. 'I am told she is rather wild. She answers the gentlemen as an equal, & roams the countryside in a pair of stout boots.'

As I looked at this Miss Elizabeth, she turned her head, & our eyes met. She quickly looked away. She is somewhat undersized, & too thin. It must be all the exercise she takes.

When the ladies left the room, I was regaled by Sir William Lucas with stories of his reception at St James's. What a prosy old bore! Nor was there anything to interest me when we finally moved to the drawing-room. One of the Bennet girls, a mousy creature named Miss Mary, in an orange gown, insisted on playing & singing. She attempted

'The Lass with the Delicate Air', distinctly off-key. I amused myself watching Miss Elizabeth Bennet. She has a bold manner, & always seems to be laughing at something or some body. Her brownish hair escapes in untidy curls round her face; her unexpectedly dark eyes sparkle with mischief— scarcely befitting a respectable young lady. Her complexion is quite brown—I daresay she is too much in the wind & sun, if, as Miss Caroline suggests, she spends her days roaming the countryside unchaperoned. Whatever the reason, she is positively weatherbeaten. I mentioned as much to Miss Caroline, who laughed heartily, showing her fine white teeth, adhering to one of which was a small fragment of some green vegetable.

October 23rd
Miss Caroline has just entered the Library, where I have been writing. She enquired about 'that tattered old moleskin book' which I carry with me everywhere. I told her it was my Diary. She wished to know if it was a very private diary. When I vouchsafed no reply, she wondered how long I had been keeping it. I told her that it had been my Mother's idea—then, unbidden, a picture rose in my mind: Mamma, on that last sunny day at Pemberley, when she called me to her & gave me my first Diary. I remember her pale arm, that pearl & gold bracelet of hers—I wonder what became of it . . . ? Try as I may I cannot clearly recall her face. I was about twelve years old, & I wished she were not so languid, reclining on the day-bed by the window. I scarcely heard what she said: I was listening for the sound of distant doors banging,

18

wondering if it was the under-housemaids playing hide-and-seek in the attics again, & whether this time they would let me join in the fun. Yet at the same time I was aware that this moment had a certain importance. I was too young to know that Mamma was expecting to be confined at any moment—& that within three days my Sister would be born & she—gone.

Keeping my Diary was the last thing she ever asked me to do. She told me gently that I should come to cherish it as a friend. After her death, I tried to be true to her wishes, & ever since have obeyed her injunction to write as frankly & fully as I could.

I believe that it was my last interview with Mamma—tho' the next day, as I rode past with Crabbe, I glimpsed her smiling at me through the window. That same night she became ill . . .

Shew this book to Miss Caroline? Preposterous!

*   *   *

Drove to Meryton today with the ladies, as Mrs Louisa wished to exchange her Library books. She tells me that Mme d'Arblay's new novel is all the rage; but I cannot bring myself to read such flummery. We met one of their new acquaintance—a Mrs Phillips, a vulgar, gossipy person of some years. Miss Caroline, who seems to know everything about the district, whispered in my ear that this Mrs Phillips is Sister to Mrs Bennet, the lady with the numbers of 'eligible' daughters. Indeed, two of the said girls were present: Miss Catriona (or possibly Catherine), a young lady with a plaintive voice,

& Miss Elizabeth, whose cheeks were red from the cold. I overhead Mrs Louisa & Miss Caroline jesting about her appearance—'no better than a bumpkin'—but to some, a rosy complexion may be no less alluring than the Bingley Sisters' freckled pallor. They should take more exercise: I must encourage them to walk round the shrubbery tomorrow.

Before dinner, billiards with Charles. Best of five frames. He goodnaturedly annoyed at the fact that I beat him every time.

Still no further word from Georgiana.

October 24

Today I have the 'blue devils' as Charles would have it: still no reply from Georgie—I was sure a letter would come today. It did not help that I have received a letter from James, enquiring anxiously as to her welfare: *'Why does not my Cousin Georgiana leave Pemberley & join you in Town? A lonely house in the wilds of Derbyshire is scarcely a congenial setting for a young lady of her years, particularly in Autumn.'* Why does not she join me, indeed! When I desire nothing better!

A walk outdoors with my two hostesses. Tho' Miss Caroline teazed me to converse with them, I scarce heeded a word that they spoke. I found a greater measure of relief in a couple of hours' hard riding. Caesar very nervous today—shied at fallen leaves, & tried to throw me three times.

This evening I have refused to play at cards, ruining Mrs Louisa's hopes of a rubber, for her Husband will never condescend either. Instead, I have been writing this—& reading Hazlitt's *Essay on the Principles of Human Action.*

October 25th

2 brace of partridges, 3 pheasants & a hare today. Edward doubled my score. I have no notion how he does it—he is always tipsy, even before we set out!

We dined this evening at Mrs Long's. All the neighbourhood invited. As always, Charles insisted on paying his attentions exclusively to Miss Bennet, whose given name, I understand, is Jane. After all, I have changed my opinion. Miss Elizabeth Bennet is rather more handsome than her Sister. Miss Bennet has the advantage of her as to classical good looks, but Miss Elizabeth has more vivacity, & finer eyes. I listened to her conversation at dinner—she was mocking the other ladies, who expressed their fondness for a soldier in uniform. She is witty & sharp—if I were only in a mood to hear her!

October 27th

To church in the morning. The Netherfield parish church is an insignificant building of dubious origins. Charles informs me that Meryton church is greatly superior, & that we should make a point of attending service there. Later that day it rained; we were all dull together.

[. . .]

November 2nd

The anniversary of my dear Father's death. Went alone to church at Meryton. I have been much preoccupied today with what might have been. Would that Papa had lived! Apart from the melancholy fact of losing a dear parent, to leave

21

me thus in sole command of a great estate & fortune! A heavy burden indeed, & I scarce more than twenty at the time. Worst of all is the guardianship of a young & innocent Sister. Knowing nothing of young gentlewomen, I have been obliged to take decisions for her welfare, of which more than one has had unforeseen & unhappy consequences. Had Papa but been here to advise me!

November 3rd
It has been a monotonous week—nothing but cards, & brief sallies outside in the intervals of rain. I would have ridden out every day, but Caesar has cast a shoe, & the farrier has a dislocated shoulder. Charles teazed me to accompany him on a visit to the Misses Bennet at Longbourn, but I could not bring myself to oblige him. We discuss the war over our Port Wine most evenings, but little of interest has occurred recently. Masséna has withdrawn to Santarem, & Wellesley encamped in Lisbon. Peebles out of sorts. He feels that his valeting skills are wasted, since I move in such undemanding circles. Nothing else worth recording the entire week.

Today, Charles insistent that we should attend the morning service at Meryton, which involved a carriage ride. I wondered a little at it, 'til Mrs Louisa whispered in my ear: Charles has learned that the Bennet family are in the habit of worshipping there, & wishes to catch a glimpse of the fair Miss Bennet. I agreed to accompany him. During the whole service Charles sat craning his neck to see the lady. Occasionally I looked in the Bennets' direction to discover how they were reacting to this attention. Miss Bennet sat with her eyes downcast, & modestly refrained from glancing towards us. Miss Elizabeth was half-hidden by one of her Sisters—the one who insists on performing on the pianoforte. All I could see was a gloved hand holding a hymn book.

At the end of the service, a churchwarden came in & whispered to the rector, who enjoined the congregation to sit, & informed us that Her Royal Highness the Princess Amelia passed away yesterday. We said a prayer, & the bell tolled. I think that Charles had intended to approach the Bennet party, but, in view of the solemnity of the occasion, his Sisters deemed it more fitting to return home without conversation, & urged that the remainder of the day be spent in sober reflection—'til, bursting with impatience, I escaped for a ride on the newly-shod Caesar.

November 8th
At last G has written, with joyous news. My relief is indescribable. She will come to London next month—as soon as Mrs Lovejoy has finished making her three new gowns. Charles has been twitting me on my high spirits, & says that such merriment is quite unlike me, since I am normally *'such an impassive fellow'*, a verdict which I must say surprized me. I burst into such laughter during the nuncheon, that Mrs Louisa murmured something in a repressive tone about *'our recent royal bereavement'*; I succeeded thereafter in mastering my unseemly jocularity.

When I went up to my chamber to dress for dinner, I found a housemaid kneeling by the hearth, replacing some fallen coals with the tongs.

A pretty wench, with dark blue eyes, & pleasing *embonpoint*. She jumped to her feet in some confusion. I chucked her under the chin, & asked her name—it is Nellie. I told her to fetch me a dish of tea later that night, before retiring, which she did once Peebles had left me. She was lively, but not innocent. The Meryton blacksmith's son has taught her everything she knows, she tells me. O, what joy to feel lightness of heart again!

November 9th
By previous arrangement, Nellie came to me again this morning with my shaving-water. I had sent Peebles forth on an errand. I untied her starched white apron, & tumbled her on my bed. Afterwards, I questioned her about Mrs Nicholls, the housekeeper: would not she suspect a serious dereliction of duty if the girl lingered upstairs for so long? She gave me a sly smile as she pulled up her stockings, & replied that she would tell Mrs Nicholls that I had sent her on a lengthy errand: 'She knows what sort of errands you young gentlemen want us to run,' she added with a giggle.

Today we had been invited to a large party at the Lucases. I expected the event to be cancelled owing to the sad death of Her Royal Highness, a thought which, I must confess, greatly disappointed me. For the first time in months I had been looking forward to an evening's entertainment—even a lecture on the cholera would have seemed delightful to me. It turned out that, despite being an *'intimate'* at St James's, Sir William was perfectly happy to host a party on a day of Court mourning. As no body else had serious scruples, we all attended.

The party was a pleasant, convivial occasion. The Longs, the Phillipses & the Bennets were all present. Miss Elizabeth looks intelligent, I think, & seems ever on the verge of laughter. I moved to stand near her to catch some of her conversation: she was discussing a forthcoming entertainment with Colonel Forster, an agreeable man, whose regiment (the 9th Warwickshires) is now stationed at Meryton. I do not recall her precise words. Later I observed her sitting to one side, deep in conversation with Miss Lucas. To my surprize, she spoke directly to me: 'Do not you think, Mr Darcy, that I spoke uncommonly well just now, when I teazed Colonel Forster to give a ball?' We had never spoken before. I scarcely know how I replied—some remark about young ladies loving to dance, I believe. I was quite looking forward to continuing the conversation, when Miss Lucas invited her to sing. She excused herself, but was prevailed upon to perform. 'There is a very fine old saying which every body here is of course familiar with, "Keep your breath to cool your porridge,"—& I shall keep mine to swell my song.' With these words she abandoned me, & moved over to the pianoforte.

I have never heard her sing before. She has a sweet, low voice; the expression in her eyes reflects the mood of her song—now sad, now merry. It is curious how varied a woman's physiognomy can be: when she sings, Miss Elizabeth is almost beautiful.

The same cannot be said of her Sister Mary, who sang for a quarter of an hour together. I heard Miss Caroline whisper to Mrs Louisa that she was disgracefully forward in first seeking to perform, then refusing to stop.

Half-way through the evening, Sir William Lucas urged me to dance with Miss Elizabeth Bennet, insisting that *'I could not refuse to dance, when so much beauty was before me.'* I was only too eager to oblige—I would have danced with anyone that evening; but for some reason the lady steadfastly refused: *'She had not the least intention of dancing.'* Doubtless her shoes pinch. Afterwards, Miss Caroline came up & required to know my thoughts. In my beatific mood, without reflecting, I murmured something about Miss Elizabeth Bennet's fine eyes. She drew back sharply. I should not have spoken my thoughts aloud. 'I am all astonishment!' said she. 'How long has she been such a favourite? And pray when am I to wish you joy?'

All my efforts to distract her failed. She continued to teaze me: 'You will have a charming mother-in-law, indeed, & of course she will be always at Pemberley with you.'

I was half-amused, but half-mortified that she should think me so besotted with this Miss Elizabeth.

In the carriage home, Miss Caroline turned her attention to her Brother, mocking at him for his continued pursuit of the elder Miss Bennet. I realized then that I had failed to observe what he was about all evening. I must remember to offer my carriage, which is more roomy, for such excursions. Sat up late finishing this.

November 10th
Nellie came this morning, in her Sunday best, without her cap. She has pretty fair hair, tied back

in a coil, & a narrow waist. I sent her away without giving in to temptation. It is the Sabbath, after all! Besides, I was expecting Peebles to enter at any moment with my coat & hat.

Mrs Louisa announced at supper that the ladies have invited Miss Bennet to dine alone with them on the morrow: 'Darling Jane! Such a sweet girl, so charming! I doat on her! If we can have the pleasure of her company without that abominable family of hers, I could wish for nothing better!' It would be premature at this juncture to warn her that the young lady could present a danger to her Brother. I have seen him think himself in love so many times; there is nothing particular about *this* flirtation. Besides, there can be no problem about tomorrow: we gentlemen will be away in Meryton, dining with the Officers.

November 11th
Early this evening came the most atrocious rainstorm, accompanied by a violent wind. We had trouble getting to Meryton, the weather was so awful. Charles, Edward Hurst & I travelled in the Bingleys' chaise; it sank into the mud up to the axle, & we made sure we should have to alight & help push it onto dry ground—which would have been quite an adventure. Charles was concerned for Weech, perched up on the box with the rain pelting down on him; but when we arrived, the sergeant in charge of the mess assured us that there would be a roaring fire & a brandy-and-water for our coachman, so that he would not catch cold. The Officers have a cosy billet in the best inn, with food & drink in abundance. Colonel Forster is a sensible, honourable man, & a fine

host: the dinner was excellent, with French wines captured by our Navy, & a good haunch of venison. We discussed the Peninsular War, which continues to provoke the anxieties of all: Forster is of the opinion that Talavera may prove a turning point; Dalby favours Corunna. I enquired whether the regiment was due to be posted abroad; but apparently they are fixed here in England, to defend the Homeland in the event of an invasion.

We reached home late & somewhat tipsy to find to our surprize that the ladies had waited up for us. They told us that Miss Jane Bennet had earlier arrived on horseback, quite wet through. Mrs Louisa had been forced to lend her dry clothing; & by the end of the evening it was plain that she had caught a severe chill: there was nothing for it but to offer her a bed for the night. She was already asleep. Charles's eyes lit up—the lady under his very roof! Miss Caroline added in an undertone that she did think that, on such a night as this, the Bennets might have harnessed the carriage for their daughter, not sent her over on horseback. Mrs Louisa murmured that it was undoubtedly a ruse on the part of the Mother, to force us to invite Miss Bennet to stay. 'Be that as it may, what is done is done; there is nothing for it but to go to bed, & hope that the young lady has the decency to depart first thing in the morning,' added she.

Peebles spent much time in my chamber, grumbling that my greatcoat & boots had been damaged by the rain, & offering to rub my chest with camphorated oil lest I catch a chill. I had to insist that I was in perfect health, & that he must leave me & go to bed. Nellie waited 'til he was gone, then came to my room. We were obliged to be very circumspect, as Miss Bennet's chamber is only two doors away.

I write this by candlelight. It is very late, but I feel full of vigour, & not at all ready for sleep.

November 12th
Far from departing, Miss Bennet has taken a turn for the worse. Miss Caroline and Mrs Louisa went to see her early this morning, & have reported at breakfast that *'darling Jane'* is very ill indeed. She is confined to her chamber. The ladies seem quite reconciled to her being in the house—they find her good company even on her sickbed, & nothing particular is planned for today. Charles is anxious about her, alternately ringing for Nicholls to make her a hot poultice, urging his Sisters to remove upstairs to find out how she does, & summoning the footman to ascertain whether Weech, who was sent to fetch the apothecary, is returned.

* * *

We could not ride this morning—the rain had left the ground in such a quagmire that the horses would have slipped, & an outing would have been no pleasure. We lingered in the breakfast parlour, amusing ourselves with desultory conversation, & reading aloud passages from our letters. It is a miracle that the post got through. Georgiana has replied to my last letter. She writes that she is chearful now, & that the news that I may likely return to London & summon her to join me there has further raised her spirits.

We were thus occupied, when a visitor was announced—Miss Elizabeth Bennet. She entered

29

suddenly, her eyes bright, her complexion glowing. She had walked over from Longbourn, she said, to satisfy herself that her Sister was not gravely ill. Miss Caroline somewhat unenthusiastically took her upstairs to the sickroom, & left her with her Sister.

Both Charles and I felt unsettled for the rest of the morning. In the end, we resolved to go out, despite the mud. As Charles said, 'If Miss Elizabeth Bennet can walk three miles in this weather, who are we to languish indoors?'

We returned about three o'clock, to meet Miss Elizabeth in the entrance hall, tyeing on her bonnet. Charles questioned her eagerly about her Sister. She replied politely enough, & even jested that her Sister must be a sore trial to the household, drinking up all the lemon & honey in the storeroom. But I could see a shadow in her eyes, which are generally so clear. She must indeed be anxious about the invalid. She declared her intention of returning to Longbourn immediately. Miss Caroline remained silent, 'til I saw her Brother nudge her from behind, when she invited Miss Elizabeth to stay in the house 'til Miss Bennet is recovered. She was scarcely cordial, but it was enough to ensure Miss Elizabeth's acceptance.

*   *   *

A provoking evening. In the earlier part of it I avoided Miss Elizabeth Bennet, tho' I confess I was ready to hear her perform on the pianoforte after dinner. But when Charles, Edward Hurst & I rejoined the ladies in the drawing-room, I found that Miss Elizabeth had returned to the sick room,

& that we were not to have the pleasure of her company again that evening. I sat down to a rubber of whist with Mrs Louisa, her Husband & Miss Caroline. The two ladies abused Miss Elizabeth without ceasing for a full fifteen minutes, deploring everything from her manners (forward) to her petticoat (muddy). Miss Caroline actually invited me to join in this sport, but I refused— indeed, I think that on the whole Miss Elizabeth looks well, so it would scarcely have been honest in me to do so. I did agree, however, when the two Bingley ladies waxed eloquent about Miss Bennet's low connections: I concur with the view that the Bennet Sisters, situated as they are, will find it difficult to catch respectable Husbands. Miss Caroline & Mrs Louisa then repaired to the sick room to help tend the invalid, leaving us to ourselves. I played piquet with Edward Hurst; Charles read the newspaper & interrupted us constantly to speculate on Miss Bennet's condition, when he was not sending for Nicholls, & issuing fresh instructions about gruel & herb tinctures. Later, while we were at loo, Miss Elizabeth came back down; at first she said nothing to us, & sat in a corner with a book. I failed to see what she was reading. Then she joined us & we chatted a little. I scarce know what we discussed.

November 13th
I have instructed Nellie to keep away while the Misses Bennet are house guests.

This morning the vulgar Mrs Bennet, accompanied by her remaining girls, came to visit her sick daughter. The youngest Sister, Lydia, a forward, impertinent girl, urged Charles to give a ball at Netherfield. 'It will be such fun! We can see all the Officers in their dress uniforms. What sport!' cried she. Somewhat to my dismay, Charles readily agreed to this proposal. Miss Caroline & Mrs Louisa were barely civil, whilst I was hard put to it to keep my countenance. However, I would not join in with their ill-concealed mirth at Mrs Bennet's expense, even tho' that lady seems to have elected me as the chief butt of her ill-humour, angrily accusing me of thinking the country *nothing at all*. She further indulged herself in vaunting her daughter Jane's extraordinary beauty, & mentioned some admirer who wrote poetry in her honour. Miss Elizabeth was unimpressed: 'I wonder who it was who first discovered the efficacy of poetry in driving away love!'

'I have been used to consider poetry as the *food* of love,' I demurred.

'Of a fine, stout, healthy love it may. But if it be only a thin sort of inclination, one good sonnet will starve it entirely away,' she retorted.

Shortly after this, Mrs Bennet & her retinue departed. It seems we are condemned to play host to Miss Bennet and Miss Elizabeth until the former is entirely recovered. The invalid is too weak to be moved, and, were she as strong as a horse, Charles would never permit her departure.

*   *   *

As Miss Bennet is now on the mend, Miss Elizabeth spent the evening with us in the drawing-room. I had started to write to Georgiana, but found it difficult to concentrate, as Miss Caroline teazed me endlessly about my letter. Miss Elizabeth was listening to our conversation; her needlework lay neglected on her lap. She looked most amused when Miss Caroline admired my handwriting, my speed of composition, &c. I was put out when Charles interrupted his Sister: 'He does *not* write with ease. He studies too much for words of four syllables. Do not you, Darcy?'

Miss Elizabeth's eyes sparkled more than ever; she murmured: 'I understand now; all is explained.'

'What is explained?'

'Why, Mr Darcy's taciturn nature: he uses up all his eloquence in writing long words, & has none left for conversation.'

Matters grew worse when Charles accused me of moodiness: 'I declare I do not know a more awful object than Darcy, on a Sunday evening, when he has nothing to do . . .' & every body laughed. How have I acquired this absurd reputation of being an unconvivial curmudgeon? I must emulate Charles, & cultivate more of an easy, outgoing temper.

Later, I hoped that Miss Elizabeth would play & sing; but it was Miss Caroline who jumped up with alacrity, and, almost thrusting Miss Elizabeth aside, moved to the pianoforte with her Sister. As we listened, I chanced to observe Miss Elizabeth. She sat a little apart, her cheek resting on her hand. She did not smile, but I could sense her amusement.

Miss Caroline played a reel. I approached Miss Elizabeth & invited her to dance. She mockingly refused me, & the opportunity passed.

November 14th

I was waiting in the drawing-room for Miss

Elizabeth to come down: I deemed it only civil in me to escort her round the park—she has scarcely left the house since she arrived two days ago. But instead Miss Caroline sought me out, wishing to walk with me. As she reminded me, I had on an earlier occasion suggested that she needed to take more exercise. No sooner had we set out than Miss Elizabeth came down the path with Mrs Louisa. On meeting us, she removed herself, & walked off alone. As soon as her back was turned, the Sisters began to speak ill of her—& to teaze me with the prospect of life at Pemberley with Miss Elizabeth as its mistress, 'til a light rain drove us in. Miss Elizabeth came in late from the garden with raindrops in her hair.

*   *   *

That evening, after dinner, Miss Bennet finally came downstairs for a short while. She is pale & looks tired, but otherwise is her usual mild, agreeable self. Charles was all eagerness to attend to her every comfort. I resolved to keep my counsel, & immersed myself in *Marmion*, my back to the company. I heard a footstep directly behind me, & resolutely kept my eyes on my book. Then came Miss Caroline's voice. She had borrowed from me the second volume of the same poem, announcing that she 'adored Mr Walter Scott', & looking over my shoulder to see how far I had got. I told her '*The Tale of Young Lochinvar*', & enquired of her how the poem was to end—but her answer betrayed her complete ignorance of the first volume. Why then is she reading the second? '*O, what a tangled web we weave, when first we practise to deceive'*, as Mr Scott writes! Looking round, I met the eyes of Miss Elizabeth, brimming with mirth. She was sitting quietly with her needlework, but I think that no word of my conversation with Miss Caroline had escaped her.

I was displeased with Miss Caroline later, when, in Miss Elizabeth's hearing, she maintained, yet again, that dancing for me is *'rather a punishment than a pleasure'*. This does not further my aim of persuading Miss Elizabeth to dance with me, if only once: so far she has eluded me. It is not that I attach any particular value to the event, but I am on my mettle now: she seems resolved against standing up with me. To this day I have never so much as touched her hand.

Miss Caroline paced about restlessly for some time—then said, 'Miss Eliza Bennet, let me persuade you to follow my example, & take a turn about the room.' Miss Elizabeth obediently rose to her feet. Though slight, she has a slender, graceful figure. She was wearing a dress of some soft grey-blue stuff with long sleeves, & a shawl about her shoulders. At her throat a plain gold chain. She would suit some fine stones, I believe. Topazes or—no, rather—rubies, with those brilliant eyes of hers. Miss Caroline continually addressed me. I replied in monosyllables: I would have preferred for her to leave me in peace to observe her deambulations. Miss Caroline has a small tear in her left stocking, just above the heel.

Miss Elizabeth then joined in the conversation. I would benefit from being mocked, said she. 'Teaze him, laugh at him,' she added, & proceeded to do that: 'Mr Darcy has no defect. He owns it himself without disguise.' At first her mockery was a novel, not uninteresting, experience; but then we fell to discussing my faults. She accused me of *implacable resentment*, & concluded '*Your* defect is a propensity to hate every body.' Her tone was jocular, but did I detect an element of earnestness beneath her wit? I am not sure.

Eventually, I began to find her criticisms irksome. Furthermore, I became concerned that our *tête-à-tête* was continuing for too long. Miss Caroline was eyeing us both, & eventually jumped up, & led Miss Elizabeth over to the pianoforte. It was quite a relief.

I was vexed when, as I was writing this, Nellie appeared in my chamber with a pot of some herb tea favoured by Nicholls the housekeeper. I mortified her by repeating my request that she not visit me in my chamber at present—then turned away her wrath by a gift of a guinea.

This evening Miss Elizabeth accused me of pride. Is this just?

November 15th

Miss Bennet's health is greatly improved. Mr Jones the apothecary says that she is ready to leave her chamber now, and, if well wrapped up, may travel home on Sunday. Accordingly, both Sisters spent the evening in our company. No longer anxious for her Sister's welfare, Miss Elizabeth was in the highest of spirits. I particularly recall one conversation: we were discussing the novels of Mrs Radcliffe, & I had ventured to disagree with Mrs Louisa's positive opinion. 'O, there is no hope for me—you always object to what I say,' cried she.

'Why is it that gentlemen's views almost invariably differ from those of the ladies?'

enquired Miss Elizabeth.

'You mean, I take it, that the ladies are always right, the gentlemen always wrong,' said I.

She laughed. 'If that be the case, why trouble to debate between the sexes? The views of the ladies should always be accepted, the gentlemen's straightaway disregarded. Then there would be an end to the matter.'

'Why, no. Gentlemen are necessary to the well-being of ladies,' said Charles.

'Because of their superior judgment?' asked Miss Caroline, favouring me with an arch smile.

Miss Elizabeth's dark eyes shone. 'No, because we need recipients for the slippers & pen-wipers we insist on embroidering,' she said mockingly.

Miss Caroline blenched. Did her fair interlocutor know of the half-worked green slippers with the lovers' knots which even now repose in her workbox?

'O, Lizzy, be serious!' said Miss Bennet. 'You need gentlemen as much as any woman.'

'Very true. If there were none to hand, I should have no body to teaze.'

'Doubtless Miss Elizabeth is proposing a republic of females,' I suggested.

'Yes,' said Miss Elizabeth. 'And all the professions would be led by women—doctors, lawyers, even Members of Parliament—even the Prime Minister!'

Every body laughed. It was the merriest evening I can remember at Netherfield.

*   *   *

Reading over the above, I see that I must take

37

myself to task. Write this down, & note it well: Miss Elizabeth is not beautiful; but she is charming, and, above all, lively-minded. Evenings spent in her company have become—I confess it—quite an adventure. Her want of connexions is of course deplorable. Were her place in society exactly as I could wish it . . .

An undersized young lady of doubtful family, however brilliant, cannot tempt *me*.

November 16th

I propose to keep my distance from Miss Elizabeth all today. It is her last day here. This morning, she sent to Longbourn for the Bennets' coach to fetch them tomorrow; the servant returned with a note from Madam her Mother to say that the coach could not be spared. I verily suspect that matron of matchmaking: she is hoping that Miss Bennet will stay here for ever, & catch poor Charles in her toils. Meanwhile, Miss Elizabeth is also present, & I have no intention of allowing *myself* to be hooked. The young lady must be made to acknowledge that her allurements have *not* succeeded with me. Accordingly, I spent the whole morning shooting. I coaxed Charles to accompany me, but he was not to be prised from Miss Bennet's side, so I went alone with Edward Hurst. I bagged three brace, Edward seven. When I returned to the house, Miss Caroline and Mrs Louisa had taken Miss Bennet upstairs to admire some new gowns lately arrived from London; Charles was attending to some estate business; Edward Hurst had disappeared (I suspect in search of his wench in the servants' hall). I was left alone with Miss Elizabeth.

We sat in the Library. I took up the newspaper, but I confess that Mr Perceval's disastrous handling of the Bank of England finances failed to occupy my attention. She sat in the window, at her sewing. I pretended to read, even remembering to turn the pages; but instead I was observing her profile, reflected in the glass of a bookcase. It gave me a feeling of power, knowing she could not be aware how I watched her. Her nose is small & straight. I could see how every passing thought shewed in her expression: often a fleeting smile would light up her face. We staid there together for half an hour. Neither of us spoke. She stitched assiduously at a piece of white stuff. Once she pricked her finger, & lifted it to her lips.

At dinner, I placed myself as far away from Miss Elizabeth as I could contrive, and turning away from her, addressed myself exclusively to Miss Caroline. Out of the corner of my eye, I did notice how well Miss Elizabeth looked in a rose-pink gown. Surely, after my coolness today, she must believe that I have little interest in her! Whether or not she views *me* with indifference, I cannot tell.

In the evening, I played a rubber of whist with Miss Caroline, Mrs Louisa & Edward. I sat with my back to Miss Elizabeth, who read a book throughout. Miss Bennet and Charles talked quietly on the sofa. On retiring, I wrote in my Diary.

I have not sent for Nellie.

November 17th

Today, after church, the Misses Bennet left Netherfield. Miss Caroline was only too delighted to see them go, & murmured to me, as we turned away from the door. 'Peace at last!'

This evening has seemed dull & empty. On retiring I rang the bell, & ordered Peebles to send Nellie up with a dish of herb tea. He replied, 'Yes, Sir,' but gave me one of his provoking looks. Nellie came, but the brief distraction of her presence did little to dissipate my melancholy. I had much better go to London, to prepare for Georgiana's arrival. I have written to my Cousin James Fitzwilliam that G will shortly join me there. There is nothing to keep me here. I have warned Peebles to be ready to pack my boxes. He is well pleased.

November 19th
I have but one thought in my mind today: I have seen *him*—whom I hoped never to meet again! He was with a group of Officers, twirling his quizzing-glass on its ribbon, that supercilious smirk on his face. I did not realize who it was until I was so close that I could not avoid acknowledging him. He had the grace to blush. The first time since— last July! In his impertinence he bowed to me, & I so taken by surprize that I actually returned his salutation!

And—the worst of it—*she* was there, in the Meryton street! With a crowd of people. She stood beside him, gazing up into his face. Does she too admire him?

*   *   *

I have spent the final daylight hours alone in my chamber. Wickham! How dare he show his face in Meryton? Surely he must purpose to discompose me by flaunting his presence here! Could it be that

Pargeter has omitted to pay him his moneys? That must be the truth of the matter: he believes that I have failed to honour my pledge, & has pursued me here. How did he find me out? Did he present himself at Grosvenor Square, & get my direction from one of the servants? Or could he have sought out Byron & obtained the information from him, if his Lordship was in the mood to communicate it? Wickham, & Byron! They are old friends—& now I find myself recalling vividly an episode I would much rather forget. It happened when Byron visited Pemberley during one of our spells of home leave from Harrow. We were about fourteen years old, Byron, Wickham & I, hiding in the shrubbery, behind the rose hedge.

'What are we doing here?'

'Wait & see . . .'

And then the footsteps. We peered out through the branches. Little Letty Hopkins with her heavy basket of wet linen. As she passed, the two of them leapt out. I shrank back out of sight. I saw them seize her, heard her screams, immediately stifled. And—O shameful memory—I did nothing. Nothing! I remained hidden behind the hedge. The roses were in flower: I remember the sweet fresh smell, & the prickles biting into my flesh as I gripped the branches. Were we really only fourteen, the three of us?

I remained there—it seemed forever. I dared not look to see what they did. Then Byron stood up, buttoning his breeches, glanced contemptuously in my direction, & strolled away with Wickham, arm in arm, laughing. There was a long silence. I parted the branches. Letty lay motionless, her skirts pulled right up to cover her face, her nether parts exposed. I had never seen a naked woman before. I felt sure that she was dead.

After a few minutes she stirred. I saw her hands go up in a hesitant gesture to rearrange her apparel. Then she sat up. Her face was flushed & tearful. She groped for her cap, replaced it on her head, tucked her hair away, stood up slowly & awkwardly, smoothed her crumpled dress, & began to gather up the wet laundry which had spilt from her basket. Then she wiped her hand across her nose, picked up the basket, and, still weeping, continued on her way towards the washing-line. She did not once look in my direction. I watched her 'til she was out of sight. There were long grass-stains on the back of her skirt.

The dinner-gong has sounded: I must go downstairs.

*   *   *

Making lighthearted conversation at dinner has been almost impossible, particularly as Charles is full of praise for *'the handsome young gentleman whom we met this morning at Meryton.'* I told him sharply that this *'gentleman'* was the same Wickham whose antics with Byron at Cambridge I had described to him on numerous occasions. Miss Caroline & Mrs Louisa immediately sought to know what scrapes this Wickham had got into during his student days; but none of the anecdotes which came to my mind were at all suitable for a lady's ears.

Luckily Charles provided a distraction, by mentioning that we had encountered another person at Meryton this morning: 'A fellow named

42

Collins. He is now a clergyman. He was up at Oxford at the same time as me, & repeatedly tried to scrape acquaintance. Impertinence itself, & intolerably prolix. What is your opinion of him, Darcy? A dull dog, eh?'

I gave a slight bow. I had not the faintest recollection of the fellow, who must have been present this morning, in the Meryton street. My eyes had been fixed on George Wickham, standing so close to Miss Elizabeth.

November 20th

I write this at dawn. All night, recollections of Wickham have preoccupied me. Aged fifteen, he stole five bottles of Papa's best Port, & insinuated that poor Harry Garnett was responsible, so that Harry was dismissed without a character. Then I remember him at perhaps seven years old, standing by Papa's chair, his curly golden head leaning on Papa's arm. He was playing with his fob & asking to see his timepiece, 'til eventually Papa made him a present of it: a chased-gold timepiece which I had always loved but would never have dreamt of claiming as a gift. I recall my feelings of jealousy & shame—jealousy of this pretty boy who could charm his way into my beloved Father's affections, and, on a whim, divest him of his valuables; shame at my mean-spirited resentment of Wickham's innocent pleasure & my Father's affectionate generosity.

Then I remembered how Wickham used to play on the orchard swing with my baby Sister Georgiana. I can see her now, flying through the air, her eyes sparkling, her soft hair tousled. She wears a blue sash; the ends flutter; she screams with delight.

I must not dwell on this.

As I dressed, paying no heed to Peebles's chatter, I resolved to take action. I must seek Wickham out, & discover what he is about. If necessary, I must make good Pargeter's oversight, & pay him his due.

* * *

I had some difficulty in liberating myself: Miss Caroline was determined to stay by my side, & had her workbox open & her embroidery silks out, seeking my help in matching the colours for my second slipper—the first one is already finished. But then Nicholls came & found her out, requesting her assistance with the white soup for the ball. She has tried it five times, & it makes lumps at every attempt.

'I daresay you have not pounded the almonds finely enough,' said Miss Caroline. She reluctantly left me, & went off to supervize the process, reiterating that she would return directly. However, I had had enough, & told her shortly that I was going out.

I found Wickham in the inn parlour, at poker with three of the Officers. Altho' the rain, which has been pouring down all night, had briefly ceased, they had the curtains drawn, & were playing by candlelight before a roaring fire. What with the smoke from their pipes & the fumes from their brandy, the air was well-nigh unbreathable.

'Why! If it ain't Fizzibuzz!' said Wickham. I could tell that he was foxed. I know my George Wickham. I requested a private interview.

44

'You can see I'm at poker,' answered he insolently.

The three Officers, equally inebriated, made an attempt at courtesy. They staggered to their feet when I appeared, & protested somewhat incoherently that they were happy to postpone their game to suit my convenience. I believe I nodded. At any rate they withdrew.

Wickham did not invite me to sit. He poured more brandy into his glass, & tossed it down. 'What d'you want, Fizzibuzz?' he asked.

I remained silent.

' 'Tis a pleasure to see you, Fizzibuzz! It brings back such happy memories!'

I cut him short: 'What are you doing here?'

'What business is it of yours?'

I moved to stand behind him, gripping his shoulder. 'Answer me!'

'Why? Haven't I the right to be where I wish?' His tone was insolent.

'If you have come to haunt me, you gain nothing by it.'

'Haunt you? How can I haunt you, when I'm not dead?' I thought privately that indeed I had never come nearer to wishing a fellow human being dead. 'Besides, I've a right to haunt you,' he continued. 'You know it as well as I.'

'Know what?'

'That you have not given me my due,' replied he. Then, raising his voice, he called to the Officers outside, 'Is not that so, fellows? He's short-changed me, with a vengeance!'

'I will not be intimidated by such empty threats,' said I.

'Was I threatening you? Hardly. I believe I was

45

merely stating the facts. You are under an obligation which you have failed to honour.'

So I guessed aright: Pargeter has not sent him the moneys. I am surprized at this: I have never known Pargeter fail in such a commission before. Could I myself, in my distraction, have failed to make the necessary arrangements? Wickham's words were a clear warning: if his money was not paid, he would spread his vile tittle-tattle abroad.

'If Pargeter has not paid the instalment I promised you, I can remedy the omission,' said I.

There was a silence. He appeared to be thinking over my words. Then he asked, simply: 'When?'

'Now, if you wish.' I took out the purse I had in readiness, & droppt it onto the card table.

'Good. I was wondering how to meet today's debts,' was all he said, as he scooped it up.

I turned on my heel & left the room. Wickham's three fellow debauchees were lounging outside on the inn bench. I believe that they attempted to rise to their feet & bow as I passed. I called for my horse. It had started to rain again.

*   *   *

The evening was spent in discussing the placement of the furniture for the ball, so my gloomy mood passed unnoticed. There is to be a small orchestra: should they be seated on a raised dais? Mrs Louisa asked me how such entertainments are organized at Pemberley; but there we have a minstrels' gallery, so no useful comparison can be made.

All this talk of balls reminds me that I had promised G that I would give consideration to the construction of a new ballroom wing at Pemberley.

Apparently our Great Hall is most unsuitable for modern dancing, & we need a parquet floor, chandeliers, &c. Destroy the Great Hall, which has stood since before the reign of Good Queen Bess! The thought fills me with dismay—but poor G wishes to move with the times, & at present I am reluctant to oppose her. I must write forthwith to Pargeter to remind him of this project, & to discover what happened about Wickham's money.

November 21st
I am speechless with fury.

Today, Charles, Miss Caroline & Mrs Louisa have ridden together to Longbourn to deliver their invitations to the Bennets. Mrs Louisa was all eagerness to see her *'Darling Jane'* once more: 'It seems an age since she went from hence. I have been positively languishing in her absence!' They urged me to bear them company, but I still so perturbed after yesterday's encounter that I could not envisage any outing with equanimity. I therefore handed the ladies into the carriage & rode out alone for a good gallop, returning after almost two hours' violent exercise in a strong, blustery wind.

On returning, I found the Bingleys in the drawing-room, discussing their morning's visit. Charles informed me that his dull acquaintance Collins, the clergyman, is staying with the Bennets as their guest. It seems that he is a distant Cousin of theirs. By a curious coincidence, he is also Rector of Hunsford, where my Aunt de Bourgh lives. The said Collins lost no time in informing Charles, in a confidential whisper, that the Bennets' estate of Longbourn is entailed in his favour. With much merriment, Charles quoted his exact words: 'Of course I wish my fair Cousins well, and, in earnest of my goodwill, I intend to make the best of them my wife.' I was taken aback when Charles added that the fellow has set his sights on Miss Elizabeth. ' 'Tis fortunate that he has overlooked the eldest Miss Bennet,' he remarked.

'Fortunate, forsooth!' exclaimed Miss Caroline. 'Why, the indomitable Mrs Bennet will have warned him off: she is determined that Jane is to have Charles, & Charles alone. That is only too evident!'

Charles blushed, laughed & turned the conversation.

Then Miss Caroline shocked me beyond description. 'Miss Lydia Bennet knows all the gossip,' she began. 'The forward little baggage! They was discussing your old acquaintance, Mr Wickham. Apparently he is fixed in the neighbourhood for the entire winter.'

'How is this?' asked I.

'Why, he has purchased a commission in the militia. That is why he has come down here—to take up his place in the regiment. Colonel Forster told Lydia that he had been trying for a commission for some months. Only in November did he procure the necessary moneys from some benefactor, for you must know that he has no fortune.'

I barely succeeded in mastering my anger. So Wickham *did* receive the payment from Pargeter! And now he has extracted the sum from me a second time. The cunning devil! My first instinct was to saddle up that very evening, ride over to the inn & take back what he has obtained through

48

deceit. But he has probably lost it already at cards.

I was so absorbed in these reflections that I scarcely heeded Mrs Louisa's next words, 'til Wickham's name again caught my attention. She was apologizing for the fact that they had felt obliged to invite him to the ball, along with the other Officers.

'I observe that you view him with disapprobation,' murmured Miss Caroline.

I see that I shall have to give some explanation to account for my repugnance—otherwise we shall have Wickham as a constant visitor to the house.

Meanwhile, I cannot escape the ball: to refuse to attend would be an unpardonable slight to my hosts. I can only hope that Wickham, well aware of my feelings for him, will have the decency to stay away. I think he will: he always was a coward at heart. Indeed, it is like him to join a regiment which does not expect to see action against Bonaparte.

November 25th
We have endured three days of continuous rain, & have been unable to set foot outside the house. Miss Caroline and Nicholls, organizing the ball, have been in a fine flurry, for the tradesmen could scarce make their way up the muddy drive. Miss Caroline is persuaded that the ice-cart will never arrive from Hertford. For me the rain has proved a relief, since it has protected me from chance encounters with Wickham. It has meant too that I have run no risk of meeting any members of the unacceptable Bennet family. Otherwise, the days have been dull indeed.

I have been brooding a good deal on Miss Jane

Bennet. I fear that she is a considerable danger to Charles. I can no longer refrain from speaking to his Sisters.

*   *   *

I have sought out Miss Caroline, who was supervizing the furniture's removal from the drawing room, where the dancing is to take place. She was in an apron & cap and, when I found her, was shouting angrily at one of the workmen: 'Thomas! Mind the fruitwood whatnot, you clumsy oaf!' For some reason she seemed annoyed at seeing me. I drew her to one side, & tactfully warned her not to allow a girl as handsome as Miss Bennet to monopolize her Brother at the ball, since she is plainly unsuitable for him. Miss Caroline pettishly brushed my scruples aside: her Brother has not shown any greater partiality for Jane than for other young ladies in the past, he enjoys a mild flirtation, &c., &c. 'Besides, the neighbourhood is insufferably empty of agreeable company, & Miss Bennet—dearest Jane—is the only bearable human being within miles! You must excuse me: they are rolling up the carpets all wrong.' With that, she hastened away.

I remain unconvinced: I worry that Charles is now seriously drawn to Jane.

November 26th
I shall attempt to give a detailed account of this last evening, to clarify my thoughts—but I fear me it will be difficult.

Let me start with this: I have danced with her. It is probably—nay, certainly—the first & only time that our hands will ever touch. She has repeatedly refused to dance with me, & yet she takes the floor, so gracefully, with anyone else who asks her. Indeed, this evening, for the first two dances, she stepped out with a clumsy, red-faced imbecile in clericals, who twice trod on her toes. Charles whispered that it was that dullard Collins, her Cousin, he who is Rector of my Aunt de Bourgh's parish. How could he be Miss Elizabeth's first choice?

I scarce dared to approach her. Formally dressed, in a golden gown which seemed to glow in the candlelight, she looked quite beautiful. I finally requested the pleasure of a dance, aware of how stiffly I bore myself. She gave me a doubtful, sidelong glance, as if she were half-minded to refuse me; but in the end she accepted—then, as if I had not spoken, continued her conversation with a lady friend. When the musicians tuned up, I claimed her hand. As we danced I did not wish to speak—but then she began her usual teazing, mocking me for not indulging in platitudinous observations about the ball, & I replying as best I could, parrying her witty attacks. She concluded pertly: 'I have always seen a great similarity in the turn of our minds. We are each of an unsocial, taciturn disposition, unwilling to speak, unless we expect to say something that will amaze the whole room.'

Anything less like my charming, loquacious dancing partner than this description can scarcely be imagined, as I informed her.

And then—I hardly know how it happened—I discovered myself in the middle of a serious conversation about, of all people, Wickham.

Again! He has been maligning me to her. She actually appears to believe that the faults are all on *my* side! Fortunately, we were interrupted; on resuming our conversation, she said, with more earnestness than I have ever heard her use: 'I remember hearing you once say, Mr Darcy, that you hardly ever forgave; that your resentment, once created, was unappeasable.' And then she embarked on a cruel analysis of my character defects. Her tongue is sharp, her intelligence keen. She seems to consider me vengeful, implacable, harsh & prejudiced. What have I done to deserve this?

After I had escorted her to a chair, I went out onto the darkened terrace, & sat in the leafless rose arbour. I needed a quiet place to reflect on what she had said to me. I leant my head against the bench & closed my eyes. But I had not been outside more than a few minutes when the French windows burst open. I saw the gleam of a white dress, followed by another, & then a flash of scarlet—two Officers. One of the girls was laughing, & I at once recognized her voice: the youngest Bennet girl, Lydia. 'I'm so hot!' cried she, fanning herself energetically.

'Surely not! 'Tis nigh on Christmas time!' came a man's voice. 'Let me keep you warm.' I verily believe that he put his arm around her waist.

'Kitty, Kitty—Mr Denny is teazing me again,' giggled Lydia.

'Well, do not you come running to me. I've enough to do keeping this one in order,' came her Sister Catherine's lighter voice. There was a slight scuffle. 'O Lord!' said Lydia, 'There's the orchestra tuning up for the next dance, & we're bespoke!

What a joke, if our partners come looking for us, & catch us out here with you!' She gave another loud laugh & disengaged the Officer's arm. The two girls slipped back into the ballroom. Unchaperoned! What was their Mother thinking of?

The girls gone, the Officers remained, strolling backwards & forwards along the terrace. As they passed before the lighted windows, I perceived that they were two of Wickham's partners at cards of the other day. They did not observe me, seated in my arbour.

One Officer took out his snuff-box & offered it. 'Fine upstanding fillies, those two, eh, Denny?'

His manner was insolent. I half rose from my seat. But then Denny said: 'They can't hold a candle to the two eldest Sisters.'

'. . . Who are all but engaged, you know.'

'Indeed? To whom?'

'O, well, Miss Lizzy—she's the second girl, the best of the bunch, in my opinion. She has more spirit than her Sister Jane . . .'

'Is she really engaged?' interrupted Denny.

'Not exactly, but friend Wickham said to me, "Hands off the fair Eliza, Sam! She's my property." You should have seen them at Mrs Phillips's supper party the other night: they had their heads together the whole evening.'

'What about the eldest Sister, Jane?'

'O, Miss Jane is practically betrothed to our host.'

'Really? Mr Bingley?'

'Ay, & she don't care a button for him.'

'And how do you know *that*?'

'Let's say it was from a reliable informant. Your

53

fine beauties are always thus: Miss Jane has her eye on poor Bingley's fortune. Still, I'll wager she'll make him a good enough wife—as long as no Officer comes along. She has a fondness for Officers. I should never have believed it, had it not been confirmed by Tully.'

'I am barely acquainted with Lieut. Tully,' said Denny, 'But I have met the lady several times. Anyone who can speak of her so in public must be a slanderous rogue.'

'Far from speaking in public, it was in confidence that he told me your Miss Jane has made quite shameless advances to him. So much for all her respectability & decorum! She is all set to gain poor Bingley, but once she has caught her prey, she will be ready for a discreet flirtation—& perhaps for more.'

'You only have his word for it,' retorted Denny.

'I said as much to him, whereupon he shewed me a letter—a short note, arranging a secret assignation. It came from Longbourn—I saw it with my own eyes.' The two Officers then re-entered the house.

It was some time before I returned to the ballroom. The first thing I observed was Miss Bennet herself, sitting apart with one of the Officers. She was smiling brilliantly at him. Then I saw Charles return to her side, & present her with an ice-cream. She gave him precisely the same charming smile: no more, no less. Surely the Officer was not mistaken: she does not particularly care for poor Charles. But she looked so calm, so virtuous. If this Tully is to be believed, all her modest gentleness is a sham, & she, duplicity itself!

Seated alone in a corner I noticed her Father,

Mr Bennet. He had contrived to provide himself with a book (could he have brought it with him?), & was absorbed in his reading, oblivious of everyone around him. He barely roused himself to move over to the supper table. A gentleman, with such boorish manners! At supper, I overheard his lady wife boasting at the top of her voice: her daughter Jane about to be engaged to Charles—*'such a charming young man, & so rich!'* Worse still, she asserted that Elizabeth is soon to be the wife of . . . that clown Collins! Which is it to be, Collins or Wickham?

I was rudely interrupted in my thoughts by that same Collins, who presumed to introduce himself, & embarked on a tedious speech extolling my Aunt de Bourgh. In the midst of his interminable prosing came Mary Bennet's voice, loudly singing her party pieces, 'The Lass with the Delicate Air', followed by 'My Mother Bids me Bind my Hair'. The people at this gathering are all, all intolerable!

Scarcely had the sound of the Bennets' horses died away (needless to say, they were the last to depart, long after the negus was drunk), when Miss Caroline turned to me and, with a broad smile, said: 'Your Miss Eliza will at length have contrived to find disfavour with you.' She paused, waiting for my reply.

I said: 'I believe you are all eagerness to inform me how.'

She took this as an invitation to pass her arm through mine, & walked me up & down as she explained that Miss Elizabeth Bennet has set herself up as champion of—Wickham! Again! I almost trod on her hem. I managed to retain some measure of composure by gazing fixedly at the feather in her headdress. It was a green ostrich plume, and, in the exertion of the dance, the quill had broken, so that it dangled, half-severed. Suddenly I could endure it no longer. I detached myself abruptly from her grasp, bowed, and, taking up a candle, wished them all 'good night'.

Though Jane appears virtuous, she is the scion of this abominable family. Did the Officers speak the truth? If it be so, & she has set her sights on Charles, my poor friend has no hope of happiness, & it is time I stepped in. Meanwhile, I shall speak to no body of what I have heard.

November 27th

After the excesses of last evening, Charles rose late this morning. He was in excellent spirits at breakfast, discoursing on the success of the evening, a Bath bun in one hand and a cup of chocolate in the other. He summoned Nicholls to congratulate her on the delicious supper (Miss Caroline took the opportunity of remarking that the broiled fowl was below standard). Then he drew me aside in the Library. Before I could begin the speech I had prepared, he confided that he was in love with Miss Bennet, & proposed to make her his wife immediately, 'If she will have me,' he added.

'Of course she will,' I assured him. It was not the moment to raise objections.

'I cannot be certain: I *believe* that she favours me with her regard, but . . .'

I had no desire to convince him. On the contrary, an idea was taking shape in my mind.

'I shall make a rapid visit to London to see about hiring a town house for the winter,' continued he. 'Then, if all goes well, we may be married in early December, & from hence before Christmas! Her Mother will wish her to remain in Hertfordshire, but I would prefer us to make a more independent beginning.' He was glowing with delight.

'This is very hasty,' said I, adopting a mildly dampening tone. 'The lady will wish for more time, to see to her wedding clothes, if nothing else.'

He jumped to his feet. 'I am afire with impatience! I will brook no delay,' cried he impetuously.

I purpose to follow him to London on the morrow, & try if I may dissuade him. Away from Hertfordshire, the lady's charms may dwindle.

After breakfast, when Charles had left for London, I requested an interview with his Sisters. I knew that I was betraying his confidence, but the situation was grave indeed. Besides, he had not forbidden me to reveal his secret, tho' a prohibition was doubtless assumed.

The quizzing-glass droppt from Miss Caroline's fingers. 'What? Me, Sister to that hoyden, Lydia Bennet? Never!'

Edward Hurst, dozing on the sofa as usual, opened one eye & said unexpectedly: 'If Charles has set his heart on her, there is very little that you can do to prevent him.'

'But the disapprobation, the censure of all those whom he respects . . .' objected his wife.

'I cannot precisely *disapprove* of Miss Bennet,' answered he.

The ladies, however, were loud in their lamentations. We have resolved to travel directly to London, to urge Charles to give up both his *inamorata* & the lease on Netherfield.

Edward Hurst has positively refused to forego his last day's shooting & travel with us. He is to join us in a few days. I daresay he is eager to be rid of us, the better to indulge his fancy for that wench below stairs.

END OF PART I

Part II

LONDON

November 28th

An uneventful journey, save that in the carriage Miss Caroline & Mrs Louisa set to & quarrelled violently. I had never heard them thus bicker before—& all about a shawl, which Mrs Louisa accused her Sister of leaving behind on purpose: 'You only did so because the colour is particularly becoming to me!' Miss Caroline retaliated that she was a horrid spiteful thing. I have never seen them behave so. Doubtless it must be the knowledge of their Brother's proposed engagement that makes them thus fretful. I could not help wondering what Miss Elizabeth would have thought had she observed a scene such as this.

I left them at their front door & drove off in some relief to Grosvenor Square, where I found Peebles, already arrived, unpacking my clothes. He too is fretful, having omitted in the flurry of our departure to wrap my spare top-boots in a cloth. He shewed me a small scratch on one heel, & averred that the boots might just as well be thrown away. He so far forgot himself as to mutter that I 'needed *a good tankin*' for hastenin' away so sudden from Netherfield.'

November 29th

Spent today catching up with my affairs in Town, to church & a visit to my Uncle Fitzwilliam.

November 30th

Called at Grosvenor Street before breakfast. Mrs Louisa met me in the hall, & whispered that her Brother was astonished at their unexpected arrival last evening but one. They had explained that they wished to visit some shops & warehouses, & at the same time to keep company with him whilst in Town. I undertook to speak to Charles without delay.

On entering the dining-parlour alone, I found Charles dressed up fine as ninepence. He desired me to share his breakfast. I declined, & as he consumed three cups of chocolate and a mound of buttered toast with an excellent appetite, I sat watching him, amazed that a man could eat so copiously at such an early hour, & wishing that I had not undertaken to enlighten him about Jane. I resolved to wait for a more propitious moment, and, for the present, contented myself with inviting him to share my bachelor quarters in Grosvenor Square: 'It will be more to your taste, I think, than your Sister's home.'

Rising to make himself yet another piece of toast, he prodded me playfully on the back with the toasting-fork: 'None of that, Fitz! I plan to marry soon, remember!'

He told me with great excitement that he had already viewed a number of establishments, & settled on a charming house, just round the corner, off Berkeley Square. He begged me to come & look over it with him. I succeeded in holding him off for the present by advising him to consult his man of business before committing himself: I must have it out with him, before he signs the lease. It was painful to sit at the breakfast table & listen to him vaunting the delights of the property: 'A pleasant, sunny parlour for Jane, and . . .' (he blushed & looked down at the pile of crusts on his plate), 'An upstairs room which would make a capital nursery.'

I have never allowed myself to contemplate married life with any woman. A picture came unbidden to my mind—Miss Elizabeth, holding aloft an infant, smiling up into its face . . . I said resolutely: 'In Heaven's name, why must you rush so at things? You have not yet sought Miss Bennet's hand in marriage.' But he appeared heedless of my words, carried away by the energy of his enthusiasm.

*   *   *

Went with Charles to the play. An unfortunate choice, as it turned out: this season, the new young actor, Macready, is playing Romeo, & the balcony scene drove Charles into a romantic frenzy. The actress performing Juliet is not without charm, but Charles seemed blind to her attractions. His preoccupation was with Romeo alone. 'O, that I had the tongue of a Shakespeare,' he breathed as we emerged from the theatre, & all the way home in the carriage he bent my ear, asking me anxiously whether his Jane would listen favourably to his proposal of marriage, whether his want of eloquence would be fatal to his hopes, &c., &c. I myself had been moved by the play, & had little desire for conversation—but fortunately there was no need for speech, as Charles filled in all my silences with his earnest queries.

December 1st
Byron called today. Once I have done the deed, I may need his help to conquer Charles's despondency. He wished me to accompany him for

an evening's entertainment, promising wine & wenches aplenty. Today I had no inclination for his sport, but instead took him down to the billiard room, & beat him soundly over five frames. He is a poor loser, and, exaggerating his limp, perambulated continually round the table during my every break—hoping, I believe, to distract me from my game.

Charles was from home when Byron came, calling at his tailor's, his shoemaker's & his hatter's to fit himself out for Jane. He returned in time for our evening's outing to Brooks's. He says he is sorry to have missed George Byron: he has scarce set eyes on him since we were all three at school together. 'He always was a devilish giddy fellow,' he laughed. 'I would fain have spent the evening with him. If, as I hope, I am soon to be settled, I must take advantage of what little freedom I have left.' Then he added, more seriously, that of course he dared make no assumption about Jane's inclinations. The rest of the evening was spent with me trying to avoid answering yet more interminable questions: Was not she far too good for him? Did I think she would really have him? &c., &c.

Peebles is vexed—he has discovered a new pair of shagreen gloves crumpled in my coat pocket. He says they are now unwearable, & that it is shockingly careless of me. I do not remember doing this—it must have been during the play.

December 2nd
To church in the morning. The text of the sermon was Love Thine Enemy (I happen to know that the vicar here has French Cousins). Spent the day at

64

home with Charles. Edwardes called, & attempted to interest Charles in a discussion of Perceval's budget, & whether it is advisable for him to act as Chancellor as well as Prime Minister (I personally continue to have the gravest doubts). Impossible to draw Charles out on this—he gazes dreamily out of the window at the bare trees in the square.

We visited the Hursts for supper. Both Mrs Louisa & Miss Caroline made haste to take me aside, on the feeblest of pretexts, to enquire whether I had already spoken to Charles. I demurred that it was preferable to wait 'til the time was ripe: he is deep in love, & may brush my objections aside. Miss Caroline humphed, & vouchsafed that she herself would perform the unpleasant task, if I could not bring myself to do it. Edward Hurst has still not returned from Netherfield: he writes that he intends to continue there a further week, to take advantage of the shooting—& doubtless other advantages too. He is not much missed here. I must ask him when he returns if he has seen any of our acquaintance in Hertfordshire.

Charles's Sisters are quite right: I am delaying because I cannot bear to dash Charles's hopes of happiness. How will he feel once all his prospects are blighted, & by me?

After supper, Miss Caroline opened her workbox, & took out her needlework, a piece of white stuff. Seeing me observe her, she told me that '*It was an altar-cloth for the church*,' & added, 'Pray have no fear! Your slippers are not forgot. Were it not the Sabbath, I should be working on them even now.'

December 3rd

Today I lured Charles to Jackson's early, & we sparred. He had wished to visit some warehouses to make further purchases for his marriage, but then realized that if he were out of condition, he should be ashamed to appear before his lady-love: 'Look here! I am acquiring a paunch! It is a repulsive sight! What shall I do?' exclaimed he, pinching an inch or two of flesh between his fingers.

I was resolved on doing the deed that very day. There was no point in putting it off. The moment came after breakfast. I had received a letter from Georgie, & removed upstairs to the Library to read it. Charles came bounding up after me, humming a tune. I believe it was 'Sir Roger de Coverley'. I turned to him, the open letter in my hand. Charles stopped on the threshold, looking from me to the letter.

'I fear I have sad news for you,' I said. My serious tone stopped him short. He fixed his eyes apprehensively on the letter. His look was pitiful, but I hardened my heart. 'I have learnt,' said I, 'that Miss Bennet's attachment to you is not entirely disinterested.'

There was a silence, in which Charles continued to stare at me as if he could not comprehend my words. Then he whispered, 'What do you mean?'

I told him then that Jane's interest was not in his person, but in his fortune, & that I had an Officer's word of honour that it was so. When he vouchsafed no reply, I gave him some further explanations. He collapsed in a chair, his head in his hands; as I moved towards him to place my hand on his shoulder, I was smitten with grief for him & shame at what I had done. I could not touch him. I am a disgraceful coward—but I am, I hope, acting for the best.

I removed downstairs to the drawing-room with my letter. I was aware that Charles had assumed it was come from Meryton. For some minutes after I had opened it I was unable to take in its import: Georgiana is arriving next week, with Mrs Annesley. She tells me to warn Bolton & Jennings that she is bringing, in addition, three servants.

December 4th
To Jackson's alone in the morning for a few bouts. On returning I half expected Charles to eschew breakfast. But he came down, heavy-eyed & mournful. He waited 'til Bolton had brought in the coffee-pots, then asked pathetically whether my information was really true, & from whom I had it. I told him, 'One of the Officers.' He did not ask which one, but nodded a few times, then lapsed into silence, toying with a piece of dry toast. I too remained silent, remembering the Netherfield ball.

*   *   *

Charles has come to me, insisting that he disbelieves everything I have told him of Jane. He waved his arms angrily. His coat was buttoned up awry. I have never seen him thus moved. I was obliged to furnish him with the details: that Jane has long since set her cap at an Officer named Tully, is already involved in a flirtation with him, & that this fact is by now common knowledge among the Officers at Meryton. He questioned me no further, but drooped visibly. I tried not to notice, but could not help observing that he was almost in tears.

I truly wish that I had not been obliged to do it—but I owed it to my poor friend. How could he have been happy, married to such as her? It is fortunate indeed that I overheard those Officers revealing the truth about her character.

But it grieves me sorely to give my friend such pain.

December 5th
Charles is sleeping late, and, indeed, has not come down to breakfast. I know not whether to go up & encourage him to leave his chamber.

*   *   *

Georgiana has arrived at last—but so changed, so thin! Even her hair seems darker & somehow more lifeless. Her face is pale, & she has scarce met my gaze all evening. At first, I hoped that she was merely tired & listless after the long journey from Derbyshire, & encouraged her to remove to her chamber to rest before dinner. But during the evening, things were much the same. She spoke but little, & appeared absorbed in cutting up small pieces of fowl to feed to Mignon under the table. Everything was '*delightful*'. That is almost the only word she has spoke—about her parlour, which I have had redecorated for her with the most modern appointments; about the dinner, for which Jennings cooked a pigeon pie & pancakes, her favourite dishes; about the new books I have procured for her, including a signed copy of Byron's poems; about the invitations & vouchers I have obtained for her. *'Delightful'*, in a small, flat voice. I had hoped that by now she would have regained her spirits, but the hurt seemingly goes far deeper than even I expected.

I took advantage of her absence to interview Mrs Annesley, whose good sense & judgment seem exemplary, tho' thankfully she remains unaware of the true nature of G's trouble. She reports that ever since she took up her post in August G has been thus out of sorts, but that lately she has revived a little. Can my Sister really have been worse than this, & for months together? I should have ignored her request that I stay away. I should have come to her at Pemberley: I could always have pretended that I was come on business.

It is only as I write that I realize that I have not seen Charles all day. He has kept to his room, & partaken of no sustenance. He did not even see fit to come down & greet G.

December 9th
The last few days have been trying ones. Charles is deep in gloom. I make strenuous attempts to keep his spirits up: my forced jocularity strikes even me as painful. From time to time he rouses himself to make some pleasant remark to my Sister, but is unable to sustain a conversation, & leaves the room.

Last night I took a box at the play (*Hamlet* this time), & coaxed them both out, making up a party with Miss Caroline & Mrs Louisa. The latter's Husband is expected back from Netherfield on Wednesday, I am told. Georgie was overwhelmed by Macready's performance. She turned to me with shining eyes & whispered, 'This is truly beautiful.'

Charles remained silent all evening.

To church today with G. Sermon on how the Lord's hand is visible everywhere in the book of Nature.

December 13th

This last week has passed in a whirl of activity. Every day I have devised entertainments for my two malcontents: in the morning sparring with Charles, or a bout of shooting practice, or fencing at Angelo's. On several occasions we accompanied Georgiana and Miss Caroline, riding in the Park. Charles is become impossibly absent-minded: three times, when I got him up on horseback, he was almost thrown; once, he forgot his hat. After the rides, we repaired home for a nuncheon, & thereafter I twice escorted Georgiana & Mrs Annesley on a visit to the shops & warehouses. G is far from indifferent to the new fashions; she visits Bond Street assiduously—tho' more inclined to go there with Mrs Annesley than with Miss Caroline, despite the latter's obliging offer to accompany her. G does not seem to value her friendship greatly—but then G is but a child.

In the evenings, I have endeavoured to procure company for G, since she cannot yet attend grown-up parties. One evening, Charles & I escorted the ladies to the play, & another day on a visit to Mr Greene's Museum. For next week, I have arranged a visit to the Royal Menagerie, where I believe they keep a giraffe, a cheetah, lions & an elephant. I am rewarded by seeing the colour beginning to return to G's cheeks—tho' I long for a solitary ride, & some peaceful reading. I do believe that the change of environment, the delights of the London warehouses & visits to her friends are beginning gradually to improve G's spirits; but even as she mends, Charles grows more cast down.

Once she is safely a-bed, it is Charles's turn to benefit from my attentions. I have staid up late with him every night: he says he cannot sleep, so I do my best to distract him. We have been to Brooks's, where we partook of a late supper of boiled fowl with oyster-sauce. We have gambled at White's; looked in at the Cocoa-Tree where we met Andrewes & Wolstenholme; visited Boodle's twice, where Charles lost heavily at piquet. Next week, Byron has promised us a visit to Watier's to see His Royal Highness the Prince of Wales playing at cards. They say His Royal Highness is about to be made the official Regent of this Realm, if it has not already happened.

I am fatigued with clubs. These nights of dissipation do not suit my humour in the least. Still, needs must. Besides, they take my mind off my own preoccupations.

December 17th
Somewhat to my surprize, Edward Hurst, on his return from Netherfield, has come to call on me early, Charles being still a-bed. I suspect that Edward is frequently thus from home; doubtless he wishes to keep away from his lady & her too-pertinent enquiries as to his activities during his lonely stay in Hertfordshire. In passing I asked him, did he catch sight of the Bennets of Longbourn while he was there? He told me that he had communicated with none of our acquaintance, and, indeed, suspected that no body knew that he

had staid behind. He concluded by offering to take over the duty of entertaining Charles for a few days, & purposes to carry him back to Grosvenor Street.

I confess that I am almost relieved to be free of my poor friend for a while. G has been invited to spend Christmas with my Uncle & Aunt Fitzwilliam. I think that she should be quite safe there, with Mrs Annesley as chaperone. My youngest Cousin, Augusta, is almost exactly the same age. I believe I may make a rapid visit to Pemberley. There is much business to attend to there; & I miss the place. Besides, it has always been my duty to bring Christmas chear to the villagers, & I see no reason to make an exception of this year. I set forth tomorrow with only Peebles for company.

December 20th

The journey has been long & cold, but I fired up by my longing to be home. As I rode in, met old Cubley, who asked me: '*Airthikaypin Sorrey*?' & drew Peebles away to drink ale in the kitchens. The house is welcoming, the Great Hall already garlanded with evergreens. The servants all lined up to greet me as if I had been absent for years. I write this seated in my own Library, by my own fire. Rufus's head rests on my knee—he has missed me all these months, Pargeter says. He is beginning to show grey hairs about the muzzle. Reynolds served up a prime sirloin, from our own cattle, fed on Hopton's new winter fodder—a marvel. I am alone & at peace. I know that I will have much to attend to, but nothing can mar this first evening. Tomorrow I do the rounds of the estate with

Pargeter. Tonight I can enjoy being alone. I have taken from the shelves an old copy of Ld. Verulam's *Essayes*—full of antick wisdom. [Omitted: three days filled with details of Darcy's visits to the cottages in the village, plans for repairs to the roofs; projects for a new village hall; provision made for the care of a newly orphaned family of children; with Pargeter he oversees the estate's efforts to grow winter wheat; he tours his woodlands with his gamekeeper, Dovedale—they wonder what to do about prosecuting poachers (Dovedale in favour of denunciation every time, Darcy prefers to consider each case on its merits); visits from neighbouring gentry; pressing invitations to join them for Christmas, all of which Darcy refuses; frequent shooting expeditions with his gamekeeper; and, every day, long rides over the peaks.]

December 24th
Hoping to meet Pargeter today to discuss business, but it being the Christmas holiday I did not wish to draw him from his family.

Parson Bright & his family invited over for dinner, after the mummers' play in the Great Hall (*St George of England* as usual), & presents for the villagers. The Parson's youngest daughter Isabella, G's friend, has turned out pretty, with very fair hair. Pert & forward, too. Waits & carol singers; posset & mince pies ('*onkins*') for all. This year, Pargeter arranged for me to give the village boys hobby-horses & the little girls hoops, whereat they all began to practise their '*baawlin*' round the Hall. Reynolds was shooing them off the polished floors, flapping her silk apron at them. For the older children, picture-books to encourage their reading. Reynolds has bought fine wool shawls for the women, & new caps for the men. After I had distributed the presents, the villagers thanked me prettily, & a small boy (I think the Tomkins's youngest) darted forward & whispered enthusiastically in my ear, '*It wer a cok-bod!*'

December 25th
Christmas Day, alone at Pemberley! I anticipate a strange but pleasant experience—utterly unlike last year's house-party, which filled every chamber in the place. I feel no anxiety for G in London with the Fitzwilliam Cousins: theirs should prove a large & merry party. And as for poor Charles—my presence would have done nothing to lighten his mood.

*   *   *

To church, quite alone, both in the carriage & in my pew. Parson Bright delivered a more pompous sermon than usual on Charity. His homilies about sacrificing all to help the poor sounded absurdly from his fleshy, well-nourished person—& I remembered the three helpings of roast beef he consumed last evening. How Miss Elizabeth would have smiled to hear him! I had banished her from my mind these last weeks. The remembrance of her smote me—I was not expecting it, had no inkling of how it would affect me. I was forced to hold my hand over my heart to still its pounding.

There has been no more peace for me this day. Evening alone by the fire with Rufus by my side & Mr Walter Scott's new book in my hand—I read

74

but little, but stared into the flames. Again she arose unbidden to my mind. I almost felt her presence.

What is the matter with me? This solitude is dangerous. I had much better return to London.

December 26th
Woke to find the country white & silent: a heavy snowfall during the night. Rode to hounds with the Pemberley Hunt. I offered the stirrup cup on our front lawn. When the snow is melted, Cucklett will doubtless be furious at the hoofprints on the grass. Belle very skittish—most unlike her usual self. She has been exercised every day, or so Young Joe assures me, but nevertheless twice refused at the hawthorn hedge bordering Rowtor Bottom, & made strenuous attempts to throw me. I daresay that it is pointless to keep a hunter when I so rarely have the opportunity to ride her; but Belle is an old friend to me. I still entertain the hope that one day I may be happily settled at Pemberley, with but few excursions up to Town, riding daily & keeping company to my animals & my household. But for that I need a Wife . . .

Today I long to stay in this place—a day's hard riding has entirely supplanted Miss Elizabeth Bennet in my mind. Yet I feel the peril of her remembrance even now. I shall depart as soon as the thaw sets in.

December 27th–January 8th
I prefer not to dwell on these last days: snowed in at Pemberley, I have been unable to rid myself of the impression that Miss E is somehow present in the house. Have attempted to distract myself:

ordered better fireplaces for servants' bedrooms; discussed tenancies with Pargeter on at least three occasions; managed to ride to the village twice; visited the Nutbeams again & made further provisions for their material welfare following their recent bereavement; engaged Corby to make ornamental railings to go round the family monument; to please Hopton, agreed to the purchase of a boar & three sows—Yorkshire Old Spots. I have also commissioned architect's plans from Cumberbatch for the new ballroom wing.

January 9th

The snow is melting, but Reynolds & Tuffnell have continually begged me not to leave Pemberley yet, insisting that it is madness to travel in such atrocious weather. Peebles shaved me this morning in disapproving silence: he has a vicious way with the razor-strop when in a fit of the sulks. But I cannot remain a single day longer. The snow having melted, I am no longer trapped. This place is too full of phantasms. Peebles muttered that such sudden disruption was too bad at his age. Indeed, his Sister lives in the village, & he was doubtless intending to spend more time with her. I asked him about her. She is still coming up to the house to mend the linen, tho' her eyes are troubling her with the fine work. I gave him some days' leave to be with her, & money for a good pair of spectacles for her. He will be returning alone by the Stage. I had difficulty persuading him: he seems convinced that I will be unequal to the task of dressing myself for a whole week! I write this in the Library as they harness the carriage, & Peebles puts the finishing touches to my luggage. I shall miss poor Rufus, who sits with his muzzle on my knee, as if to pin me down & prevent me from departing.

January 16th
It has been a long & difficult journey. The weather turned cold again, the snow came down, & on the first day I battled through the blizzard for nigh on six hours, & took the only sleeping quarters I could find along the road. Poor Smalley well-nigh frozen to death that evening, after a day's sitting on the box; the horses not much better. After spending the night in a wretched inn, I woke to find myself snowed in. Unable to move for a full five days. At least I could read, with profit, Verulam, which I had brought with me.

On reaching London, I find G much improved; she has enjoyed a convivial Christmas & New Year with her Cousins. We have dined together, alone save for Mrs Annesley, who continues sensible & trustworthy. Charles of course has spent Christmas with his family in Grosvenor Street, so he cannot dampen our spirits by his mournful presence.

G's pleasure at my return distracted me from my imaginings of Miss Elizabeth; after dinner I sat but a short while alone with my Port Wine; afterwards G performed on the pianoforte, which completed my cure. I am persuaded that my phantasy represented the dying throes of a most ill-judged infatuation. I shall not think of Miss Elizabeth Bennet again.

January 17th
London still cold, tho' the snow turns to slush almost as soon as it falls. To Jackson's for an

hour's sport, where I met Algy Fitchett & learned of the scandal of the proposed Regency Bill. Apparently, the Prime Minister has informed His Royal Highness that his powers as Regent will be subject to those of Parliament; naturally the Prince is not best pleased.

I thence repaired to Grosvenor Street to see how Charles does. They were all at home, & invited me in to breakfast. I had forgot how tall Miss Caroline is—I was quite surprized when she rose from the table. I now recollect her perambulation around the drawing-room at Netherfield, arm in arm with Miss Elizabeth . . . She made a discreet sign to me to follow her. There was indeed little need for such caution, as Charles sat with eyes downcast throughout the repast. He seems even harder hit than I feared, & taking an inordinate time to recover his spirits.

I followed Miss Caroline to the chilly back parlour, where the fire had only just been lit. She invited me to sit; then, with an air of importance, took from her reticule a letter, & handed it to me. I began to read, then stopped, in some dismay. Suspecting who the correspondent was, I turned over the page to see the signature: *Yours, &c., Jane Bennet*. It is too bad. No sooner have I resolved to put the Hertfordshire episode behind me than I must be reminded of it.

There was worse to come. On perusing the whole of Miss Bennet's letter, I found no mention of her Sister, but instead some most alarming news: by the time her letter arrives she herself will already be in London!

'What is to be done?' asked Miss Caroline. 'Jane will undoubtedly pay us a call.'

78

'The bad weather may have prevented her journey.'

'I believe it was accomplished before the cold came down: her letter has taken some time to reach us.'

'Could not you pretend to be from home?'

'That is what Louisa suggests,' she replied, ringing for a servant, whom she dispatched to find her Sister.

We three discussed the matter at length. Miss Caroline was steadfast in her refusal to *'insult a lady with whom they had been on intimate terms'*.

'But what are we to do about Charles?' asked Mrs Louisa. 'If we encourage the connexion, we shall be obliged to inform him that she is in Town.'

I was against this notion. Charles is already so perturbed, that this further twist would distress him beyond measure. At the back of my mind was a more disturbing thought: once Charles set eyes on his Jane, would not he forget all my warnings, & forthwith renew his suit? It is imperative to preserve him from the scheming Miss Bennet.

Louisa is clearly of the same mind. 'Remember that monstrous Mother of hers, those loud, vulgar Sisters!' she insisted. 'Do you wish his infatuation to continue? Be reasonable, Caroline!'

How great a change of attitude, coming from one who had been the most ardent champion of her *'dearest Jane'*!

We have finally agreed on a compromise: Miss Bennet's presence in London is to be kept secret from Charles; Miss Caroline will receive her alone when she makes her visit, on which occasion Miss Caroline must adopt a discouraging manner, in the hopes of preventing any further calls. She must furthermore delay returning Jane's call, to show how little she values the friendship. 'It helps that Jane will be staying in Gracechurch Street, a part of London with which you are unfamiliar,' added Mrs Louisa.

Miss Caroline rose & paced about the room, twisting her hands together anxiously. 'But if she comes to this house, how shall we prevent Charles from catching sight of her?' asked she.

'He had best come back to stay with me,' said I, suppressing a shameful reluctance to take on the burden of Charles once more.

Mrs Louisa clappt her hands together. 'That is a capital notion!' she exclaimed. 'I only hope he will agree to it.'

There was little doubt of that: at present Charles shows but scant enterprise. He dolefully obeys every injunction, with a continuing want of spirit.

We left it at that. Jane will surely not call for a few days; in the meantime we can effect the removal of Charles to Grosvenor Square.

Who knows, the presence of Georgie under the same roof may eventually distract him from his thoughts of Jane! That would be my dearest wish—& I suspect that his Sisters may share my hopes. But that must be in the distant future. G is still so young, poor child!

January 18th
Peebles is returned, & has lost no time in pointing out that my unseemly haste to leave Pemberley gained me no more than an extra day in London. *His* journey from Derbyshire was rapid & uneventful, *mine* fraught with difficulty. I cannot

deny that I am pleased to see him.

Today, after some target practice, I went round to Grosvenor Street to invite Charles to stay. I found him in the small parlour, sitting over some documents. 'My man of business has called with these for me to deal with,' said he fretfully. 'I cannot seem to fix my attention on such matters.'

'Let me assist you,' I offered. We spent the next hour attending to his papers, which, despite his neglect, are in good order. His late Father seems to have left his affairs in the hands of an excellent agent—which is fortunate both for Charles & for his Sisters.

Afterwards I coaxed him to return with me to Grosvenor Square. 'You will be more at ease there, & we can plan our days together.'

He shrugged. 'What's the use of planning? One day is much the same as any other.'

'It would be a pleasure for me to have your company.'

He looked up then, & gave me a twisted smile. I was surprized at its bitterness. 'Very well. It's all the same to me,' said he.

I persuaded him to instruct his man to pack his effects, & took him straight back home with me.

G did not dine at home this evening. She was visiting at my Uncle Fitzwilliam's, & has informed me that our Cousin James is expected home soon on furlough. G is often abroad these days. Her newly found appetite for enjoyment gives me nothing but pleasure. I believe her to be well supervized by my Aunt. I took Charles off to Jackson's, then we visited the Cocoa-Tree. Bullivant was there. He has heard that His Majesty continues mad: the Prince of Wales's appointment as Regent is imminent.

Charles revived somewhat after a few glasses of hot toddy, & sang snatches of 'The Lincolnshire Poacher' on the way home.

January 19th

G out early with Mrs Annesley to buy a new bonnet. She says she feels very grown-up having her own milliner, & proudly showed me that lady's bill, which seems very large for a young girl, not yet Out; but G has her own fortune, & may spend her money as she pleases. Charles & I to Cox's for marksmanship practice. I note that exercise always improves his mood, so we went riding 'til dinner-time. To the Opera in the evening in Lady Redwood's party. I have not seen the theatre since it was rebuilt: it is now very fine, & the boxes lined with red velvet. We saw one of the late Herr Handel's operas—*Rolando*—or some such name—followed by a performance on the tightrope by Madame Scacchi. Charles shewed some interest in this performer, who wore a revealing flesh-pink spangled costume.

January 20th

I really do detect a lightening of Charles's mood—at last! He sparred with enthusiasm at Jackson's, & ate almost his customary quantities for breakfast, during which he mentioned Madame Scacchi twice (G being from the room).

Byron came. Charles reminded him that they have not met for years. Byron told us that he is thinking of making his maiden speech in the Upper House. When that happens, he says he intends to invite us to attend in the Visitors' Gallery. He further suggests that I too might consider standing for Parliament. When I mentioned that I have a Pocket Borough in my gift, he instructed me to give it to myself! Charles warmly seconded him. Part of me is attracted by this proposal; but my duty is surely to Pemberley. If I undertake to represent Hognaworth, I must be always at Westminster instead of supervising the management of my estates. I am interested to know why Byron thus advised me: his actions always have an ulterior motive. Maybe he desires an ally in the Commons? I do not think that I shall act on his suggestion.

Byron accompanied us to White's. Afterwards, he announced that he was about to visit his favourite house of fornication, & carelessly suggested that we might accompany him. Charles seemed almost inclined to accept; but he finally refused, and, since I am humouring him these days, we both returned home unsatisfied.

And *she*—how her eyes would have sparkled at the absurdity of my electing myself as Member of Parliament for my own Borough!

January 21st
On returning from Jackson's before breakfast, as Peebles was helping me into my coat, Bolton brought up a card: Miss Caroline. What could she be thinking of, visiting alone, at this hour? I thought we told her yesterday that Charles would be abroad all morning. He is gone to Angelo's for fencing practice.

Bolton had shewn her into the morning-room. She was seated on the edge of an upright chair, tyeing & untyeing the ribbons of her bonnet.

'Alone, Miss Caroline?' I asked. Such a want of propriety was astonishing in a lady so punctilious.

She made a gesture, as tho' brushing aside my scruples, & began untyeing her bonnet-strings again. 'Louisa has an engagement, & the business cannot wait.'

'Why? What has happened?'

'Jane paid a call on me yesterday.'

I managed to say, with a tolerable show of indifference: 'How fortunate then that Charles is staying here with me.'

'I know. He could easily have dropt by—indeed, I was half expecting him yesterday. I was in such a flutter, you cannot imagine. I made sure I should faint on the spot.' She leant forward & laid her gloved hand on my arm.

'What happened then?'

'I was so discomposed that I was quite unable to collect myself. I attempted to explain away my confusion by attributing it to extreme surprize, & pretended that her letter had not reached me. I could think of no better solution on the spur of the moment.'

'What did Miss Bennet tell you?'

'That she is staying in London 'til March. How are we to keep them apart?' Her voice was shrill.

'Oh, London is a big place, & we frequent very different circles, I daresay,' said I reassuringly.

'You do not know the half of it. She mentioned that she is going to the play this very evening. *Romeo & Juliet*!'

This is grave news indeed. Charles has been so insistent that he wishes to see the play once more, that I have bespoken a box for him & me this evening also. I have done so with some reluctance:

I find his fascination for this play somewhat morbid. I understood now why Miss Caroline had defied convention to come to me.

'What must we do?' asked she, at the ribbons of her bonnet again. They were growing sadly creased.

'Let me think.' I rang for Bolton, & ordered ratafia for the lady. In truth, I had no notion how to proceed.

'I could pretend to be ill, & summon him to my bedside,' she suggested.

'But how could you sustain the pretence? Your illness would have to be as acute as it is sudden.'

'I could tell him that I had fallen downstairs.'

I suppressed a smile. 'Would you then simulate a limp for days together, & paint yourself all over with bruises?'

She fell to wringing her gloved hands. 'Do you have any better suggestion?'

I considered the possibilities in my mind. Fill him so full of brandy that he is too befuddled to go abroad? Pretend that I am ill or distressed myself, & wish to stay at home? Request his presence as G's escort to some evening function? Each option seems more absurd than the last. I said; 'Leave everything to me,' but try as I may, I cannot find out what is best to do.

As she rose to leave, Miss Caroline murmured, 'Jane looked much as usual. She certainly did not appear to be languishing after Charles, tho' she did enquire after him—& after Louisa & Edward, of course.'

In the doorway she paused again, & said, 'She was wearing a pink bonnet. Imagine! Pink! This season! It looked ridiculous, for all she is a pretty girl.'

I escorted Miss Caroline to the door, & handed her into her carriage. As she seated herself, she said, 'Seeing her has quite unnerved me, Mr Darcy. In appearance she is so gentle & unassuming, that it is well-nigh impossible to credit her with licentious behaviour such as you have described. Indeed, the situation pains me—for all her manifest iniquities, I cannot help but feel as though I am deceiving a friend.' She pressed my hand. I stared at her in some surprize, remembering her former vituperations against Jane. Despite her fair words, her face shewed but little compassion. Nevertheless, I agree with her. It is demeaning to have to behave so ill.

*   *   *

More through luck than judgment, I have succeeded in keeping Charles & Jane apart. In the end I could think of no better solution than to seek him out & inform him that Macready is indisposed, & the performance cancelled. Charles questioned me, & I was obliged to pretend that I had got it from someone at Brooks's. I told him I did not know the fellow's name. It is mortifying to have to lie to a friend—as Miss Caroline says.

I gave him a good dinner, & promised him tickets for the next available performance. He was quite chearful this evening. He tucked into a joint of Pemberley beef with horseradish which Pargeter sent up with Peebles. I must congratulate Jennings: she roasted it to perfection.

Let us hope that Miss Bennet's hosts have the good sense to keep her from public places in future. These machinations are far too complicated & far too risky—but cannot be avoided, since an unexpected meeting would undoubtedly exacerbate poor Charles's distemper.

January 22nd
Charles still a-bed. To church alone with G, she clad in a most becoming pelisse of midnight blue, with matching bonnet, & a muff to protect her hands from the cold. She grows into a fine-looking girl; I observed that she was much admired by several young gentlemen in church: they are of course unaware that she is scarce sixteen. It is a great relief to see her once more in looks, & to know that her spirits are so improved. I only hope that nothing occurs to dampen her new-found chearfulness.

Yet another sermon on charity, after Parson Bright's homily on Christmas Day. G, who really seems quite merry today, whispered to me that *'Charity begins at home, & she would very much like a dappled mare like her Cousin Augusta's.'* I smiled, & agreed to purchase one for her. I shall have to ask around for a good, tractable animal. G is an accomplished rider, but the streets of London are always full of unexpected hazards. Only yesterday I heard that Tom Bullivant's horse, taking fright at a street-crier, bolted & threw its rider, who has three fractured ribs & a broken collar-bone.

January 23rd
I have resolved that Charles must have more substantial distraction to banish his thoughts of Miss Jane Bennet once & for all. I am wondering whether to take him abroad for a spell of foreign

travel. Have sent to Byron, who knows about such things after visiting Greece & Arabia, requesting a private interview to discuss the matter, & have received a curt reply: *'Let me come to you. You must not see what establishment I keep.'* I take it he refers to a woman, whose presence he wishes to conceal.

* * *

I have set the problem before Byron. He grew very mirthful: 'So Charles fancies himself in love? He always was a sentimental fool. We'll wean him of his grand passion in a trice!'

He gave as his opinion that to journey to the continent would be impractical. The whole of Europe is so unsettled, with Bonaparte rampaging over country after country, that travellers can nowhere be in surety. We would need to cross to Belgium, from thence to Switzerland & Italy—& Boney is known to have designs on Italy. For my part I should welcome the experience, but with Charles in his present state, it would be difficult.

Byron proposed instead to introduce Charles to some charmer who will prove an effective distraction, & undertook to find one out. 'However, we shall not resort to the *bordello*. Charles wants a more serious romance with a young lady who will at first seem propriety itself, but later will know when to succumb to the urgings of a young man of fortune. He may then set her up in an establishment of her own, & lavish on her all the affection he has hitherto reserved for this— Jane, was not that it?'

I was so taken aback by this suggestion that I

could find no words. What an exploitation of a young man's innocence! Poor Charles—at Byron's hands, he may well be transformed into a libertine like his Lordship himself. Furthermore, there are other, practical disadvantages to this cynical plan: the 'charmer' is very like to fleece my poor friend of considerable sums; my hopes that Charles might some day acquire an interest in Georgiana will likely be dashed; & then, how to keep such a development from his Sisters?

In one respect & one alone Byron's plan leaves me happier. I have been dreadfully uneasy at the thought of travelling abroad, leaving G alone but for Mrs Annesley.

As I can think of no better solution at present, I have reluctantly allowed Byron to proceed. He purposes to approach an actress of his acquaintance, & seek her help in procuring for Charles the ideal mistress.

January 24th
Last night I dreamt I saw a figure in the distance, walking away from me down a moonlit country road. When I caught up I saw that it was Miss Elizabeth. She glanced at me sideways, without turning her head. Her dark eyes were so beautiful they gave me pain. I dared not address her, but walked on, leaving her behind in the shadows. When I woke I was sensible of a void inside me. Must she thus preoccupy my thoughts?

Out of sorts all morning because of my dream.

*   *   *

A note from Byron, inviting Charles & myself to a

89

dinner in Town. He plans a sumptuous repast—he says it ought to be sufficiently lavish to seem memorable to Charles. I offered him 50*l.* as a contribution—I know that he is deep in debt. He refused my money with something like contempt.

Of course I cannot take Miss Caroline into my confidence *re* Byron's scheme. Such matters must not be put baldly before ladies. It will perhaps be sufficient to inform her that we are acting for the best. Would that I could be certain that it is so!

*   *   *

The lady destined for Charles turns out to be dangerously alluring. Before presenting us to her, Byron whispered to Charles that she is a Mrs Winter, *'a young widow of independent means'*. Later, in private, he will doubtless tell *me* a different story. Mrs Winter was accompanied by her Cousin, an equally handsome young woman. We dined at a Lady Foxton's. I am informed by Byron that this lady is not above lending her presence to gatherings of a doubtful character, but her establishment has all the outward appearance of gentility. I suspect that Charles has no notion of the reality of the situation. The dinner was elegant: we were served lobster, ices & fine French wines. By candlelight, Charles's widow is ravishing—a dark beauty with golden-brown eyes & a white skin, infinitely more spirited than the placid Miss Bennet. She monopolized Charles for the whole evening, he proved suitably attentive, & I heard him laugh aloud on several occasions. Meanwhile, I was entertained by the Cousin, Miss Anstruther, who, as I could not help observing, was wearing a becomingly low-cut gown, with a striped turban over her dark curls. She has a strong cleft chin. She teazingly accused me of an excess of gravity, but, indeed, I have little inclination for levity these days. She finally grew quite put out at my want of sociability.

Afterwards, we three gentlemen climbed into Byron's carriage (an abominably ostentatious equipage, upholstered in crimson velvet) to take a late-night drink at Brooks's. I murmured to Byron: 'Confess it, George! You intended Miss Anstruther for me.'

He vouchsafed no reply, merely shrugged.

'You will not catch me so easily,' I informed him.

Charles & I eventually left Byron at Brooks's & repaired home to my house. Charles was a trifle foxed; he held my arm to steady himself. Walking down King Street, he said: 'If you imagine that I am so taken with that young lady, Mrs Winter, as to forget Miss Jane Bennet even for one minute, you are greatly mistaken.'

It was the first time he had mentioned Jane to me since I convinced him that she must be given up. Poor Charles. If only his Jane had been worthy of him!

January 25th
Yesterday I neglected G, occupied as I was with Charles. Today I resolved to make up for my want of attention. After I had put in some fencing practice at Angelo's, my Sister & I ate breakfast together & rode in the Park. She is now much improved: indeed, I fear that she outdoes me in spirits.

I have been catching up on my own affairs. I

91

have written at some length to Pargeter & to my bankers. I have also received a letter from my Aunt Catherine, reminding me that I am expected at Rosings in two weeks' time—I am under orders not to fail her. She writes that she is, as usual, planning improvements to the house, which she has postponed 'til after my departure. I have mentioned to G that she might care to come down to Kent with me; but she is reluctant to part from my merry Cousin Augusta, and, besides, she does not deal well with my Aunt de Bourgh or with my Cousin Anne. During my absence, she & Mrs Annesley are to move into Fitzwilliam House.

January 26th
Today visited the late Dr Hunter's curious collection of medical specimens. Byron told me about it the other day. I alluded to it in passing to Miss Caroline & Mrs Louisa. After that I had no peace 'til I undertook to arrange a visit for them. At present the collection is housed in an ill-lit basement—but a Museum is planned soon.

It has been a most disturbing visit. The collection is wholly unsuitable for ladies' eyes. Again & again I attempted to shield my two companions from the glass cases. I had them one on each arm, they uttering little cries of alarm at the macabre specimens. I could only thank providence that I had excluded G from this expedition. I think I shall never forget Miss Caroline's distressed face turned towards me and, behind her head, a row of glass jars, in each of which floated an unborn child.

As we passed a half-dissected arm, the tendons skilfully laid out for our scrutiny, she remarked that the time was long overdue for returning Miss Bennet's call. 'I do not wish to be discourteous,' she added. I nodded, distracted by a lump of yellow matter in a bottle. I fell to wondering what it might be—a growth? A wen?—then realized that Miss Caroline was waiting for my reply. When I remained silent, she continued: 'I dread having to pay Jane a courtesy call, which would undoubtedly involve lying about Charles; yet I fear that postponing my visit would seem unpardonably discourteous.'

I peered over her shoulder at a statuette of a Chinaman. Clinging to his waxen body was a curled-up infant. I could not help myself—I moved forward to read the label, which informed me that image was the perfect likeness of a poor soul born with his own half-developed twin attached to his body. As he grew to maturity, so the little succubus remained in place, neither dead nor alive, feeding off his blood. Presumably it lived with him and, at his death, was buried with him.

'Do not you look at this,' I begged them. I saw Mrs Louisa's eyes turn towards the statue in an involuntary movement. She looked away again immediately. 'Imagine what it must be like, dusting this collection,' she whispered to her Sister.

I endeavoured to distract them by bringing their attention back to Miss Jane. 'In my opinion, it would be as well to delay returning her call for a further week,' said I.

'But why is that? What can we gain by an act of wanton discourtesy?'

'It will make it plain to the young lady that you are far from eager to continue the acquaintance.'

'Poor Jane! She will be surprized & hurt at our

want of manners,' observed Miss Caroline, unusually considerate. I wondered if the specimens were affecting her. She need not feel such concern: Miss Jane Bennet has, I am sure, other suitors in the offing, & will forget Charles when there is no further intercourse between them.

January 27th
Byron has contrived a second meeting between Charles & the widow, Mrs Winter. It is to happen *'by chance'*. I am to persuade Charles to visit Astley's Royal Amphitheatre this evening. He is a great lover of horseflesh, & Byron has told him that the performing horses are remarkable in every respect.

Unfortunately, G, on hearing of the proposed expedition, expressed a strong desire to accompany us. This will not do at all: she cannot be permitted to keep company with the likes of Mrs Winter & her fair 'Cousin'. Fortunately Mrs Annesley reminded her that she is already engaged to spend the evening with her Cousin Augusta.

G was quite put out. She said: 'I have never been to Astley's! Cannot I come with you, Fitz? I can see Augusta any day.'

Mrs Annestley ventured that Lady Augusta would rightly be affronted at such cavalier treatment: 'It is now too late for her to make other plans for the evening.'

'O, could not we invite Augusta too?'

Worst was to come when Charles joined in the conversation, offering to put off the visit to another day, when G would be free. I have had to agree to go again with her to Astley's next week. I told Charles that I particularly wished to go this evening, as there was to be a special demonstration of dressage with Lippizan horses from Spain.

G, who is a docile child at heart, has acknowledged that engagements must be kept.

*　　　*　　　*

G has set off for Augusta's with Mrs Annesley. Byron will shortly come to fetch us.

*　　　*　　　*

The new Amphitheatre is very large & crowded: you can scarce see the horses cavorting in the distance. I had no notion how we should meet with the ladies. However, Byron arranged everything. They had seats not far from us, & very prettily expressed their astonishment at the fortunate coincidence of our meeting. Somewhat to my surprize, I was very taken with the performing horses, fine beasts which can canter & even turn on one spot.

We prevailed on the Widow & her Cousin to take some refreshments afterwards; Byron had bespoke a private dining parlour for us, & the ladies made no objection to being of our party.

During our supper I overheard Mrs Winter expressing a desire to visit Vauxhall Gardens, & Charles offering to escort her there the following evening. I believe he sounded almost eager. I managed to avoid including myself & Miss Anstruther in the party.

On the way home, Charles told me seriously that he is attempting to cease his repining over Jane, &

is using Mrs Winter as a distraction. 'You will see me dance attendance on her from now on. Let us try if it can help me,' he murmured. I hope that this means that the situation is progressing as Byron would wish it.

January 28th
Charles has gone to take his Widow to Vauxhall Gardens—a most absurd excursion—a pleasure garden, in January! There is a hard frost tonight. Doubtless the Widow plans to entertain Charles in the privacy of his carriage, & will not set foot on the ground. G & Mrs Annesley are at a family *soirée* at the Fitzwilliam Cousins'. I am quite alone.

It is my first solitary evening since I was at Pemberley for Christmas—& again, to my dismay, I find myself recollecting Miss Elizabeth. A new thought disturbs me: if Miss Jane Bennet is a fortune-hunter, what of her Sister? Was she too dangling after a rich man? Were the cruel wit & vivacity that captivated me assumed as a ruse to ensnare me?

And then, there is the Mother. What moral values can daughters have, brought up by such a parent?

*   *   *

G has returned from her evening, full of enthusiasm. She urges me to come with her next time. Apparently my Aunt Fitzwilliam regularly entertains those Officers from my Cousin James's regiment who are on furlough. G insists that they are all delightful, & that she & my Cousin Augusta greatly enjoy their company. I am surprised &

disturbed at this. If the girls are not Out, they should not be spending the evening hob-nobbing with Officers! Should I have words with my Aunt Fitzwilliam? But she has brought up five daughters before Augusta—surely she must know what is proper! I further reflect that it is as well that G speaks of *all* the Officers with such enthusiasm. If she singled out but *one*, I might have greater cause for anxiety.

January 29th

To church with G & Charles. Miss Caroline & the Hursts also attended, as did the Hetheringtons from up the road & other families of our acquaintance. The sermon was on the sins of idleness. Truly I felt that it was aimed at me, who have been doing little else but indulge in *idle* dissipation & dreams these last weeks: Satan has indeed found mischief for my *idle* mind to do . . . If only I could relinquish my responsibilities here & escape to Pemberley! But it cannot be—at least not for the present. Besides, Pemberley has its own dangers.

January 30th

To Angelo's with Charles for fencing practice—& to prevent *idleness*. Later, Miss Caroline & Mrs Louisa came to call on Georgiana. She was from home, but it turned out that they knew they should not find her: the real purpose of their visit was to see me. Miss Caroline revealed that she had ignored my advice to delay, and, last Saturday, had returned Miss Bennet's call: ' 'Twas irksome indeed. The house—in Gracechurch Street!—was small & poky, with a deal of little children running about on the landing-place. We had trouble finding a quiet parlour in which to sit. I did not meet the Uncle & Aunt. Jane was as courteous & gentle as ever, & received me kindly; but it was evident that she was disappointed in me.'

'But did you succeed at least in disabusing her as to Charles's attachment?'

'Indeed I did. I do believe that she is thoroughly discouraged, & will not seek to pursue the friendship further. It pained me to do it, but I was as cold as it is possible to be. I repeatedly implied that Charles has forgot her. I mentioned his free & easy life here in Town, & strongly suggested that another lady had captured his interest.'

'And who may that be, pray?' I asked curiously. Surely they know nothing of the Widow?

Mrs Louisa coughed slightly. I saw a glance pass between the two Sisters.

'Oh, no body you know,' said Miss Caroline dismissively.

I wondered if there were yet another lady waiting in the wings of whom I have not heard. I concluded that they must mean G. If only she were older! I have observed them together, but tho' Charles has been living in this house for some time, I can detect no sign of particular interest on either side.

'Jane mentioned your Miss Eliza,' added Miss Caroline.

I schooled my countenance to betray nothing.

Miss Caroline continued: 'Jane tells me that her Sister is to pay a visit to Hunsford this spring. She is to be the guest of her Cousin, Mr Collins, the Rector of that Parish. It seems that this Mr Collins is newly wed to Miss Eliza's friend Charlotte

98

Lucas. It has all been most sudden. Jane only recently heard of it herself.'

So Miss Elizabeth is not married to Collins, as her Mother wished! Scheming minx tho' she may be, she deserved better than *him*.

'She is to be at Hunsford for Easter,' continued Miss Caroline. 'Hunsford is very close to your Aunt Lady Catherine de Bourgh's country seat, is not it?'

'Rosings is about half a mile from the Parsonage of Hunsford, I believe,' I replied.

'But you shall be spared the company of Miss Eliza, since I understand that you are due to make your visit to Lady Catherine very shortly, is not that so?'

'In scarcely more than a week from now.'

'You will be long since returned to London by the time Miss Eliza arrives there,' remarked Mrs Louisa, with a complacent smile.

A wild scheme was taking shape in my mind. I merely bowed.

The ladies chatted some more about Miss Jane. I sensed that Miss Caroline is a little ashamed at the part she has been obliged to play. Mrs Louisa is more sanguine; but then she did not have to pay the call.

After the ladies left, I settled in the Library, to brood on what Miss Caroline had told me. Collins married to the Lucas girl! So he failed to engage Miss Elizabeth's affections. On reflection, how could he ever have done so—that pompous booby: Miss Elizabeth would have seen through him in a trice. There still remains the blackguard Wickham. But if Miss Elizabeth is ready & willing to abandon Longbourn on an extended visit, it is scarcely probable that she is engaged to Wickham either: if she were, she would be unlikely to leave him behind—why am I writing this? What possible interest can I have in the fortunes of Miss Elizabeth Bennet?

*   *   *

I have evolved a plan so rash that I amaze myself. I purpose to write immediately to my Aunt, delaying my visit to Rosings 'til Easter. Why should not I see Miss Elizabeth once more? What harm can come of it?

*   *   *

Charles from home this evening. I escorted G to the play at Drury Lane (an absurd farce named *Croaking; or, Heaven Send We May All Be Alive This Day Three Months*). I found it irredeemably tedious, but it pleased her well enough.

January 31st
This morning I sent my letter to my Aunt, seeking her agreement to delay my arrival at Hunsford. Went to Jackson to spar. I find the violent sport takes my mind off my preoccupations.

Charles away this evening. I scarce have the opportunity to exchange the time of day with him. I kept my word & took G to Astley's to see the performing horses.

February 1st
Attempted to rouse Charles from a heavy slumber to carry him off to Angelo's to fence; but he was

not to be waked. He mumbled that he did not get home until four in the morning. Went to Angelo's alone.

Afterwards, to Weston to order a couple of new coats, some pantaloons, & 3 pair of breeches. His order-book is already overfull, but I have insisted.

*   *   *

Dined alone—G at the Cousins' again. Charles, as ever, absent. My unquiet thoughts kept me busy all evening.

February 2nd
To Jackson in the morning. Afterwards to Hoby's to order boots & evening pumps. The new gloves & shirts I have left to Peebles.

G & I dined with Miss Caroline & the Hursts in Grosvenor Street. Charles sent his apologies. After dinner, they implored G to play. She proved somewhat bashful, but acquitted herself well. When she was finished, Miss Caroline clappt her hands for an age, then showered her with compliments. I am happy that my Sister is so well appreciated by our friends.

February 3rd
Byron called this morning. I confess I was relieved to hear in the distance G playing scales on her pianoforte—I have no desire for her to become acquainted with Byron, who, by all accounts, exerts a dangerous fascination on all young ladies. Undoubtedly he is handsome, with his tight white pantaloons, his black coat, & that lock of hair falling over his brow. I suspect that, for the ladies,

even his twisted foot must add to his charm. As usual he called for brandy, telling Bolton to bring the *'Good stuff, not that rubbish he served up last time.'* I mentioned my uneasiness about Charles, who is now entirely taken up with Mrs Winter. He has been with her every evening this week.

Byron gave his strange smile, the corners of his mouth seeming to turn down. 'It is what you wished, Fitz,' says he.

'I know it, but I wonder sometimes whether it has been entirely prudent. Will not the young lady make inroads into his fortune?'

Byron shrugged. 'That is a risk that he must run. I cannot pretend that debauchery comes cheap. But at least it is enjoyable.'

'How can you speak so? If things go wrong, we could even be responsible for our friend's ruin!'

'He himself is responsible. We merely placed the means for it within his reach.'

Byron lounged in the chair, his fingers playing a tattoo on his leg—white, tapering fingers, a small, almost feminine hand. In the background came the sound of G's scales—up & down, up & down. Outside, a street crier screeched 'Scissors & Razors to grind ho!' I could not think of a sensible remark to make.

Byron has proposed no stratagem for detaching Charles from his new charmer, saying cynically, 'All I can recommend is that you reintroduce him to that Jane who caused all the trouble in the first place.'

On escorting Byron to the door, I observed Peebles lurking in the entrance hall to glimpse the great man's apparel. I daresay he will again plead with me to order a black coat & white sharkskin pantaloons like his noble hero's.

February 4th
I have been impatiently awaiting my Aunt Catherine's reply to my letter, but now that it is come, it proves far from welcome:

'It will not be at all convenient for you to visit Rosings at Easter,' she writes. 'I have undertaken the refurbishment of the bed-chambers, and, as your Cousin James Fitzwilliam is already invited for that period, I should not have comfortable rooms for you both. The Yellow Room is to be freshly papered, the Duke's Bedroom needs new bed-curtains, & the Crimson Room will be without a dressing-room. I must therefore insist on your keeping to the original plan, & beginning your visit next week.'

Not only am I to be deprived of a sight of Miss Elizabeth, but my Cousin James is to be thrown into her company! A man of taste & discernment, he will be unable to withstand her wit & charm. And she—if, as I surmize, she is on the hunt for a good Husband, the Honble. Colonel James Fitzwilliam, an Earl's son, will surely prove irresistible!

My Aunt's letter irks me. I dislike the thick cream-coloured paper, the big looped letters, the violet ink. I have written again to her, insisting that I will be unavoidably detained in Town until Easter, so have no alternative but to come then, & professing my readiness to sleep in a small back chamber if necessary. I know full well that there are at least ten good chambers at Rosings: her scruples are absurd.

Charles tells me that he purposes to be abroad again tonight. His assiduity in pursuing the Widow makes me more & more uneasy.

I am ashamed of my irritation with my Aunt. How petty-minded of me to reproach her for wishing to receive me in the best possible conditions! I must not let her foibles irk me.

February 5th
The text of the sermon was 'Thou shalt not covet thy neighbour's goods'. Listening to it, I had a sudden, terrible thought: is Charles the victim of a plot between Mrs Winter & Byron? Will Byron regard it as fine sport, that Charles be fleeced of his money? Could Byron be so corrupt as to watch an old schoolfellow be despoiled? I tell myself that it is impossible. But today I have deep misgivings.

February 6th
Miss Caroline & Mrs Louisa came this morning to call on G, who has been permitted to ride in the park with my Cousin Augusta, & Mrs Annesley following in a carriage. Miss Caroline expressed astonishment at finding me at home: 'I made sure you was already in Kent, visiting Lady Catherine!' she exclaimed.

I realized that it was incumbent on me to explain: 'My plans have changed; I am now supposed to be arriving rather later,' said I.

'O, really? I was hoping to arrange an evening at the Opera, & would wish to include you in the invitation. Might I enquire when you purpose to make your visit?' she enquired. I could hear the strain in her voice. I believe she is suspicious: of what I know not.

'My Aunt has not yet told me precisely when she expects me,' I replied shortly.

Miss Caroline shrugged.

February 7th
Spent all morning at Jackson's. Sparring is an excellent distraction—indeed, the only effective distraction. Byron was there, & we fought a bout. As usual, he defeated me roundly. He tells me that Jackson regards him as one of the finest pugilists of his generation.

February 8th
This morning, sought to amuse myself by riding with G in the park. We passed a pair of Officers who saluted her. She tells me that she met them at my Uncle Fitzwilliam's. They are Brother Officers to my Cousin James, it seems. I am unhappy at her fraternizing with young Officers, but she assures me that *'All her friends' Mammas permit it.'*

February 9th
Why has not my Aunt de Bourgh replied to my letter? Surely it is not too much to ask to be allowed to visit her for Easter?

February 10th
At last my Aunt Catherine's letter has come; more purple ink:

'My dear Nephew, Since you are clearly resolved on coming at Easter with my Nephew James, I can

make no further objection. I shall naturally give you the best bedroom, so it will have to be on yr conscience that James is lodged less comfortably than I should have hoped. I shall write to him to this effect.'

There follows a list of commissions that she wishes me to undertake for her in London—matching wallpapers & paints, arranging for the upholstery of her new dining-room chairs, & other such chores—I am to delegate this duty to *'some lady equal to the task'*.

So I am after all to be at Rosings at Easter! I shall, of course, do my utmost to oblige my Aunt. I wonder if G can be prevailed upon to assist me with the chores?

February 12th
To church with Georgie—Charles from home again. The sermon was on reflection: we should think out the consequences of our actions, not perform them on impulse. I should never have thought it before, but at present I fear that in my case these warnings are only too apt. I must return to Verulam, & put aside *Romeo & Juliet*, which I have been reading of an evening.

February 13th
Miss Caroline came to call on G this morning. G sought her advice in attending to my Aunt Catherine's list of errands. Miss Caroline immediately insisted on offering her assistance. Indeed, she has taken the whole list off our hands, claiming that she has far too little to do in London: 'At Netherfield, I kept house for Charles; here I am

106

merely a guest in my Sister's house. The enforced idleness is irksome to me. I shall be grateful for the occupation, & delighted to be of service to Lady Catherine.' She really is a most obliging creature. She has asked me to call on her regularly to check that the tasks are being performed as my Aunt would wish.

This evening, to Brooks's with Charles. It is rare for us to spend the evening together, for these days he is constantly occupied with the Widow. He almost seems like his former merry self, but is a trifle pale. When addressed, he daydreams before vouchsafing an answer. He is moreover taking more wine than was his wont. However, we spent a convivial evening, in the company of a group of his old friends from Oxford.

Bullivant was present, his broken arm still strapped up. He tells me that the Regency Bill has been passed. His Royal Highness is, however, dissatisfied with its terms, which are such as to curb his spending. The general view was that the Regent is shockingly extravagant. He keeps a mistress & ten or eleven children, & builds houses & palaces all over the country. His annual tailor's bill alone would be enough to maintain a small town in comfort.

February 15th
To Jackson's with Charles, then shared a nuncheon alone with him. Jennings had prepared a fish in corbullion. Charles took one mouthful, then laid down his fork & sat with his cheek in his hand, gazing into the distance, with so melancholy a look that I enquired what ailed him.

'Why, we ate just such a dish at Netherfield on

the day that Miss Bennet first dined with us after her illness. I myself caused it to be ordered, for I thought the fish would be wholesome for an invalid. It was November 15th, a Friday. Three months since!'

I could think of no suitable reply. He still pines for her, despite the constant presence of his Widow!

What is the use of his dalliance with that lady, if he does not even care for her? But I suspect that he is in far too deep to turn back.

February 17th

Called round at Grosvenor Street to see Miss Caroline about my Aunt's commissions. She scolded me for not having been before—tho' it seemed to me unlikely that she would have anything of import to tell me as yet. However, this is far from being the case, as I have discovered—to my dismay. She informs me that she at once called on her own upholsterer, Rawlins, to check on the cost of dining-room chair-seats. Finding his prices much more reasonable than those of my Aunt's upholsterer Mortimer (who had the chairs in his possession, waiting for her to make up her mind about the trimmings), Miss Caroline has taken the liberty of removing my Aunt's chairs from Mortimer, & giving them to Rawlins.

I happen to know that my Aunt cherishes Mortimer—not because he gives value for money, but because he learned his craft in the workshops of the late Mr Sheraton. Moreover, he has executed commissions for St James's Palace. She would be affronted at having the work carried out by an unknown upholsterer with no pedigree: she particularly enjoys vaunting the glorious history of her interior furnishings to her house guests. Miss Caroline has upset the whole arrangement. What is to be done? I cannot quarrel with her: she meant well—she was not to know of my Aunt's foibles, which, harmless in themselves, are not without causing difficulties for those around her.

February 18th
Charles has spent the entire night away from home. I sought to carry him off to Jackson's for a bout of sparring, but a housemaid informed me that his bed had not been slept in, so I went alone. He did not appear at breakfast, but returned late in the forenoon. He has been unusually silent all day.

I had been intending to take him to a lecture at the Royal Institute; but he refused to accompany me, so I went alone. Mr Davy gave a most instructive talk; he requested a volunteer from the audience, & administered to him a certain Laughing Gas from a tube which made the fellow chuckle & laugh fit to split his sides. It was as much as I could do to keep a straight face.

February 19th
To church with Georgie. The sermon was on the mote & the beam. It is true that we tend to judge others more severely than ourselves: I have been censorious about Miss Bennet's attitude to Charles, but my own behaviour towards him is by no means beyond reproach. I fear me he has been drawn into an entanglement with a clever, scheming woman.

February 20th
This morning, a first fitting at Weston's for my coats. The new assistant there, a red-faced fellow with moist lips, filled his mouth full of pins before attending to me, taking them out one by one to pin the cloth on me.

Afterwards, called on my Aunt's upholsterer to apologize for the 'misunderstanding' of Miss Caroline's removing the Rosings dining-room chairs from his care. He would not be pacified 'til I had made a substantial purchase: a very costly *escritoire* with tapering legs & fine marquetry detail. It has moreover a cunningly-concealed & capacious secret drawer. I believe that I shall keep it in my own rooms. It may yet prove useful.

*   *   *

Charles has come into the Library dressed for his evening's entertainment in breeches & black silk stockings & a very fine new blue coat. He now favours high collars & ties his cravat in the new style. He clappt me on the back, almost his old self.

February 22th
Charles has again slept away from home. It is fortunate that G is most unlikely to discover what he is about: Mrs Annesley is of the opinion that young ladies should rise early & occupy their morning hours with useful activities; accordingly, G mostly breakfasts alone with her, & then is shut away at her pianoforte 'til it is time to walk or ride in the park. My own breakfast (and Charles's when he is not playing truant) is normally accompanied by the distant sounds of arpeggios, exercises &

repeated passages from a sonata by Herr Haydn which Georgiana is learning at present.

*   *   *

It is almost dusk, & Charles has only just returned home. Today he seems in low spirits, & is dozing on the Library sofa as I write.

February 24th
Miss Caroline has matched the paint for my Aunt, who has chosen a cherry-red border to go above her drawing-room dado, & wishes for canary-yellow walls. I find the colours glaring, but Miss Caroline says that she understands the effect that my Aunt wishes to achieve. I hope she is not mistaken—tho' 'tis true that my Aunt has always favoured bright colours. Miss Caroline asked me to accompany her to the warehouse to purchase the paint, which I will then take with me to Rosings.

We duly went there. It has been a cold, frosty day, & Miss Caroline clung tightly to my arm, claiming that it made her feel warmer. On the way, she asked me how I found her Brother, of whom she has seen but little recently.

I looked down at her. Her eyes were red-rimmed, the tip of her nose faintly pink. It is the cold weather. I advised her to speak to her Brother herself. I could see that I had disappointed her.

February 25th
I have been anxious to see how Georgie spends her evenings these days: tonight I visited my Uncle Fitzwilliam in Berkeley Square. I also wished to question my Cousin James about his proposed stay

111

at Rosings—he is now returned to London. I do not understand what G sees in these evenings. The Berkeley Square mansion, while spacious, is freezing; all the older people seem to me lugubrious; the food is atrocious. We were served whiting which must have been fished weeks ago; the mutton too was elderly, & boiled 'til all flavour was gone. My Aunt puts on regal airs, & expects to be addressed as Your Ladyship. However, the younger people are merry enough, and, after dinner, repaired to their own sitting-room so as not to disturb their elders at cards. There they proceeded to dance & make merry. Numbers of extra guests arrived, among them Officers in regimentals. G is shy in company, & of course much too young to dance; but to my surprize, my Cousin Augusta, more forward & spirited, actually danced, not just with her Brothers, but even with occasional Officers, family friends. And she not yet Out! It all seems much too free for young people— but I daresay I am too old-fashioned—we gentlemen are woefully ignorant of such matters. Augusta is grown into a lively young girl, inclined to plumpness, with pleasing dimples & a chuckle. The perfect companion for raising G's spirits.

Spent much of the evening talking to my Cousin James. He much pleased that we are to visit Rosings together, & dismissed my suggestion that he take my place & make the earlier visit in my stead. He said: 'By all means let us go together, Fitz. It can be dull at my Aunt's. Your presence will make all the difference. At the very least we can amuse ourselves after dinner, if we abandon my Aunt & my Cousin, & retire to the billiard-room. Besides, I must return two days from now to my

Regiment, & will not be free again 'til shortly before Easter.' In his red coat with the gold frogging, Miss Elizabeth may find him irresistible.

February 26th
The vicar has been preparing us for Lent: a rather tedious sermon on taking these forty days seriously. G twinkled at me over her muff in a most disrespectful manner; then when I looked a trifle disapproving, blushed & hung her head. I felt sorry: I had not meant to intimidate her.

February 28th
Shrove Tuesday—& Lent begins tomorrow. Georgie loves Pancake Day, & asked Jennings to make piles of pancakes for supper. She has been in a happy mood all day, & prevailed upon Charles & me to play forfeits with her afterwards. For once Charles was at home for the evening. He informed me in an undertone that Mrs Winter had gone to a private party with some other friends. I wondered if he was in the mood for such trivial pursuits as youthful games with G, but he good-naturedly obliged. As I write this, they are enjoying a noisy game of cribbage. He is due to go out later to meet his Widow, by which time I hope G will be tucked up in bed—& I free to sit by the fire & muse.

March 1st
Ash Wednesday. Forty days 'til Easter.

March 2nd
At breakfast Charles informed me that he is thinking of setting Mrs Winter up in an establishment of her own. 'It will be expensive, but

113

she is so entertaining that it is worth the money,' he told me. 'There are others moreover besides myself who have designs on the lady. I must move fast if I am to keep her.'

'Will you then take up residence with her?' I asked.

'She does not wish it. She is an independent woman. She would not desire my continual presence.'

The woman is clever indeed. She plans to have him in thrall, while remaining free to indulge herself as she pleases. He is spending considerable sums, & leading a life of dissipation, as Byron intended. Is he more content? I am not convinced. I hope that I will not be obliged to extricate him from this new entanglement, & this one more serious than the last. At least it is not for life—it is not a marriage.

March 4th

Charles away from home all night. It is becoming a custom with him. If I thought that G might be tainted by it, I would send him back to his Sister's house; but it is plain that she has noticed nothing, nor is like to do so.

March 5th

The sermon today was on abstinence, since we are now in Lent. We have all been urged to give up something important. I looked at Charles, who appeared solemn, then gave me a sidelong glance, & suppressed a smile. G too shews increasingly high spirits these days. When the Vicar spoke of the evil of indulging in pleasures during this time, she gave an impatient sigh.

March 6th & 7th
Visits with G to St Paul's, & a private viewing of Sir John Soane's collection of Antiquities & Curiosities (soon to be opened to the public), have failed to curb my impatience. On Monday evening, I was obliged to keep my promise & accompany Charles to see *Romeo & Juliet* a second time. I had hoped he had forgot all his romantic nonsense. The play is no less powerful on a second viewing.

March 8th
We have 'scaped disaster by so narrow a margin that I tremble to think on it.

Before dinner Charles came to find me in the Library. I was reading Pargeter's letter about the problems of lambing in this cold weather when he walked in, but I could tell by the very sound of his footsteps that he was deeply perturbed. He threw himself onto the sofa, & I put by my letter. He looked white & shaken, & when he passed his hand over his face I saw that it was trembling.

'What's the matter?' I exclaimed.

He attempted to speak, but then, to my dismay, a tear rolled down his cheek.

'What, man?' I repeated.

'I . . . I have seen her . . .' he faltered.

'Seen whom? In Heaven's name, whom?' I began to guess at it.

'I saw her—I could swear it was she!' Then he appeared to collect himself, & amended: 'If I did not know that it could not be so, I could have sworn it was she.'

I breathed again. 'Who, Charles? Who was it?'

'Miss Bennet . . . Jane.'

'Impossible!'

'I know it.' By now he had control of himself, & went on more quietly: 'This morning I spent a couple of hours at Angelo's, & afterwards walked down Bond Street. Mrs . . .'—Here he paused as if he was forgetting the name—'Mrs Winter has been coaxing me to purchase some bauble for her, so I went to look for it. And there, in the distance . . . The very way she walked . . .'

'Did not you approach her?'

'I stood motionless, staring helplessly. She turned the corner into Piccadilly, & disappeared. I roused myself then, & ran after her.'

'And it was not she?'

'I do not know. She had disappeared.'

'It cannot have been Miss Bennet. Why should she be in London at this time?'

'I know it. Besides, if she had been in Town, she should surely have called on my Sisters, & I must have learnt of it.'

There was a silence, then he continued: 'I can still picture that pink bonnet bobbing away in the distance. O, that it had been the real Miss Bennet! O, that I could once more be . . .' He broke off, as if ashamed.

By the end of our conversation he had convinced himself that he had been mistaken. He left me, & repaired upstairs to sit alone in his chamber.

*   *   *

If he discovers how he has been deceived, I fear that neither his Sisters nor I will be forgiven.

March 9th

This morning, a fitting at Weston's, followed by a visit to Hoby's to collect my new boots. They are of very fine, soft black leather with a tan cuff. Peebles has taken possession of them, & purposes to grease & black them thoroughly before I wear them.

*   *   *

This evening, Charles has staid at home. When I enquired why he was not diverting himself with his Widow, he replied somewhat sheepishly that he felt like a quiet night in, & had sent word that he was indisposed. He is spending the evening leafing through a book of Mr Wordsworth's poems.

March 10th

Today I have been walking out with Mrs Louisa & Miss Caroline. I told the ladies of Charles's near encounter with Jane.

*   *   *

Miss Caroline's grip tightened on my arm. 'How very fortunate that Miss Bennet was too far away for Charles to be certain it was she!' she exclaimed. 'If by some mischance they should meet, what a ruination of all his friends' hopes for his prosperous marriage!'

'And, we hope, to a truly disinterested lady!' added Mrs Louisa.

I made no reply. I am too acutely aware of the disastrous situation in which Charles finds himself at present with his Widow—& of the threat that a

meeting with Jane would pose to his affection &
his trust in us.

March 11th
Charles has spent the evening quietly at home.
Georgie too at home, & played & sang to us. I
once glanced at Charles & saw he had his hand
over his eyes, shading them from the lamplight. I
did not like to peer too closely.

March 12th
To church in the morning with G & Charles. The
sermon on 'Do as ye would be done by'. Avoided
looking at Charles.

G once more at home for dinner—she tells me
that my Aunt Fitzwilliam prefers to restrict social
gatherings during Lent. 'It does not stop Augusta
& me from diverting ourselves,' added G with a
giggle. Charles too at home this evening—yet
again. Has his Widow left town? As we sat at our
Port Wine, I wondered whether to enquire about
the situation, but felt my curiosity to be indiscreet,
so said nothing. We joined G & Mrs Annesley in
the drawing-room, & played at whist together—
very pleasant.

Charles's presence in the evenings, & his new-
found serenity, bode ill. Either he has parted from
his Widow, or he is irrevocably committed to her. I
infer that it is the latter. How indeed could it be
otherwise? She would never have allowed him out
of her clutches unless she were entirely sure of
him.

March 13th
The newspapers are full of a great battle fought at

118

Barrosa. Our regiment of 500 men held off 7000 Frenchies! We have captured a regimental Eagle. The newspapers claim that this victory will mark a turning-point in the war, but I note a certain reluctance to number our casualties.

Charles & I dined alone tonight—despite it being Lent, G was at the play with my Cousins Augusta, James & the rest of the Fitzwilliams. After dinner, we removed to the Library & sat on either side of the fire.

'Fitz, I have something to tell you,' said Charles.

My heart sank. I made sure that the wedding date was fixed. But to my surprize & delight, he said: 'I have decided to part from Mrs Winter.'

I remained silent for a space, savouring the news. Then I schooled myself to say, soberly: 'I think that you have made a prudent decision, Charles.'

We sat together, gazing into the flames. I felt the greatest relief. Eventually, I questioned him further: 'Might I be so bold as to ask the reason for your decision?'

He made no reply, & I added hastily: 'Of course I have no desire to pry into your private affairs. Pray do not feel obliged to tell me if you do not wish it.'

'I have no objection to telling you, Fitz. It is just that my heart is too full . . .'

And then he told me: it has happened because he saw Jane, on that day in Bond Street! And yet he is unaware that it must really have been she! 'It was that young girl I saw in the distance,' said he. 'She reminded me so of Miss Bennet, that I received a violent shock, a kind of blow to the heart. Over the next few days, I realized that I have truly loved but once. Mrs Winter is an entertaining & charming woman, but I feel nothing for her. She has been a distraction, no more—she can never replace Miss Bennet in my affections.'

I could not help asking: 'But how did you extricate yourself?'

'I have long been aware that she is not the respectable female that she seemed to be at first acquaintance. She is an adventuress, who uses her charms to make her way in life. It has taken me some days to make up my mind; in truth, I was so shaken by my glimpse of that unknown girl, that I was unable to think clearly. I simply knew that I had no further desire to see Mrs Winter. It was not 'til yesterday that I told her that I was no longer willing to support her. I have paid her a reasonable sum to keep her in funds 'til she finds a new protector. It is all over, & I much relieved.' Then he added, with a smile, 'Byron will be most put out. I am persuaded that he counted on her to make his fortune, on the grounds that it was he who introduced me to her.'

I too had formerly shared his cynical view of Byron: his Lordship has long been deeply in debt, as is well-known. But I have since realized my mistake: Byron is very proud, & more like to make grand, extravagant gestures which plunge him still further into the clutches of the money-lenders, than to attempt to trick a friend out of his fortune.

Still, now was not the time to argue the point. I leant forward & put my hand on Charles's shoulder. 'I am so glad that you are free of her! I own that I was never happy at your entanglement with the lady.'

On reflection I am astonished at what he has

told me. I have been thinking of him as innocent, almost child-like. In truth, he is probably more of a man of the world than I. Am I then a poor judge of character?

March 14th
Charles has been acting like a man reprieved. Today he rose early, & from my chamber I could hear him singing as Gunn shaved him. He ran downstairs two at a time, & was waiting for me in the hall in his greatcoat. At Jackson's he sparred energetically, & later partook of an excellent breakfast. He then offered to accompany Georgie wherever she wished to go, so they set off in the highest spirits for a morning's shopping. Afterwards he has consented to take her to the Ranelagh Gardens in Chelsea, tho' Augusta has told her that they are no longer worth visiting, as no body fashionable has gone there for years.

*   *   *

G & Charles are returned from the Ranelagh Gardens. They drove all the way to Chelsea, only to find a barren, frozen space, where no body walked abroad but a few veteran soldiers, whose leers & hoarse greetings greatly alarmed my Sister. 'And the rough ground scratched my shoes, & the mud splashed my stockings,' she complained, holding out her foot in a most unladylike manner for me to see. She is such a child! Mrs Annesley looked shocked.

'I acted without reflecting. It is madness to visit such a garden in this weather,' added Charles.

'Well, *I* shall not go back there again,' said G

pettishly.

March 15th
Tonight have agreed to escort G to a grown-up party at my Uncle's. It is to be a low-key affair, as we are in Lent, so my Aunt felt that it would do no harm for Augusta & G to attend if well chaperoned. G has been chattering about her *toilette* for days, & has told me details of several of the Officers who should be present; but I confess I am somewhat *distrait* these days.

It is months since I attended such a gathering. Indeed, I remember the precise date: November 26th, at Netherfield. I have not danced with a woman since. I managed to avoid it at Christmas. Today, as Charles's Sisters will also be present, I shall be obliged to stand up with the ladies.

March 16th
Yesterday's ball was as I feared. Miss Caroline kindly offered to sit out with me, *'knowing how I hate to dance'*. But I could not 'scape standing up with Augusta, & then did so again with Miss Caroline & Mrs Louisa, then with Georgie, who, despite being solicited by several Officers, danced only with the family. She continues much less forward than she is at home with me & Charles. Indeed, she seems positively shy outside her most intimate family circle, of which I am glad.

March 19th
To church with G & Charles. The sermon was on the Lost Sheep. It made me reflect on the fact that Charles's rejection of Jane is solely my responsibility—a heavy burden. Who am I to judge

her?

March 20th
My Aunt Fitzwilliam has sent word that she wishes to see me tomorrow, alone. I am not to mention this to G, as it concerns her. I am greatly discomposed. Has she learnt something? What will she say?

March 23rd
To Berkeley Square in the morning. I was ushered into a freezing parlour, where my Aunt Fitzwilliam, muffled up in shawls & mittens, was waiting. As I entered, she called to the footman to fetch her a hot brick for her feet.

It transpires that, far from discovering anything to G's disadvantage, she wishes to bring her Out with Augusta.

'Poor dear Georgiana needs a London Season, you have no suitable chaperone, & His Lordship feels that as her Uncle it is his duty to attend to her future.'

I bowed. 'Thank you, Aunt. That is extremely generous of you.' My breath came out in a frosty cloud.

'Not generous at all,' she snapped. 'You know how threadbare we grow—& now Rupert wishes to marry, which will put us to colossal expense. *I* shall help out with the chaperoning & the procedures; *you* shall pay for both the girls. You can well afford it, Fitzwilliam.'

'I shall require to discuss this with my Sister,' said I. 'If it meets with her approval, the financial side of things need not trouble you.'

'Pho, pho! Georgiana is a mere chit. Just

arrange the whole thing, & she'll do as she's told. I'll find them both eligible . . .' She broke off as the footman returned with the brick, which he tucked under her feet, wrapping her legs in a shawl. The room was so cold that I could have done with the same attentions myself.

I told her that I would consider the matter carefully, & took my leave.

*   *   *

This evening I spoke to G about her Coming Out. She flushed deeply. 'Do you think it would be suitable?' she whispered.

'Indeed, yes, my dear, if you wish it.'

She hung her head. 'I do not know. It is too soon . . .'

I put my arm about her. She rested her head against my shoulder, then pulled away and, without a word, left the room.

When she was gone, I touched the shoulder of my coat: it was damp.

She is less well recovered than I had hoped.

March 24th
I have written to my Aunt Fitzwilliam to say that Georgie is as yet undecided about Coming Out, & promising an answer nearer the summer. I took G out to Hatchard's Bookshop, hoping that the possession of several interesting new volumes would take her mind off her present griefs.

March 26th
All week I have been wrestling with my conscience. I cannot exonerate the Bennet family. Their

manners are on occasion reprehensible. They would not have been a worthy connexion for Charles. Truly I cannot blame myself. I confess that I was so preoccupied with these thoughts that I could not recall afterwards what today's sermon was about.

Having been unusually cold, the weather is now unseasonably fine. At Rosings the primroses & daffodils will soon be out.

March 28th
I have received a note from my Aunt Fitzwilliam:

Lady Fitzwilliam wld. be obliged to Mr Darcy if he would make haste to resolve his Difficulties & reach a Decision as soon as possible about Miss Darcy's Coming Out. A London Season requires months of Preparation. The Young Ladies will be expected to Hold a Joint Ball, & to be Presented at Court; numerous Soirées *must be arranged, both at Home & Elsewhere. In addition,* Toilettes *must be bespoke for every Occasion. For Her Majesty's Ball White Dresses & Plumes—different Ballgowns for each of the other Events. Mr Darcy will Acknowledge that all this requires Time & Effort to arrange.*

Lady Fitzwilliam will be greatly Inconvenienced if Indecision on the part of her Nephew & Niece prevents her from taking the Necessary Steps at the Appropriate Time.

Aunt Fitzwilliam is an old-fashioned and, dare one say it, overbearing matron. I am amazed that her son James is so easy & unassuming—the ideal travel companion.

We travel to Rosings in less than a fortnight.

April 1st
April Fool's Day. Georgie played a trick on us. She had procured some bottled plums & had Jennings prepare them, coated in a brown sauce, for a nuncheon. She served us herself. We set to, taking the plums for kidneys. She & Charles laughed merrily. Truly, they are both in spirits these days. For myself, I feel unsettled.

April 4th
Charles has moved back to Grosvenor Street. While I am from home, Georgie & Mrs Annesley are to live in Berkeley Square with my Uncle & Aunt. I must confess that I pity them: tho' the weather continues fine, the house is freezing. However, G is anticipating the removal with pleasure. She is very fond of my Cousin Augusta. I cannot but feel uneasy when G is out of my sight— but I tell myself that life must continue, & that I cannot forever be dancing attendance on my Sister.

I read in *The Times* that a new Tunnel between Marsden & Diggle has opened today, after 15 years of digging. It is over 5000 yards long!

April 5th
Peebles has been asking me about my apparel; I know not what I answer him—my mind is elsewhere. G explains about her arrangements— five minutes after she is gone, I have forgot what she has told me. Only three days more.

April 6th
Peebles unwontedly tiresome. I mentioned in

passing that I wished him to pack my new coat & the other garments which I have recently purchased. He objected that it was surely not necessary to fit myself out so fine for a visit to the *'back of beyond'*. I am sorry to say that I snapped at him to obey my orders without question. He sulked all day as only he knows how. Once he actually came down to the Library to ask, *'Did I really want the new beaver & the new gloves for trudging through muddy fields?'* I could not bring myself to reply, so annoyed was I. He retired, muttering 'O, very well, very well' under his breath.

April 7th
I have resolved to control my anticipation. I can never think seriously of her. She is to be seen once more, for a few days, then put out of my mind for ever.

I purpose to see little of her, & to observe her with the utmost coolness. Surely I have been exaggerating her attractions in my mind. The reality will prove a disappointment, & I shall be happily cured of my absurd preoccupation.

Tomorrow James & I leave together for Rosings.

END OF PART II

127

Part III

ROSINGS

April 8th

We set off in the early morning. I was anticipating some difficulty in concealing my impatience. As it was, my conversation with my Cousin proved so absorbing that I well-nigh forgot my own preoccupations.

After an exchange of commonplace politenesses which lasted 'til we reached Bromley, he opened his heart to me. While they changed the horses we took breakfast at The Bell. As we sat in the inn parlour James enquired abruptly: 'You have no plans to marry in the near future, have you, Fitz?'

I was taken aback. Far from planning matrimony, I have spent the last months fighting against any thought of it. I replied in the negative.

' 'Tis all very well for you,' he remarked.

I was at a loss to understand him, but he vouchsafed no further explanations, & a short interval was spent by both in reading the newspapers which we had brought with us.

It was not 'til the coffee & rolls were brought that he again took up the conversation: 'I have lately been thinking . . .' He stopped, & would not continue without prompting. I had no notion of what was in his mind. Finally, he confessed that for these last few months he has been wondering whether to take a Wife. He feels the need for a family & children; would sell his commission tomorrow & settle; but is lacking in two essentials: an agreeable lady to wed, & the means to support her.

'Here I am, an Earl's son, without so much as two coins to rub together,' he concluded ruefully.

We discussed his problem at some length. It seems that my Uncle is even more penurious than I had imagined, having settled a considerable sum on my Cousin Rupert as the eldest son. Poor James has no money & no prospect of ever obtaining any. His Godfather, the Bishop, had given him reason to hope, but is recently deceased, leaving his entire fortune to a distant relative. I thought of offering James a long lease on Darnley Manor, without payment. He refused, pointing out that my gesture would represent a significant sacrifice, & would in any case be inadequate for him, since he needs not only a house but an income.

' 'Tis all very well for you,' he repeated.

'Explain yourself!'

'You lucky dog: money a-plenty, fancy-free—& yet you show no signs of settling down. Is not this a paradox?'

'What you imagine is far from being the case,' I replied, somewhat nettled at his bland assumption of my heartlessness. 'Tho' I confess that, from mine own observation, an entanglement with a lady can prove so dangerous that I am, in truth, nervous of burning my fingers.'

'O, really?' He was all agog to hear more. Finally he coaxed an explanation out of me, & I found myself telling him about Charles's unfortunate involvement with Jane. As I omitted the names of the parties concerned & gave him only a portion of the story, I believe myself to have been discreet enough. I merely told him that the misfortune had befallen a friend of mine, & explained my part in detaching this 'friend' from the unworthy object of his affections.

'Your poor friend! A misfortune indeed for him!

132

Has he recovered from the blow?'

'Only partly, I believe.'

'And is the lady really quite as unsuitable as you claim?'

'Utterly unsuitable. The match would have been a disaster. Everything about her—family, upbringing, character—makes her unfit to be his Wife, besides which she is virtually penniless.'

After breakfast we set off again. Soon James was back on the subject of his own prospects. We have concluded that his only hope is to find a pleasant & amenable lady of considerable means, & willing to link her fortune to his. I sincerely wish him well.

As we turned in through the carriage gates, I looked out, wondering if I should see anyone in the Parsonage. But there was no body at the windows. Then I beheld Mr Collins, the red-faced Rector whom I met at the Netherfield ball, standing by the lodge, doffing his hat. I looked out for the ladies; but they were nowhere to be seen.

The house is greatly improved. The lime avenue has been newly pollarded, & some ailing trees replaced. My Aunt, who came down the steps to greet us, pointed out this work to us immediately, explaining that she had employed a craftsman recommended by her friend Lady Charteris. She gave both of us a peck on the cheek, then bade us make haste to enter, as it was cold. My Cousin Anne has not appeared. My Aunt says that these days she is frequently too fatigued to venture downstairs 'til nightfall.

We immediately sat down to a nuncheon. My Aunt informed us that she has purchased a new billiard table against our arrival. She invited us into the breakfast-parlour, whose chairs have been recovered in a shiny blue & yellow satin, & questioned us closely about every body in London. She has given us a deal of instructions to pass on to the family when next we write.

Eventually my Cousin Anne came downstairs with her companion, a Mrs Jenkinson. She grows more delicate every time I see her; but my Aunt's assessment of her condition is robust: 'O, Anne will do very well. There is nothing the matter with Anne. She is no different from other young girls—a trifle more sensitive, perhaps.' And she gave me a sidelong glance. She cannot be prevailed upon to relinquish the hope that I will one day offer for my sickly Cousin. She expects me to honour an agreement she reached with Mamma when I was but nine years old, & Anne a mere infant in arms!

*　　　*　　　*

At dinner I mentioned having seen the Rector by the Lodge gates, & explained that I had previously met him in Hertfordshire.

'He is always here in the house,' replied she. 'I can scarce keep him away. But he makes himself useful, & keeps me in touch with the parishioners. I daresay you will see him tomorrow.'

Not a word about any visitors. Is she here?

'Is not he recently married? I believe I also met his Wife,' says I. 'A pleasant, unassuming young woman. Miss Lucas, was not it?'

'O, so you know Mrs Collins as well, do ye?' says my Aunt. She sounded quite put out: I know that she takes great pleasure in effecting introductions, & must feel it that in this case she is become unnecessary.

'O yes,' I replied, 'But I was a trifle surprized to hear that they were married. I had been told for a fact that Mr Collins was set on wedding one of his Cousins, the Misses Bennet.'

My Aunt drew herself up: 'I do not chuse to be party to the matrimonial projects of a Mr Collins. Suffice it to say that the Wife he has brought back with him has proved equal to the task of serving this Parish.'

Then my Cousin Anne murmured: 'But there is a Miss Bennet staying with them at the Parsonage even now.'

So she is here. I shall see her. 'O indeed? Which Miss Bennet is that?' I asked, wondering at the calmness of my own tones.

'Why, a Miss Elizabeth Bennet. A pretty, forward sort of girl. Doubtless she too is among your acquaintance,' said my Aunt crossly. 'You seem to know every body in Hertfordshire.' She paused. 'In fact, I do now seem to recollect Mrs Collins mentioning that she had met you. I had quite forgot.'

April 9th

It is over. I have seen her. It happened thus:

Scarcely had we finished breakfast, than Mr Collins was announced. Apparently he comes almost every day to discuss parish business with my Aunt. Today, however, it transpired that his purpose was to pay his respects to me, as an old acquaintance—I, who have addressed not above three words to him in my life. After bowing & scraping to me, he staid for a full hour, talking with my Aunt in the Library. I lingered in the same room, listening to their conversation. It was of the dullest possible nature, concerning the turnip harvest, & whether the children in the village school should be disciplined with a cane or merely with a shoe, &c. It concluded in this way:

'So, why was old Runcible not in church last Sunday, Mr Collins? Have you found it out yet?' asked my Aunt in her sharpest voice.

Mr Collins, standing before her, gave a low bow: 'Your Ladyship was only too right to draw my attention to his case—else I might not have bethought me to pay him a visit. The venerable parishioner has a severe case of gout. That is what prevented him from attending Divine Service last Sunday. Moreover, he fears that it will do so again on Good Friday & Easter Sunday.'

'Nonsense!' exclaimed my Aunt. 'His nephew Harold must push him in a bathchair. We cannot have our parishioners playing truant from church!'

'I doubt me whether he possesses a bathchair,' objected the Rector, with another bow.

'My dear Mr Collins, you are as feeble as he is! There must be some vehicle that can be pressed into service. Failing everything else, there is always a wheelbarrow. Go & tell young Harold that I expect him to push his old uncle to church in a wheelbarrow!'

'Indeed, dear Madam, I shall be only too happy to do your bidding,' replied Collins. 'Your Ladyship's word is my command.' So saying, he rose to leave the room.

'Might I have the honour of accompanying you, to pay my respects to Mrs Collins?' I asked him.

He turned quite red, I think with pleasure. 'The honour is all mine . . .' he began, bowing in my direction this time.

'Why, Darcy, there is no need for all this ceremony,' interrupted my Aunt. 'Mrs Collins will quite understand if you are too fatigued by your journey to do her the courtesy of paying a call today. Leave it for now. You will see her in church on Friday.'

'I am not in the least fatigued,' I replied. 'The exercise will be beneficial to my health & spirits, & will, besides, give me an appetite for the excellent nuncheon which you have no doubt bespoke. Will not you come with me?' I asked, turning to James. It had occurred to me that his presence might give me countenance.

'With pleasure,' answered he.

'Then, Mr Collins, pray wait five minutes while we make ourselves ready, & we will accompany you.' We went off to find our hats. I was not sure that I had done the right thing in soliciting James's company—but it was too late to draw back.

During the walk to the Parsonage, I spoke but little. Mr Collins conversed volubly with James. Having ascertained that James is both a Colonel in the army & the son of an Earl, he seemed beside himself with joy at the honour of bringing such a visitor back to his house. I was wondering whether I had been foolish in refraining from wearing any of the new garments I had had made precisely for this occasion. This morning, on rising, it seemed too ridiculous to dress like a fop merely to meet a young woman whom I have not seen for four & a half months. Accordingly, I told Peebles to lay out my everyday country apparel. When the house came into view, I almost turned back.

But it is done. I have seen her—& now that I

have done so, my fears seem absurd & groundless. She is indeed charming—her skin a darker, more golden colour than I remembered, becomingly set off by a peach-pink gown; her hair curling about her temples in rather longer elf-locks than before; her eyes as sparkling as ever. As for her wit, which filled me with dread as well as longing, I had very little opportunity of admiring it, for she said almost nothing. Upon our entering their small dining-parlour, she rose & curtseyed prettily, in silence; then she sat quietly in a corner. Her friend Mrs Collins was also present, & a rather sharp-eyed young woman, Mrs Collins's Sister. I scarcely noticed them.

There was but one moment which caused my heart to miss a beat: when I enquired, as I must needs do, how her family kept, she raised her dark eyes to my face, and, looking directly into my eyes, asked, *'Had not I happened to see her Sister Jane, who had been in Town these past three months?'*

I managed to sustain her gaze without flinching, & replied, truthfully enough, that I had not had that honour.

And now, as I sit in my chamber writing this, I can say in all honesty that I felt nothing on seeing her. Nothing but a common admiration for a pretty woman. It is over. I am free.

On the way back, James was all amazement at *'The bewitching Miss Bennet.'* Let him admire her! Let him woo her if he will—tho' she can never be for him: apart from every other disadvantage, she has no fortune.

April 10th
To church, but without my Cousin Anne. She is

visible here only in the evenings. In the mornings she keeps strictly to her chamber. Her companion, Mrs Jenkinson, sits with her much of the time. When they join us, Mrs Jenkinson hovers over her anxiously, & is far too assiduous with offers of assistance. It must surely be bad for a young lady's character to be thus indulged!

Today my Aunt has been interrogating me about the errands she asked me to run for her in London. I have been hard put to explain away Miss Caroline's removal of her dining-room chairs from her upholsterer.

'What! Took the chair-seats away from Mortimer? The interfering chit. What was she thinking of?'

I felt most embarrassed—considered from my Aunt's point of view, I can see how unacceptable Miss Caroline's behaviour must seem. I explained lamely that Miss Bingley was hoping to save my Aunt a considerable sum, & was able to vouch for her own upholsterer, who achieves excellent results.

'It is not up to your Miss Bingley to decide who is to be my upholsterer. I will thank you in future to make sure that she keeps her nose out of my affairs,' replied my Aunt indignantly. Poor Miss Caroline! She was only trying to help. I said as much to my Aunt, who growled something which I did not catch, & was quite out of temper for the rest of the day. She was only slightly mollified when I presented her with the paint for her drawing-room dado. She grudgingly acknowledged that the colour would do, but refused to give poor Miss Caroline any credit for the choice.

April 11th

Today James decided to pay a morning call at the Parsonage. He claimed that it was on parish business on behalf of my Aunt; but I suspect that it was also to pay his respects to Miss Elizabeth Bennet. I did not chuse to accompany him. On his return he came to find me, full of praise for his new friend. 'I was aware of how pretty she is, but had not realized the extent of her liveliness & wit!' said he.

I am astonished at my own want of concern: I would not care if James were to announce tomorrow that they are engaged! How can a powerful attraction dissipate itself thus instantly? I can only conclude that I was in reality less smitten than I myself believed.

While James was absent visiting Miss Elizabeth, my Aunt opened her mind to me about a boldly innovative plan: she intends to install the latest water-closets at Rosings. Owing to her reluctance to refer to them by their name, & talking earnestly of *'nature's way'*, & *'unmentionables'*, I found it difficult at first to comprehend her scheme. She learnt of the closets from her new young architect. She told me his name, which I forget; he has been recently in the employment of His Grace the Duke of Devonshire at Chatsworth. Apparently this water system is currently in use in the Captain's quarters of a few of our most modern ships, but could also be applied to houses, & is a great improvement on the old Bramah closets. His Royal Highness the Prince Regent is planning such an installation in the Palace which he purposes to build at Brighton. My Aunt immediately resolved to do the same. The water for the guests' chambers is to be pumped from the well in leaden pipes, & carried up to the top of the house to fill a large cistern. From thence a pipe will carry it down to the dressing rooms, where it will pour automatically into basins—& the water-closets. From thence, more pipes will carry the foul water away to a midden. If they perfect the system, I might consider it for Pemberley. In return, I discussed my own scheme for a new ballroom wing with my Aunt, who expressed the hope that it would be sufficiently grandiose *in view of my standing in the county*. I wish I could summon up more enthusiasm for this project.

As he laid out my evening apparel before dinner Peebles was muttering indignantly: he has all but come to blows with James's batman, Cobby. The latter insists that as servant to the son of an Earl he should take precedence at meals in the servants' hall.

'I gave him what for,' growled Peebles. 'Earl's son indeed! My master's is one of the oldest families in England on both sides, so I told him, came over with the Conqueror, & can his gentleman boast a country seat to compare with Pemberley? With its acres, its park . . .' He rambled on in this vein all the time I was dressing, & tweaked my hair angrily as he combed it.

April 12th
Yet again, James has walked over to the Parsonage. As before, he invited me to accompany him, but did not seem at all put out when I refused to go—in fact, almost the opposite. He has known Miss Elizabeth but two days, & already seems besotted.

I had nothing particular planned for the rest of that day. I would have welcomed the opportunity for a walk with James. Why must he always be bending his step towards the Parsonage? As it is, I had no body to keep company with, & wandered alone in the garden. It is too bad—my Aunt should keep at least one decent horse, suitable for a man to ride. Even the shooting season is over. There is nothing to do in this God-forsaken place.

When James finally returned, a good two & a half hours after he had set out, he again waxed eloquent about Miss E. Bennet & her charms. I would that he held his tongue.

This evening, dinner was tedious in the extreme. Afterwards, I refused to play at cards with my Aunt, but instead beat James soundly at billiards. We discussed our Cousin Anne over the billiard-table. I mentioned to James that I feel uneasy at the way she is spoilt. She is no longer a child—indeed, I believe she is nineteen years old—& should be encouraged to be somewhat more independent.

'My Aunt makes little of her pretensions to ill-health, yet she permits all this misguided cosseting by Mrs Jenkinson.'

'My Cousin is delicate, I believe,' answered he.

'Why, surely it is nothing that cannot be cured by a brisk walk in the fresh air?'

' 'Tis her breathlessness that is the problem. If you observe them closely, you will see that Mrs Jenkinson frequently holds the salts to her nose.'

'She does have a quiet, almost whispering voice,' said I. 'I am ashamed that I have always attributed it to affectation, not ill-health. I did not think.'

April 13th
This morning, James actually suggested visiting the Parsonage yet again before matins. My Aunt had to remind him that as it is Good Friday, to pay such a call would be most unseemly. We went to church twice—& I saw Miss Elizabeth both times. She curtseyed gravely, & passed by in silence. Today the sacred words of the Scriptures filled me with emotion. The reading was Our Lord's betrayal by Judas. Even the absurdity of Mr Collins in the pulpit failed to lighten my mood. In the carriage, I felt incapable of responding to my Aunt's questions about the repairs to Pemberley Chapel—& annoyed her by confessing that I sometimes chuse to worship in the village church instead: she said that it was unworthy of me, & that I should not allow myself to forget my station in life.

Fish for dinner. I felt a sudden urge to play billiards with James, but we recollected ourselves, and, instead, sat in virtual silence in the drawing-room with my Aunt & my Cousin Anne. I have been observing the latter since James mentioned her ill-health. She does at times seem to fight for breath. In addition, James has revealed to me that she has problems in the bones in her legs, & has drawn my attention to the fact that she walks with a slight limp, which I had also failed to notice.

April 14th
In the forenoon, I took a long ramble with James round the perimeters of Rosings Park. At one point my Aunt's land borders on Parsonage Lane. When we passed in front of the Parsonage itself, James exclaimed: 'I wonder if we shall catch a

glimpse of the ladies?' & began peering over the wall. I refrained from participating in this activity.

My Aunt's Butler, Simpson, seems a tactful fellow: he has healed the rift between Peebles & Cobby, by seating them at the head of the table on alternate days. Peebles objected that the man who sat there first would be regarded as the superior. Simpson promptly drew a coin from his pocket & made them toss it for the privilege. I did not venture to ask who had won the toss, for fear of setting Peebles off again.

After dinner I beat James at billiards. The ladies played desultory card-games upstairs in the drawing-room. They implored us to make up a four with them, but we were not in the mood.

April 15th
To church in the morning. I succeeded in keeping my eyes averted from the Parsonage pew: I could not say what colour pelisse Miss Bennet was wearing. On emerging, we met with the Parsonage party in the church porch. After the customary salutations, my Aunt invited them to spend the evening at Rosings: I suspect that she is desperate for a game of whist, & James & I are proving a sad disappointment.

So I am to spend the evening in the company of Miss Elizabeth! I knew that it must be. I shall emerge unvanquished. I am sure of it.

*   *   *

I write this late at night, in my chamber. I might have known that my resolution would be fruitless! The signs were not good: I made Peebles lay out my new coat, on the pretext that it was a festival day. He was not deceived, & gave me a quizzical look which irritated me beyond measure. Looking at myself in the glass before going down to dinner, I found my own countenance sullen & disagreeable.

When she arrived, I kept to the background, & allowed James to monopolize her in conversation. She was so brilliant that even my Aunt was grudgingly drawn into the dialogue. I still sat removed, & heard not above half of what was said. But then—then she began to play & sing. I could not help myself: I came to stand beside the pianoforte. And then she ceased playing & said, provocatively: 'You mean to frighten me, Mr Darcy, by coming in all your state to hear me. But I will not be alarmed.' I had forgot how she mocks me, so wittily & charmingly that one could not possibly take offence. I replied as calmly as I could that she knew full well that I would never alarm her, & that she was saying the opposite of what she knew to be the truth.

She turned laughing to James: 'Your Cousin will give you a very pretty notion of me, & teach you not to believe a word I say. I am particularly unlucky in meeting with a person so well able to expose my real character, in a part of the world where I had hoped to pass myself off with some degree of credit.' She proceeded to teaze me for my well-known reluctance to dance. Again! And concluded with an attack on my awkwardness in society, which she attributes to want of effort.

Anne is so pale & small, she dwindles almost to nothing beside Miss Elizabeth. If the latter could see how she outshines the poor girl, she would surely feel compassion. Everything about Anne is dull & quiet: her hair has no shine, but hangs limply about her face; her cheeks are waxen-white. She always wears a shawl—I suppose to protect her weak chest—& sits by the fire.

Miss Elizabeth looks more beautiful than ever, with her longer hair, & perhaps a trifle more slender than before. I had forgot the small pulse at the base of her throat. I had forgot how delicately formed are her bare arms.

April 16th
I slept almost not at all, & woke heavy-hearted & weary. I must see her again: I cannot keep away. Immediately after breakfast, I took up my new hat and, without telling any body, left the house. On reaching the Parsonage, I loitered a while inside the Park gates, not daring to approach. Then, to my delight & terror, I saw Mrs Collins & her Sister leave the house with shopping baskets & direct their steps towards the village. She must then be inside the house, alone. Giving myself no time to draw back, I hastened up the path & knocked on the door.

The servant shewed me into the parlour. E sitting at a desk, writing. When I entered, she looked startled, but rose to curtsey. I made some excuse about expecting to see the other ladies, & not wishing to intrude upon her solitude. She replied civilly enough, & we sat down together. For the life of me, I could not think of anything to say—& allowed her to chuse a topic. This was unfortunate, for she immediately began to comment on Charles's removal from Netherfield (& from the clutches of Jane, thought I).

'I think I have understood that Mr Bingley has not much idea of ever returning to Netherfield again?' she asked.

'It is probable that he may spend very little of his time there in future,' said I in some embarrassment.

'It would be better for the neighbourhood that he should give up the place entirely, for then we might possibly get a settled family there.'

I assumed that she was thinking of her Sisters' prospects, & of the possibility of another, more eligible tenant taking the house.

That subject being exhausted, we lapsed into silence. I have never known myself so tongue-tied. Finally we managed some halting conversation about the amenities of the Parsonage—I scarce know what I said. Gradually growing more confident, I ventured to raise my eyes to her face—& she looked so beautiful that I found myself blurting out the hope that she would be willing one day to leave her home at Longbourn—at least, that is what I meant to say. Happily, I believe that it came out so garbled that she did not take my meaning.

This imprudence stopped me short. I know not what I had been on the verge of saying. I was relieved when, shortly afterwards, Mrs Collins's Sister walked in. I took my leave almost at once.

A narrow escape! I must be more careful. In future, I must absolutely refrain from visiting her. Let James have his fill of her!

A letter arrived from Georgie today—she has seen Charles, & says he is in tolerable spirits. She herself is pleasantly occupied in London, chaperoned by my Aunt Fitzwilliam.

After dinner, when we two gentlemen were alone together over our Port Wine, James enquired if I was still bent on returning to London on Wednesday—because he was greatly enjoying himself, & would welcome an extension of our stay. 'By all means,' said I. 'Let us leave on Saturday.' I have no objection to his indulging himself with Miss Elizabeth, & will readily sacrifice a few days to his pleasure.

James is continually kind to my Cousin. He sometimes accompanies her when she feels well enough to go out in her phaeton. It is a pleasure to see her mournful little face light up when he makes her smile. This evening, he offered to play at cards or at Mah-Jong with her, leaving me in a *tête-à-tête* with my Aunt, who amused herself making disparaging comments about Miss Elizabeth. I have always felt affection for my Aunt, & dismissed her 'foibles' as the endearing eccentricities of a matron somewhat advanced in years. But now that I recollect the gist of her remarks to Miss Elizabeth last night, I find them insufferable. She asked intrusive & impertinent questions, & patronized her at every turn. She presumed to judge her performance on the pianoforte—& actually ordered her to come to Rosings to practise on a spare instrument, adding that '*She would be in no body's way, in that part of the house.*' At the time, I was so preoccupied that I failed to observe how insolent were her words. But in retrospect, I am ashamed of her.

The Parsonage party have again been invited to the house in two days' time.

April 17th

Today I resolved not to visit the Parsonage. However, I felt the need to stretch my limbs, so took myself off on a lonely walk. My steps did unaccountably direct me towards Parsonage Lane, but I had no intention of calling, & repeating the humiliating experience of yesterday. Instead, I veered off along the Park boundary. There is a very pretty walk there, & now that the primroses are out, it is a most agreeable spot. Indeed, Miss Elizabeth herself mentioned it to James on our last visit.

I wandered a while along the path, then spied a figure in the distance—it was she, walking briskly towards me. I noted the start of surprize that she gave as she caught sight of me. I attempted to explain that I was in that spot purely by accident. She eyed me gravely, & said: 'This is my favourite of all the walks in the neighbourhood.'

We walked & talked—or at least, she talked. As usual in her presence, I was tongue-tied. I know not how long we were together. Eventually she told me that she must return to the Parsonage. I escorted her home, her hand resting on my arm. It is the first time she has touched me since November 26th. I left her at the gate, & walked home in a daze. I think I picked a bunch of primroses, then tossed them away.

She has told me where she prefers to walk. It is tantamount to an invitation to join her there. If she wishes it, why not? There can be no harm in meeting her in that beautiful place, & walking with her again.

April 18th

All day I have restrained myself. I did not go to walk with her. I did not visit the Parsonage. I sat all morning in the Library & construed Cicero's *In Catalinam*. The vituperations contained therein echoed my troubled mind.

Today Anne greatly surprized me. My Aunt & Cousin joined me in the Library after our nuncheon. My Aunt was shewing me the plans for her new water system, & I congratulating her on her ambitious project, when Anne, from her corner by the fire, said quietly: 'You should not encourage Mamma, Cousin. She spends a fortune on extravagant architectural innovations, when she should be attending to the welfare of the estate.'

I was astonished at such words from my little mouse of a Cousin. She had often seemed morose, but never ill-mannered. I was even more surprized when, instead of quelling her with a dampening reproof, my Aunt bit her lip & remained silent.

'Why? Is the estate in need of improvement?' I asked. I was indeed curious to learn what this semi-invalid girl could know of such things.

'Yes, indeed,' replied she. She then exposed to me the need for more extensive arable farming, according to new methods about which she has been reading. 'I have not the energy to read very much—perhaps an hour after the cold meats,' said she. 'But I feel it behoves me to acquire some understanding of such matters.'

I moved over to sit beside her—tho' the heat of the fire was suffocating—& asked her for further details. I too have heard much of the new approach, & have for some time been of a mind to try it at Pemberley. I am utterly amazed at her

150

knowledge of such topics, & equally astonished at her authority. By merely whispering, she can bend my Aunt to her will.

On reflection, I believe I have the answer: I dare say that the considerable wealth enjoyed by my Aunt is actually Anne's. My Aunt cannot have brought much of a dowry to her marriage—one has only to look at the penury of her Brother, my Uncle Fitzwilliam, to realize the truth of this. My Cousin will doubtless come into the enjoyment of her fortune when she is twenty-one—& then my Aunt may be dependent on her approval for financing her wilder schemes.

April 19th
I went to bed calm & free of emotion—then dreamed of E all night. It does *not* mean that I am about to give in to my weakness for her. On the contrary, I find myself able to control my emotions. I plan to walk out with James, & will insist on guiding our footsteps in the opposite direction to the Parsonage.

*   *   *

To my surprize & dismay, during our walk James has reminded me that we are now supposed to be leaving Rosings this Saturday. I cannot go. Not yet. I have told James that I propose to stay another full week after this one, & leave on the last Saturday of the month. He has made no objection, & appears convinced by my mendacious explanation—namely that, contrary to my expectations, my man of business has written that I am not needed in London 'til the end of the

151

month.

I went back with James, & immediately ventured out again, alone. Miss Elizabeth's favourite walk—once more I met her there. I am now persuaded that she meant me to find her. Can she care for me? Unexpectedly, I find the thought too sweet to bear. Walking alone with her, I imagined how it would be if I could always be thus in her company. I found myself picturing a visit to Hunsford in which we would both be guests at Rosings. I murmured a few words of this to her. It could only happen if I made her my Wife . . .

April 20th
This morning James & I visited the Parsonage together. I cannot refrain from shewing my face there: it would look particular, since I have hitherto been a regular visitor. Today her back hair is gathered up into a loose knot. Untie the ribbon, & it would cascade down over her shoulders . . . As usual, I could find no words. To my dismay, James began to teaze me & to draw everyone's attention to how tongue-tied I was, commenting that I am not normally so silent. Mrs Collins & her Sister stared. E appeared to take no particular note of James's remarks, but half-turned her head as if to look at me, & instead turned back smilingly to him. Is she too timid to meet my eye?

April 21st
I managed to keep my footsteps from wandering towards the Parsonage all morning—& then learned to my dismay that James had been less discreet. What does he say to her when they are alone together?

This evening, the Parsonage party came over to take tea, & she was asked to oblige us with some music. As she played she smiled at me. I am convinced that she paid more attention to me than to James.

Watching my Aunt as she sat reading, I was suddenly reminded of my Mother, who had the same aquiline profile (which I too have inherited). For the first time in my life, I wonder about Mamma—could she possibly have been as proud & arrogant as my Aunt now seems to me? I begin to feel embarrassed at her manifold discourtesies. Is she truly as overbearing as she seems? And if I have never noticed it before, am I too guilty of the same fault? Am I proud?

April 22nd
I must not think of her.

April 23rd
Dreamed of her all night, & woke in a ferment. I must go to her! I can no longer hold back. I could eat nothing, & am unable to recollect what Peebles said when he came in to attend to my *toilette*. I took no sustenance, but seized my hat & left the house. I walked fast through the park, & arrived at the Parsonage dishevelled & out of breath. At the door I met her, dressed to go out. How her eyes sparkled! I cannot live without those eyes . . . She waved me in, telling me that she herself was going for a walk, but that Mrs Collins was in the parlour, & would be happy to receive me—then left the house. I was obliged to sit for a whole half-hour with Mrs Collins & her Sister, who, as usual, stared me out of countenance. Just as I felt I could

153

without offence take my leave, the door opened & the Rector came in. It was altogether impossible to escape from his salutations & compliments; it was a full hour before I could withdraw. As soon as I was out of the house, I searched for her everywhere, but she was not to be found on any of her favourite walks. I had to return to Rosings, already shamefully late for the nuncheon, & listen to my Aunt's complaints about my irregular habits.

Later: I have concluded that I have been fortunate indeed not to find her at home alone. I could not have held back—I would irrevocably have bound myself to a woman whose connexions I cannot approve, whose family I cannot respect.

April 24th

To church. She was hidden from me for most of the service by Mrs Collins's Sister, who, I understand, is called Miss Maria Lucas. Only once did the annoying child move to one side. Then I caught a brief glimpse of E's pure profile, her lowered eyes as she read from the Hymnal. On emerging, she curtseyed to us, & waited politely with the other ladies while Mr Collins paid his tedious compliments to my Aunt. Then they all turned away towards the Parsonage. I watched her go. She has narrow shoulders & an elegant, fragile form—& yet she is a robust walker!

I was roused from my musings by James, enquiring of me whether I had a sore throat. I told him no.

'Then why did not you join in & sing the hymns?'

I invented some excuse. In truth, I had not been aware that there were any hymns.

I know not how I lived through the day. She is to be with us at dinner tonight: I can think of nothing else. Received a letter from Miss Caroline, & one from Pargeter. I could not even bring myself to open them. I paced about the Library all morning. In search of a dry volume, picked out the Essayes of Monsieur de Montaigne, & opened the book at random. The first words I read therein were: *'Passion penetrates even into the secret of reason, infecting & corrupting the same . . .'*

My Aunt castigated me for my restlessness: 'Cannot you sit in one place for a few seconds, Nephew? Your perambulations exhaust me.'

I apologized, & sat down, only to find myself on my feet again a minute later.

April 25th

Dinner last night was a nightmare—I conscious only of her presence, unable to respond to the simplest remark. I should have left the room.

This morning I feel no different. The urge to be with her is still upon me. It is too difficult to seek her out alone—but I must let her know my true feelings. I shall write to her.

LETTER

April 25th

My dear Madam,

You must by now have become aware of the assiduity of my visits to the Parsonage. What I have to say may therefore come as no surprize to you. You must know that I hold you in the highest regard. I ask nothing better than to make you mistress of my heart & of Pemberley. Your want of connexion means nothing to me.

My Aunt has long cherished the hope that I may wed my Cousin; other equally glorious matches have been proposed for me; but I am prepared to relinquish all for love of you. I have been struggling to come to terms with the disadvantages of this match, & find that I can face them with equanimity. My mind is made up. Your want of fortune is perfectly acceptable—I have enough for both.

I herewith offer you my hand & my heart. Dare I be so bold as to hope that you may look kindly on my proposal?

Your devoted servant &c.,
Fitzwilliam Darcy.

I read over this epistle twice before I realized how absurd it is. To pretend that her disgraceful family does not matter!

I shall have to leave Rosings soon: today James has received a letter ordering him to regain his regiment within the week. He purposes to leave Rosings in three days' time. I do not see how I can linger on after his departure.

April 26th
I have scarcely slept. I write these few words in the Library. Today, I purpose to commit myself irrevocably. I cannot pretend that she is my equal: tongues will wag. But I cannot live without her.

I have been up since dawn. Peebles came in with my shaving water to find me in my shirtsleeves, surrounded by discarded papers.

I continued in this way all morning, & was hoping to put my courage to the test later in the day; but James has just now poked his head round the Library door to inform me that he is intending to visit the Parsonage & invite her out on a walk, & to enquire whether I have any objection to his going alone.

Alone? Is he then undaunted by her poverty? Has his imminent departure fixed his purpose? If she will have him, I shall have missed my only chance of happiness, & by a paltry couple of hours. Had I but gone earlier this morning!

*   *   *

James is returned, & I can tell from his face that nothing untoward has occurred between him & her. His face wears not the glow of a man successful in love. I shall dress for dinner with the utmost care: the Parsonage party are all expected to take tea tonight. I hope I may succeed in drawing her away from the company & speaking to her alone.

*   *   *

Shortly to go down to dine, I write this in haste. Peebles has touched me by his fatherly concern. When he came up to help me with my *toilette*, he first busied himself about the room; then smoothed my coat carefully over my shoulders, knelt down to burnish my boots with a clean silk handkerchief, then, still kneeling, said, without looking up: 'I wish you very happy, Master Fitz.'

I stared down at him. He did not meet my eye. Finally, after a long silence, I said 'Thank you.' He offered me a rosebud for my buttonhole. 'It is the first rose of summer, from her ladyship's glass-house,' he told me. I refused it gently, & left the room.

Half an hour before they arrive: I am in the Library, attempting to calm myself by concentrating on Gibbon's *Decline & Fall of the Roman Empire*. Peebles must still be upstairs as I write. I hope that his wish comes true, & that Elizabeth & I will be happy together.

LETTER

April 27th

~~My dear~~ Madam,

Do not alarm yourself: this letter is not to be a reiteration of the proposals which so ~~distressed~~ disgusted you ~~this~~ last evening. I merely seek to address some of your remarks, & to justify myself against the accusations which you have seen fit to make against me.

Why continue? She has rejected me, with contumely. Why did I leave the party at Rosings, & make my way to the Parsonage, where she had remained alone? I had far better forget everything that has passed this evening.

Forget? I can never forget her words. She has told me that I am the last man in the world she would ever wish to marry! That I am ungentlemanly! That I am unjust to Wickham! Surely I must rebut this last charge. Let me at least

158

try to explain about Wickham. I have never told it, nor written it to anyone. She shall be the only one to know. May she think the better of me for it!

I must in all justice explain the nature of my hostility to treatment of relations with Mr Wickham. It is true that my late Father loved him like a son, & wished to make generous provision for his future as a man of the cloth. However, when it fell to me to execute my dear Father's wishes, Wickham expressed such strong reservations about a career in the Church that I made him a handsome financial settlement instead. That money he rapidly gambled away.

I can fill in the details of his attempts to extract more & more money from me later. Let us get to the heart of the matter:

The chiefest of my grievances against Mr Wickham I have told to no body 'til this moment. It concerns his behaviour last summer, & involves my Sister Georgiana, then but fifteen years old. I need scarcely add, that I count on your discretion not to reveal what I am about to write: no body knows it, but the three persons concerned.
Until last summer, Georgiana, nervous of the close proximity to France, would never venture near the sea which separates us from that country. Now that the danger of invasion seemed less immediate, she was spending a few weeks in Margate with her chaperone, Mrs Younge, enjoying the sea air. I decided on a whim to pay her a visit.

In my letter I cannot explain it all—how I reached the Queen's Promenade to find the house in an

159

uproar, & luggage piled up in the hall. The hired butler told me that Miss Darcy had unexpectedly departed but two hours since. Mrs Younge was due to follow her within the hour: she was in her chamber packing. He made to go upstairs to announce me, but I forestalled him, & ran up quickly myself. Mrs Younge emerged from her chamber, carrying what I immediately saw was Georgiana's jewel-case. At the sight of me she turned pale; I had to help her to a chair. She had the wit to pretend that her alarm was caused by the shock of my unexpected arrival, & informed me that my Sister had wished to go to London with her dear friend Miss Rosalind Goulding. She herself was to follow as soon as the luggage was packed up.

I had never heard of any Miss Goulding; and, moreover, Mrs Younge had been strictly enjoined to apprize me of any decisions concerning G's movements.

'O, you know how Miss Georgiana can be: hasty & impetuous. She will brook no contradiction once her blood is up. There was no holding her,' said she, speaking more confidently now. The portrait she painted of my Sister was palpably false, for G is a gentle, biddable girl. I had a strong sense of danger threatening my Sister.

I seized Mrs Younge by the shoulders & shook her. 'Tell me the truth, woman! Or it will be the worse for you.'

'It is the truth,' she answered, attempting to thrust me away.

I shook her still harder. 'It is not,' I cried. 'You cannot deceive me. If you do not explain everything immediately, I shall have you brought before the magistrate.'

I had not reckoned with her impudence. The woman continued insisting that she was telling the truth, & even threatened to call for help in her turn: it was scandalous that a gentleman should presume to lay hands on her in this manner, &c., &c. As she spoke, she glanced anxiously over to the table, where I perceived a letter. I snatched it up: my name was on the envelope.

Mrs Younge reluctantly disclosed that she had in her possession a letter to me from my Sister, who had eloped with Mr Wickham. Mrs Younge, in whom I had been sadly deceived, refused at first to reveal their destination. At length she reluctantly let fall that the couple purposed to stay at —, a village about two hours' journey from Margate.

I do not care to remember how the woman first lied to me, leading me to believe that they were on the road to Gretna Green, & then offered to tell me their true destination in return for payment, which I handed over. I recovered G's jewel case from her, & sent Smalley to find me a fresh saddle-horse.

I was on my way within ten minutes, on a fresh horse ~~I might possibly overtake them, since in a carriage their progress must be slow.~~ *I had to acknowledge however that there was little prospect of overtaking them before irreparable damage was done. After a number of delays, I reached the inn at —.*

It took me just over an hour to reach the inn—it would have been quicker, but that I lost my way &

had to make enquiries. I tethered my horse outside & hastened in. The landlord ambled slowly out of a back parlour, wiping his hands on his apron. When I implored him to lead me to the young gentleman & lady, he denied any knowledge of them. I had to resort to bribery before he grudgingly pointed with his thumb to a small staircase at the back of the room.

This is the moment which I prefer to forget. Indeed, over the last eight months I have made strenuous attempts not to recall it. I must do so now.

I ran up the stairs, then proceeded quietly along the corridor. I put my ear to the door. I could hear weeping—my Sister's voice. I tried the door, which was not locked. I tiptoed inside. The curtains were drawn, & a candle burned on the table. They both lay on the bed. She was . . . she was only half-clad. She was weeping. Propped up on one arm, he was looking down at her. Then he laughed, & reached out a hand to touch her. She shrank from him. I strode over to the bed & hauled him off. He was in a disgusting state of undress. She averted her face, covering herself with the bedclothes. He looked up at me from the floor & grinned: 'Too late, Fizzibuzz. Too late. Your timing's perfect. I was hoping you would find us out, but not 'til I had secured her. Now you can arrange a regular marriage for us. It will look so much better than an elopement! Think of Lady Catherine, & your noble Fitzwilliam relatives. I would not have them turn my dear Wife & myself from their door!'

Mr. Wickham & my Sister were alone in the room. He told me that I had no alternative but to permit them to marry.

'Marriage? Marry her to a scoundrel like you?' I exclaimed.

'She's ruined otherwise, I tell you! Do you understand nothing? Dullard!' Then he added: 'At any rate her fortune is now mine. That will teach you to blight my hopes & baulk me of my legacy from your Father.'

The mention of my Father enraged me; but I controlled my temper, told him contemptuously that he could have none of her money without my agreement, and, walking over to the bed, sat down beside Georgiana. 'Do you love him?'

Still weeping, she shook her head.

I asked quietly: 'Did he force you, my child?'

Then she nodded. I turned & struck him with my fist—I could not help myself. Wickham has always been a coward in a fight. He cringed away from me, all his complacency gone.

I went back to the bed & bent over Georgiana. I stroked her hair & wiped the tears from her cheeks. She trembled, but did not push my hand away. 'Do you love him, Georgie?' I asked her again.

'No, no! Not now!' she sobbed. 'I thought he was my friend. I trusted him, 'til he . . . I hate him. I hate him!'

'What you want me to do?'

'Please take me away,' she whispered.

But my Sister indicated to me that she had repented of her rash elopement, & now viewed him with the utmost repugance. Eventually, he agreed to remain silent in return for a handsome annuity. It is that

163

money which bought him his commission.

His only response when I offered him the money was: 'Not enough. I need ready cash now, for my travel expenses.'

'Not a penny. You have my note.'

'Then I can't leave.' He was abject, but insistent. I tossed him a few coins, which he actually picked off the floor.

'It is not enough. I need a more substantial sum.'

'Very well,' I said through my teeth, & gave him 10*l*.

'But what about the rest? Can I trust you?'

I shrugged. 'Trust me or not—you'll get nothing more from me now.'

He snatched up his coat & made to leave. At the door he turned: 'O well, if I can't have her, I can't. At least I'll be better off for this day's work.'

I need not describe in detail how I helped my poor Sister to safety, & how I hushed the matter up. Suffice it that no body suspected that aught was amiss. But worse was yet to come—poor Georgiana feared that she was with child unwell [?] *about to suffer the consequences of her rashness. September went by, & October; it was not until November that she knew that she was safe. The relief was indescribable. Now my concern is to repair her shattered life. She is very young—a mere child; she will, I hope, succeed in restoring her ruined happiness. I hope too that she may one day find peace with another, worthier man.*

On reflection, I wonder if I have been wise. I know that I can count on Elizabeth's discretion—

164

whatever her feelings for me, she would never be so dishonourable as to gossip about our family misfortunes. But however much I may trust E, it would be improper in me to expose my poor Sister, by letting a written account of her disastrous mistake go forth into the world. I will have to change the letter.

Instead, I think I should tell her what I told James at the time: I shall say that I arrived at Margate before the elopement, & that G told me all, so that I was able to prevent Wickham's villainy. The pretence is thin, but it will have to do. I will have no time to draft a rough copy: it is dawn—almost time to deliver my letter into the indifferent hands of Elizabeth. I shall write my new account straightaway, give it to her, then leave this place, never to see her more.

*   *   *

I scribbled my letter, sealed it, waited impatiently 'til the time came for her usual walk; then I went out alone, hoping to find her in the Park, & deliver my envelope. Before long, I heard someone approaching from the road. It was she. She looked pale & ill, with dark shadows beneath her eyes. When I called her name, she raised her eyes briefly to mine, then lowered them immediately, with an expression of resentment such as I have never before seen. I feared for my letter. When I held it out to her through the bars of the great gates, I was afraid lest she push it away. But she reluctantly took it from me, & at once turned to leave. Through those bars, the visible signs of the insuperable barrier between us, I watched her go.

No sooner was I back at my Aunt's house than James told me that he is shortly to walk down to the Parsonage and take his leave of the Collinses & Elizabeth. He seems to assume that I am to accompany him. He is right, of course: it would look strange indeed if I failed to behave with ordinary courtesy, & make my farewell visit. Everyone would start wondering why—which is the last thing I would wish. Besides, I am most preoccupied as to the effect of my letter. Will she have softened at all towards me? Perhaps it will show in her face.

*   *   *

I am expected to dress for dinner, but instead reach for this Diary. It is my only confidant. Here I will confess what I can tell to no living soul: that I went with James to the Parsonage today in the hopes of catching one last glimpse of her.

But she was not there. They said that, contrary to her usual custom, she was still out in the Park. Reading my letter? Determined to keep away lest I call? I shall never know. I sat for a few minutes in the very parlour in which she rejected me—'til I could bear it no longer, & took my leave.

Elizabeth, farewell.

END OF PART III

Part IV

LONDON & NEWSTEAD

April 28th

Six a.m. Awake all night—I rose, lay down again, lit my candle, read some of Wordsworth's new volume, recently recommended to me by Byron. I am ashamed to own that the poems made me weep. *'The still, sad music of humanity . . .'* This morning we leave for London. I cannot stay a day longer in this place. How shall I endure a four hours' journey alone with James, & not betray myself?

*   *   *

I managed the journey somehow. I was forced to pretend that I was unwell. It helped that I looked fatigued: I have scarce slept for three nights. Stared out of the carriage window. Blue skies, trees in blossom, black mud splashing up from the wet roads. James left me to my thoughts, but in his presence I could not allow myself to dwell on them: I must wait 'til I am alone.

Arrived home. My one consolation is Georgie, surprized & delighted at my unexpected return. She hastened back from Fitzwilliam House to be with me, & offered to play & sing for me last night, which meant I had no need to converse with her or with Mrs Annesley. When the ladies withdrew after dinner, I sat alone for an hour together, thinking dismal thoughts, & consuming far too much brandy.

April 29th

I must have been exhausted, for I slept well, &

woke feeling more sanguine. I shall weather this shock—I am determined not to permit her ingratitude to destroy me. I rose betimes & called for Peebles. He very quiet, and, after shaving me, pressed my shoulder as he removed the towel. I do not wish for his pity, nor for anyone else's.

Could not bring myself to attend matins this morning. Instead, to Jackson's for a mill. Bob said to me as he bandaged my fists: 'None of the other gentlemen is here today, Sir, it being the Sabbath. You'll have to work with the punch-bag.' The *other* gentlemen! If I am to believe *her*, I am not worthy to be counted among their number. The thought enraged me: I hit the punch-bag so hard that I split my knuckles. Bob obliged to fix me up with a dressing. I shall be unable to box for days.

April 30th
Had she studied for years together how to humiliate me, she could not have devized a more painful torture. Every minute of the day I revolve in my mind her most cruel words: *'Had you behaved in a more gentlemanlike manner.'* How dared she thus attack me? How am I not a gentleman? What did I say that was so 'ungentlemanlike'? Was it my frankness in acknowledging that she is an unworthy bride? Was I supposed to play the hypocrite with the woman I wished to marry? I do not know what she would have had me do. However I expressed myself she would doubtless have found fault with me.

*   *   *

Still angry. I have resolved to cease moping &

brooding at home. To Brooks's this evening. Several of the fellows told me I was looking *'devilish poorly'*. Why do not they believe my insistence that I am perfectly fit & in good spirits?

May 1st
I must keep my mind off E & her cruel attack. I have been in Town for four days: why, because I have been insulted, may not I lead a normal life? A call on Charles & his Sisters is overdue. They will be vexed to learn that I have failed to notify them of my return.

*　　　*　　　*

I found them all at home together. As I walked into their drawing-room, Charles rose, exclaiming anxiously, 'What's the matter, Fitz? You look out of sorts.'

'I have been unwell, but am now in excellent health,' said I.

'You don't look it. What has been the matter?'

And I was obliged to invent a specious explanation. I must indeed look woeful, if even Charles has observed it—he is not generally wont to see such things.

As for Miss Caroline, she has absolutely overwhelmed me with her solicitude, & insists on sending round a recipe for beef tea which Jennings is to serve to me every day. She would not listen when I told her that I dislike beef tea—but unwelcome tho' her beverage may be, it is a comfort to feel that I am not abhorrent to *all* my acquaintance.

Charles took me on one side to say that he has

emerged from the doldrums, & is now endeavouring to enjoy himself. 'I cannot forget what I have lost, but I am attempting to divert myself. I daresay that with time the hurt will fade.'

I can only hope devoutly that the same thing will one day be true of me. At present the pain is sharp indeed!

May 2nd

I need to remind myself of the things she said to me. It will be hurtful, but I must refute the accusations she has levelled against me—at least for my own satisfaction. There can, of course, be no communication with *her*, ever again.

1. She said that my affection had been unwillingly bestowed on her. It is quite true—but how should it be otherwise, when her younger Sisters, her Mother, nay, even her Father, are all guilty of gross impropriety? Any man who allies himself with such a family, let him have but the lowest standing in society, will find himself obliged to endure the scorn of his friends. I wrote as much in my letter to her. I hope that it was tactfully phrased. I feel sure that my riposte must have hit home.

2. She accused me of ruining her Sister's happiness. But I had also to think of the happiness of my friend! E was doubtless unaware of Jane's clandestine letter to her Officer. Imagine Charles marrying for love, against the advice of all his friends & family, only to discover the true character of his new Wife! I am not ashamed of what I have done. I told E so in my letter.

3. She attacks me for causing the 'misfortunes' of Wickham. I have given a partial explanation in

172

my letter, which, tho' it is far from detailing the full perfidy of the man, is nevertheless amply sufficient to ensure that she sees the scoundrel in his true colours.

4. She takes me to task for not being a gentleman: 'Had you behaved in a more gentlemanlike manner.' This I cannot bear. I cannot reply to it: if I protest that I am indeed a gentleman born, I seem absurd—& yet I cannot swallow this insult without feeling the pain of it.

5. She attacks my character with merciless cruelty. I am, she tells me, arrogant, conceited, selfish & inconsiderate of others' feelings! If that is what she thinks, what is the use of wasting further time? I had much better forget her.

As I cannot box because of my bad hand, I plan a long ride, & afterwards to the play with Charles & some of the fellows. But I recall that it is the Sabbath. Will attend Evensong.

* * *

As he prepared me for bed, Peebles continued to exhibit a solicitude which enrages me. He said not a word, but the very way he unfolded my nightgown exuded concern. Why cannot people leave me alone?

May 3rd
I AM FURIOUS. Not content with refusing my hand, she has insulted me in every possible way. She took my honourable proposal of marriage, & flung it in my teeth. To crown it all, she told me that I was the last man in the world she could ever marry. And I, *not gentlemanlike*! To think that I

173

ever thought that I loved her!

Today I could not stay indoors. Called on Charles. He was from home, but Miss Caroline received me. She was wearing a gown that she had worn one day when E was staying at Netherfield. I recalled seeing them together, & finding E's soft blue attire more becoming than Miss Caroline's harsh green. In the middle of my musings, I realized that Miss Caroline was impatiently repeating a question. It turned out that she was inviting me to escort her & her Sister to Vauxhall Gardens. 'Now that the weather is improved, it would be a pleasant trip,' she said. But I cannot—I cannot go about with this woman who has spent time with Elizabeth, & who, at every turn, reminds me of what I would prefer to forget.

I must control this impulse to run away from everything that reminds me. Why should *she* carry off such a victory over me? I must fight back. I therefore escorted Miss Caroline on a shopping expedition to Bond Street.

This evening I sat alone in the Library, reading & drinking Port Wine. Despite all my good resolutions, I put down Boswell's *Life of Dr Johnson*, & picked up *Romeo & Juliet*.

May 4th
Having gone to bed with thoughts of E for company, I slept but little, & remembered her for most of the night. Today my rage is spent: I fear that all her accusations against me are justified. I am indeed cold & insensitive—else how could I have misjudged her feelings? I truly believed that she was encouraging my suit. I had no expectation of her refusing me.

I shut myself away in the Library all day, not at home to callers. I went over & over her words. It must then be true that I am no gentleman. I must be selfish. She is right to hate me, & I am indeed the last man in the world who deserves to wed her.

Evening. I feel worn out & wretched. I wish that I could ask Georgie to keep me company after dinner, but, not wanting to tell her my sorrows, I must pretend that everything is as usual. Thus it is that she has again gone out to spend the evening with Augusta & her Brothers, with Mrs Annesley as chaperone. I am quite alone. I have resolved to occupy my mind, & to construe some Latin verse.

*　　　*　　　*

I took down a Virgil, & opened it. I swear I did not chuse the passage—it fell open of its own accord at the lament of Dido, abandoned by Aeneas. O, the agony of her suffering! Her anger & her pain!

> *quid loquor? aut ubi sum? quae mentem insania mutat?*
> *infelix Dido, nunc te facta impia tangunt?*
> [Editor's note: Dryden's translation of Virgil (which Mr Darcy must have known) renders this as: 'What have I said? Where am I?' Fury turns / My brain, and my distemper'd bosom burns.']

When I finally put down the book, I was more disturbed than I have been for days.

May 5th
Too low to write today.

May 6th

Charles called again this morning. He says he is anxious about me: he has never seen me so out of sorts. He was commanded by his Sister to bring me back with him for breakfast. Afterwards, we went for a stroll. He attempted unsuccessfully to draw me out. I cannot confide in him: how would it seem to him, to learn that I have been paying court to one Sister, while barring him from all intercourse with the other? And yet I long to speak . . .

May 7th

To my surprize, G's little friend Isabella has arrived on an extended visit. I have no recollection of having discussed this with G, but from her demeanour I deduce that I must have done so. I cannot continue like this, oblivious of my surroundings & my actions. I was obliged to seat the young lady beside me at dinner. Luckily, she seems somewhat intimidated by my presence, & spoke but little.

My Aunt Fitzwilliam has sent word to remind me that she is still waiting on my answer about my Sister's confounded Coming Out. I cannot occupy my mind with such trifles—not at this time. I have therefore written to her that Georgie is too young, & that her Coming Out must wait 'til next year. I mentioned this to G herself, who said, 'Of course you must not bother with such things Fitz: not at present, while you are so cast down.' I had hoped that I was concealing my distemper from her at least, but evidently my efforts are wasted.

May 8th

I have been too ready to shoulder the blame for my disastrous proposal. Elizabeth too was abominable, treating my honourable offer of marriage as an insult. I awoke yesterday with a strong sense of injury, & brooded all day on the wrongs which she has inflicted on me. *Ungentlemanlike*, forsooth! I have resolved to have nothing more to do with women. I even went so far as to cast aside this Diary—which I have been writing all these years at the behest of a woman, tho' she is my own dead Mother.

Last evening, in a gesture of defiance against all gentlewomen, I visited the *bordello*. I asked for Esmeralda, but was told that she has left. In her place they gave me one Dulcinea, a small girl with but little flesh on her. Still, she was merry, with yellow curls, & made me laugh when I asked whether she had really been named after Cervantes's beloved. She replied that at home she was known as 'Mopsy' but that her employer, Madam Flint, had required her to chuse a more alluring sobriquet.

My evening proved enjoyable enough 'til I took her to bed. With my eyes shut, my arms clasped round that little body, it came to my mind that E is just so—slender & small. It might almost have been she whom I held in my arms. I was forced to turn my head aside, that Dulcinea might not observe my tears.

Then home, & dreamed of E, & awoke this morning feeling utterly alone.

I caught sight of myself in the glass as Peebles combed my hair. As a result, I spent the day wrestling with the conviction that I am the most undesirable of mortals. She told me that I was the last man in the world she could ever marry. Can one wonder at her reluctance? I am pale & grim-faced, with a great beak of a nose which shews me to be proud no matter how I behave. I have always been conscious of my height, which I felt conferred additional standing on me. Now I see I am a great, lumbering, dunderhead. Of course she could never love me! What arrogance to have presumed that she could!

Later, I went riding, wishing that my hand were healed so that I could spar or fence, or even shoot, instead.

I was expecting an evening alone, sitting dully in the Library; but Charles came, & carried me off to Boodle's, where, for once, I played at cards for money. I won a considerable sum, which pleased me not at all. Helmsley was there, & invited me to stay next month. He has a place near Ascot & has invited a large party of fellows for the races. I refused—I am no company for any man.

May 9th

To church with G & her little friend Isabella. I must begin to lead a normal life: it would seem very strange in me to miss the Divine Service for two weeks in a row. The text of the sermon was James iv.6: '*God resisteth the Proud, but giveth grace unto the Humble.*' The vicar spoke with feeling on the folly of pride & arrogance. It might have been Elizabeth castigating me. I felt bruised & saddened. Am I really as proud as she suggests?

All day I have been pondering this question. For the first time, I begin to wonder about my complacent assumption that I have a right to my superior position in society. To whom do I owe this conviction? To those responsible for my upbringing? I have been remembering my Aunt's manner, her patronizing behaviour towards Elizabeth, her insolent comparisons between her own lordly position & that of her inferiors. When we were all at Rosings together, I did begin to have an inkling of how deplorably she must strike a dispassionate observer such as Elizabeth.

And now I come to think of it, my Aunt Fitzwilliam is no better. Yesterday I met her in the porch after matins, & she complained at the top of her voice that the coal merchant's Wife had presumed to give her 'Goodday' in church—to her, Countess Fitzwilliam! Did the woman not know her place? &c., &c. Previously I should have smiled indulgently. Nowadays, such arrogance disgusts me.

During my earliest childhood I was made aware that Mamma was the daughter of an Earl, & that the name of Darcy was a proud & ancient one. Who was it suggested to my childish mind that these things were important? Who but mine own parents? I cannot bear to think on it.

I have sneered at Elizabeth for her family's shortcomings, & proclaimed that an alliance with her would turn me into a laughing-stock! But in insulting her family, was not I forgetting the shortcomings of *my own*?

May 10th

In his latest letter, Pargeter upbraids me gently for my recent neglect of my estates. He is right: I cannot spend the rest of my days repining. I must move on! Henceforward, I shall occupy my time constructively: I plan to catalogue my Library in Town—& later to do the same for the Pemberley books, which are considerably more numerous. I shall begin work in earnest on the new ballroom wing—there are chandeliers to be found, furniture to be chosen, &c. I shall resume my sparring at Jackson's—or, if my hand is still too damaged, shall go to Angelo's every day to fence. A brisk ride afterwards, & a session with my accomptants—& the day is profitably employed.

Began with Angelo's: my hand is still rather stiff where the skin was broken. I managed a bout against Andrewes, but have decided that it is too soon. Instead, I shall practise shooting for the next week or so. Ran into Bullivant, who tells me that the Luddites are wreaking havoc in Nottingham, breaking machines. I am glad now that, having discussed the matter with my tenants & noted their antagonism, I decided not to invest in stocking-machines.

On returning home, I began my attempt at a catalogue. I started with large sheets of paper, but soon found that I would be forever shuffling them around, & inserting titles which I had forgot to include. I therefore resolved to write the details of each book on a separate card. Off to Riley's on Ludgate Hill to purchase the cards. I shall have to have a cabinet made to hold them. When I got home, there was just time for a ride before supper. After supper, I sat in the Library alone, & catalogued twenty books, listening to the distant sound of G at the pianoforte. I believe that we have about two thousand books here in London— so at this rate I should be finished in less than four months.

On completing the twentieth book, I realize that I have not yet made contact with Batchelor to bring me over the detailed accounts that I may examine them. Tomorrow! There is scarce time to write this before retiring. I feel quite exhausted.

I have not thought of her today—not once.

May 11th
To Cox's for shooting practice. Byron was there. His lame foot scarcely interferes with his sporting activities. In addition to his boxing & fencing, he is a crack shot, & hits the target every time. I remember him playing cricket at Harrow, & recall once or twice making the runs for him when he was batting—for running is the one thing that defeats him. Afterwards, he lured me to an ill-famed coffee shop in Douro Street, crowded with shady characters. I never meet him but he inveigles me into situations I had liefer avoid.

He wishes Charles & me to come with him to Newstead, his country seat. It is not so far from Pemberley. I know not if I wish to go, but will discuss it with Charles.

Batchelor came. We have agreed that this year the income from my London properties is to go towards the new ballroom at Pemberley. He attempted to dissuade me from this project, on the grounds that it will do little to enhance the value of the house. I cannot but agree—but there is Georgie's preference to consider. It is, after all, her home as well as mine. She herself seems to have spent a happy day at the warehouses with Isabella & Augusta. Poor Mrs Annesley looks quite worn out with so many young ladies in her care!

May 12th

Today called on Charles to hear his opinion of
Byron's invitation. Miss Caroline intercepted me,
& asked me eagerly what my Aunt de Bourgh had
thought of the paint she had chosen, the chair-
seats she had arranged to have upholstered, etc. I
really knew not what to reply—my Aunt was so
incensed at poor Miss Caroline's *'interference'*, that
she made no attempt to write & thank her, nor did
she even ask me to do so verbally. Poor Miss
Caroline! I fudged it as best I could, but she looked
quite crestfallen.

Charles has no objection to visiting Byron at
Newstead. Accordingly, I shall send word that we
accept his invitation. What with that & my
projects, my life has become very full. I spent the
afternoon over the accounts Batchelor left with
me, which seem in good order. I have a fair sum
invested with Child's, but am wondering if it would
be wise to move some of it into the modern
industries. Is this an acceptable departure for a
gentleman? Am thinking of the local collieries—or
perhaps a foundry. Then there is the cotton trade.
I must enquire further into this. Carruthers has
been regretting the law prohibiting the slave trade
with Jamaica. By operating discreetly, one can still
make handsome profits: he urges me to invest; but
at that I draw the line.

May 13th

To church with G. Isabella claimed a headache, &
staid at home. G confided that her friend was not
really indisposed but is suffering from a surfeit of

sermons, her Father being a clergyman. I myself failed to attend to the sermon—to my shame. I was thinking about the bay mare Andrewes was riding yesterday in the Park, a fine animal, of Arab extraction. He has offered to take me to the stud, a day's ride outside London. I wonder if there would be a horse there suitable for G? I have not forgot that I promised her a new mount some time ago.

May 14th
My Aunt Catherine writes to remind me that she is intending to come up to Town early next month. She adds that she is planning to supervize the redecoration of all her reception rooms. Her wish is for *'marble-effect scumbling.'* She adds: *'We shall be rubbing shoulders with craftsmen & tripping over ladders all day long, unless some kind friend be willing to take us in.'* I take that for a veiled plea for an invitation to stay in Grosvenor Square—but how to respond perplexes me. G finds my Aunt's peremptory manner exceedingly trying, & I have come to feel somewhat embarrassed by her *hauteur*—& furthermore I am loath to spend my days with one who cannot but remind me of E at every turn—tho' she may have news of her from Mrs Collins, which I could possibly elicit on discreet questioning.

I have shewn my Aunt's letter to G, who tossed her head & said, 'I don't care a rap for my Aunt. She is always disapproving of everything I do. Why should we entertain her here? I shall have no freedom—& I am sure Isabella won't like it either.'

I protested that it was the least we could do for our nearest living relative.

'What nonsense!' answered she. 'My Uncle

Fitzwilliam is just as close, & much less tiresome.'

Eventually I persuaded her to put up with my Aunt for a brief visit. I have written accordingly to invite her up to London.

Spent the day poring over my accounts & cataloguing my books. By the evening I was exhausted & out of temper. This pretence is sapping my energy. For how long must I struggle to delude myself that my life is normal? The instant that I allow my mind to roam, it fixes on the cruel words with which she rejected me—& I remember that I am never to see her again.

May 15th
Spent the day with Andrewes, looking over the horses at the stud farm near Farnborough. They are beautiful beasts. I am tempted by an unbroken gelding. Young Joe would like nothing better than to break him in for me at Pemberley—but how to get him there?

Augusta to dinner, escorted by her Brother James, on a short furlough. Over the Port Wine, he mentioned E with a sigh: 'I still think of Miss Elizabeth Bennet. That young woman is likely to make some lucky man a delightful bride!' I quickly turned the conversation, & invited him to play billiards. He did not mention her again.

Afterwards we listened to G, Isabella & Augusta singing in harmony. They finished with a lively canon:

My dame has a lame tame crane,
My dame has a crane that is lame.
Pray, gentle Jane, let my dame's lame tame crane
Feed & come home again . . .

The name of Jane has staid with me all evening. I remember, on that terrible evening, E accusing me of ruining her Sister's happiness, *'perhaps for ever.'* I remember the indignant look in her dark eyes as she spoke the words. I have been selfishly preoccupied with my own misfortune, & have spared but little thought for her Sister's. Perhaps it was not true, perhaps Jane did not write to any Officer, but there is no going back. If I was mistaken, & she loved Charles after all, it is too late now, but I am responsible for suffering which, as I now know to my cost, is past bearing!

May 16th
No sleep last night. Felt sore & dismal all day.

May 17th
Great news! We have defeated the French in a great battle at Albuera. I read it in the newspapers. Later, met Carruthers at Boodle's—he was full of the victory. They say that we have suffered great losses. Carruthers tells me that Whiting is much perturbed, waiting anxiously for news of his Brother Jack, who is in the Lancers, at present stationed in Spain, & must have been fighting. I remember Jack Whiting at school—a little imp of a boy, two or three years below us. He was always in trouble with the Beaks. I recall the whole school being given a detention because some mischief-maker had stuffed old Ponsonby's ink-bottle with live worms. When it transpired that Whiting Minor was the culprit, I, as Monitor, was obliged to thrash him. I can only hope that he did not hold it against me in later life—& that he survives to tell me so.

May 18th

This morning at breakfast, Georgie wished me a Happy Birthday. Twenty-eight years old today—I had quite forgot. Later, she came to me in the Library, & enquired timidly whether I wished to ride out with Isabella & her, or whether I was still as low as ever. I regret that I snapped at her angrily, ordering her to leave me alone. Poor child—this is not her fault!

Catalogued thirty books today, & wrote to Pargeter about the proposed new dairy at Pemberley.

May 19th

Gave up cataloguing today, & went to Boodle's to discover what is happening on the Peninsula—the newspapers say very little to the purpose. Sad tidings! Jack Whiting severely wounded at Albuera. They are now saying that the battle-plan was faulty, & that Marshal Beresford is to blame. Whiting has no notion when or how Jack will be brought home.

This afternoon, obliged to take G & Isabella to Astley's. The clowns especially made me mournful. Isabella too wanting in liveliness. Afterwards, G assured me in private that she is wont to be more entertaining. 'It is your brooding presence that frightens her, Fitz!' I try my best, but evidently that is not good enough.

May 20th

My Aunt has replied by express to my invitation. To my dismay, her letter says: '*We shall be arriving next Saturday. Kindly provide a private parlour for Anne & Mrs Jenkinson—Anne finds it too fatiguing to spend all day in company.'* In truth, it had never occurred to me that Anne & her companion were to be of the party. I had assumed that my Cousin, being patently unfit to travel, would remain quietly at home. I cannot refuse to receive her—my Aunt is well aware that there is ample room in this house for two extra guests, & it would seem excessively churlish to object to my Cousin's being of the party.

After reflection, I have reached the conclusion that my Aunt is bringing her daughter as part of her sustained effort to arrange a match between the two of us. She should have realized by now that I have no interest in her schemes. For the duration of their visit, I shall be obliged to be frequently from home. On no account must I encourage any *tête-à-tête* between my Cousin & me.

May 21st
I have finally decided to accept Helmsley's invitation. I am off to Ascot tomorrow for a long weekend. The races start early this year. The Gold Cup is to be run next week. I have been watching a filly named Jannette, a very sweet runner—my odds are on her.

Luddite problem much discussed at White's this evening. Carruthers of the opinion that one must move with the times, & that it is absurd to hold out against the advance of the machine.

May 25th
If I was hoping for a congenial interlude to distract me from my troubles, I was sorely deceived. The

party was convivial indeed, but I have been unable to share my friends' high spirits. My horse's win at 5/4 scarcely raised a flicker in me. My stay at Ascot has been blighted by what happened on the first night.

I slept fitfully that night, & woke in the small hours with the realization that I must marry my Cousin Anne. It is the answer to everything: I shall no longer be able to pine for E, for ever out of my reach; I shall be fulfilling my duty to the family; I shall enable my Cousin to enjoy the role of Wife & Mother, which I fear would otherwise be denied her. I feel nothing for her, nothing. But it is of no account: as I can never love another woman, I might just as well make the sacrifice. It is all the same to me.

I rose, lit my candle, & sat on the edge of my bed, contemplating my future. It filled me with gloom; but what must be, must be, thought I.

Next morning, I viewed matters in a very different light, & was astonished at my own folly. Imprison myself in a loveless marriage, on some self-destructive whim! It cannot be . . . Every day I seemed to change my mind—now resigned, now rebellious; but the impression slowly grew that my sacrifice was inevitable.

As the week went by, my resolution gradually came to seem irrevocable; nevertheless, I have not had a moment's happiness since I took it. Must I really destroy myself thus, in the interests of I know not what? I think I must: I can see no means other than marriage of ridding myself of my unhappy passion. Once I am married, I *must* forget E. Such illicit thoughts become out of the question.

My dilemma is as ridiculous as it is distressing:

only by shackling myself to an unloved woman can I free myself of an unattainable one.

May 26th
My Aunt & Cousin have arrived. In addition to herself, her Daughter & Companion, my Aunt has brought her maid, Anne's maid, her coachman & footman, & another coachman to drive a second vehicle packed with portmanteaux, trunks & packages. My Aunt insisted on supervizing the servants as they unloaded all this baggage, & on ordering where everything should be put. She has brought us several jeroboams of Kentish cider made from her own apples.

After nuncheon, during which she maintained that our dining-room is too old-fashioned & needs to be redesigned, she declared her intention of issuing forth at once to inspect the work in her own house, with the parting words: 'You may look after Anne, Nephew. Kindly make sure that she is comfortable.' G was not there to support me: she has carried Isabella off to spend the day with Augusta.

My secret resolution very much on my mind, I observed my future bride closely. Anne was very pale & so fatigued that she was almost speechless. I sent her & Mrs Jenkinson upstairs to their apartments. I observed that Mrs Jenkinson had to assist her to mount the stairs.

May 27th
Jack Whiting has lost an arm, but is otherwise safe, & on his way home from Spain. So his Brother told me today at Angelo's, where we fenced. Afterwards he invited me to take coffee with him,

189

but I felt it incumbent on me to return home speedily to partake of breakfast with my Aunt. She has been at Hatchard's, *'equipping her Library'*. She always contrives to display the latest publications at Rosings.

After she had finished practising on her pianoforte, Georgie came to find me in the Library, & whispered that she found our visitors tedium itself. I have changed my mind: why do not I abandon this wretched plan, which will make not only myself but my Sister unhappy? Felt less heavy-hearted for the rest of the day, & celebrated with a bout at Jackson's, & a visit to Brooks's with Charles, who was pleased to find me somewhat merrier.

Anne kept to her room all day.

May 28th
Poor Anne so quiet & diminished in London. She keeps to her apartments, & only occasionally creeps downstairs like a little mouse, to sit in a sheltered corner of the drawing-room, with Mrs Jenkinson muffling her up in shawls to keep out the draughts. And to think that I had fixed on her to be the next mistress of Pemberley! I can scarcely endure the thought. What would Georgie have said?

May 29th
I found Anne in the Library, reading the newspaper. She asked me my opinion of the Luddites. She says that she herself is inclined to invest in the new machinery, & is looking into mechanical cider-presses for Rosings. She is well on the way to becoming a forward-looking &

prosperous landowner in her own right. I find this enterprizing character-trait sits oddly with her mouse-like demeanour.

Accompanied my Aunt, G & Isabella to visit Lady Howlett. G, as ever, shy in the company of strangers; Isabella fidgeted very much in her seat, & kept giving me sidelong glances. Anne as usual remained at home.

May 30th
My Aunt wished to attend matins, & packed Anne into the carriage also. I preferred to walk, & G walked with me, tho' she complained that her new pumps became scuffed & dirty. 'Still, anything is better than sharing a carriage with Aunt & Anne,' said she. Isabella also came, fearing my Aunt's disapproval. Walking briskly, we arrived at the church just as my Aunt was alighting from the carriage, complaining about the abominable London traffic, which had kept them motionless for nigh on a quarter of an hour. I assisted my Cousin out of the vehicle. She is so light & thin that her arm resting on mine seems almost weightless. I glanced down at her, & saw that she was looking up at me, with a mournful expression on her pale little face.

'You seem a trifle out of sorts, Cousin,' said I.

'O, it is nothing.' She brushed the back of her hand across her face in a dismissive, sideways gesture.

She fills me with pity. It must be hard for her to preserve some independence against such a strong-willed Mother—tho' her mind is as robust as my Aunt's ever was.

May 31st

Anne has seemed more chearful today, so much so that G invited her to drive in the Park with the young ladies—but she refused with a shudder. Instead, I sat with her for a large part of the afternoon, making desultory conversation—'til the topic of my proposed new dairy arose, when she produced several helpful suggestions for a new sluice system which she has shewn me in a book. She even sketched a diagram to shew how the system could be adapted to suit my needs. I could do worse than follow her advice.

June 1st

Anne's presence begins to oppress me—my pity for her knows no bounds. She does not complain: indeed, she frequently remains silent for hours together. Mrs Jenkinson seems to know her wants without being told. What ails her? Is her weakness the result of an illness, or is it attributable to low spirits? I have started attempting to draw her out, talking to her when I find her sitting alone. Tomorrow I have offered to take her in my phaeton to the Park, if the weather continues fine. To my surprize, she has accepted. G quite put out—she claims that I never take *her* up in the phaeton. I have had to promise to do so some day next week.

June 2nd

Drove in the Park with Anne. The pink parasol she held lent her face more colour: she looked almost pretty. I entertained her by pointing out some of the eccentrics who like to walk there. She caught sight of Sir Horace de Zouche, immense in his bright blue caped cloak, & I told her how he once tried to fight a duel, but was prevented from brandishing his foil by his enormous stomach. She laughed out loud. I realize to my amazement that I have never heard her laugh before. Poor child!

June 3rd
This evening we are invited to a ball at my Aunt Fitzwilliam's.

'Anne will stay behind with the girls & Mrs Jenkinson,' announced my Aunt Catherine. But to everyone's surprize, a quiet voice from the corner said, 'No, Ma'am. I think I shall come with you tonight.'

For her part Georgie made no response, but I could see that she looked mutinous. She is just come to find me, complaining bitterly about my Aunt's high-handedness: 'She flattens everything before her like a great garden roller. Why must I obey her?'

'You know that you may not attend a ball, Georgie,' said I mildly.

'It is so unfair! Fanny is allowed to go, & she is only a year older than Augusta. Why must we be always banished to the nursery, like babies?'

'Wait until next year, when you are Out.'

G fixed me with angry eyes, then stalked out of the Library, slamming the door.

*　　　*　　　*

Anne did accompany us this evening. She wore an elaborate pale-blue gown, with a matching turban. Her arms, emerging from the lacy sleeves, are painfully thin—never before have I seen them bare. She appears to have no bosom at all. At the ball she soon tired, & sat quietly in a corner, watching the other young people enjoying themselves. She scarcely smiled. I made sure that she was well supplied with food & drink, tho' I observed that she ate only a mouthful of trifle. My Aunt Fitzwilliam never serves ice-cream at her parties. I suspect that she finds it too expensive. I was obliged to stand up three or four times with my Cousins.

In the carriage home, poor Anne seemed so worn out that she could not speak. I actually carried her into the house & upstairs to her chamber, & laid her on her bed.

Afterwards I shut myself in my own chamber with my recollections of dancing with E for the first & only time.

June 4th
Took Georgie out for a drive in the phaeton to make up for missing the ball. She has forgiven me for that, but was annoyed that I refused to allow her to take the reins. She is developing a decidedly wilful streak.

*   *   *

G's uncertain temper these last few days has forced my hand. She appears to be on the verge of misbehaviour, & badly needs a Sister to guide her. I have taken a momentous decision: I must make my Cousin Anne an offer before I lose courage. Since I can never love again, I may as well bring some comfort to my Cousin's melancholy existence. Anne may be better off with a Husband than with her Mother, & G will eventually learn to accept her as a Sister. Though sickly, Anne is sensible, & will doubtless manage G better than I can. I had best act quickly before I change my mind.

June 5th

I have been trying to screw up my courage to speak to Anne—but I cannot do it. The sight of that little, pinched, unsmiling face chills me. It is not that she is bad, or foolish, or in any way reprehensible. It is just the thought of living forever with that wan presence in my house, day & night . . .

June 6th

This morning I resolved more firmly to ask Anne for leave to approach her Mother. Accordingly, after matins (which she did not attend), I found her sitting in Mamma's old parlour, gazing out of the window at the square garden opposite. Her small hands lay palm upwards on her lap, the fingers curling up like little dead claws. I enquired how she had come to chuse this deserted room, which has never been used since my Mother's death, sixteen years ago.

She turned her head slowly. 'Why, I sit here every morning,' answered she.

There was no sign of any occupation—no embroidery, no book. The old harpsichord was shut. How did she entertain herself every morning, alone in this chill little room? She was looking back at me now, her head turned away from the window. Behind her, the tall trees in the square shone green & gold in the sunlight. The dark

shape of her head seemed to stand between me &
the world beyond. I felt the need to be outside,
away from the house, in the fresh air. I excused
myself, & ran downstairs. Pausing only to pick up
my hat, I hastened out into the square.

I paced about on the pavement. I had let a
valuable opportunity slip. With her back to the
light, her face in the shadow, I had been unable to
read her expression: I might then have been
emboldened to speak.

O, how I wish I had not resolved to do so!

June 7th
This morning Charles came to call, complaining of
having been 'short-changed' on hiring a hackney
carriage. The term reminded me of something, I
could not recollect what. Later it came to me—it
was used by Wickham when he extorted a double
payment from me, that day in the inn at Meryton.
When I realized how he had cheated me, I had
thought of returning to the inn & confronting
him—but then I disdained to do so, & put the
affair out of my mind. What then had he meant
when he accused me of short-changing him? Of
course, the thing Elizabeth blamed me for, during
our last terrible conversation: depriving him of the
living that was his due. It had never occurred to me
that he might conveniently forget that I had given
him a generous payment in its stead. The man is
doubly dangerous, in that he appears to believe his
own monstrous fabrications.

June 8th
News has reached us that Badajoz is again under
siege. This war is indeed discouraging! No sooner

is a city captured than it is again attacked. Will they resist the enemy this time?

*   *   *

This afternoon I again forced myself to seek out my Cousin Anne. This time I found her in the Library alone—Mrs Jenkinson is accustomed to taking a nap after the cold meats. When I enquired what book Anne was reading, she held it up for me to see: *Annals of Agriculture & Other Useful Arts*. I had not known that I possessed such a volume; it must have belonged to my Father. We fell to discussing the different varieties of wheat which thrive in Kent & Derbyshire respectively, & thence to speaking of the more general difficulties relating to the management of a farm from a distance, as an absentee landlord. Conversing thus of our home farms, I found myself much more at ease with her, & began to wonder if this was the moment to make her my offer. The thought immediately caused me to become tongue-tied. My silence seemed like a contagion: it stopt her mouth, & we found ourselves sitting at a loss for words. After a lengthy, awkward silence, I finally sought refuge in a mention of the lime-trees but lately added to the avenue at Rosings, & enquired how they did. She responded that, according to the books, if the winter was like to be a hard one, they had much better have been planted in March than in November; the leaves of three of them were beginning to drop in a manner that boded ill. We discussed different methods of tree-planting for another ten minutes, by which time my awareness that I could not further delay my proposal again made my words dry up. Even my mouth was dry. I silently chid myself for my cowardice, & launched straight into my speech.

I have no notion what I said, nor how it sounded to her. I suspect that it was done without grace & without any show of feeling. However, she accepted me at once, and, before I knew it, we were engaged.

When I understood what I had done, I felt the need to be away from her presence. I rose abruptly and, bowing before her, lifted her hand to my lips. It was cold, a little damp. The bones felt thin & small, as if I were holding a small amphibian, which I could easily crush in my fist. The thought flashed through my mind that I had never held Elizabeth's naked hand in mine. Had my inopportune recollection of her shown in my face? I hastened from the Library, leaving Anne in possession of my fortune, if not my heart.

And now, as I write, I know that I have condemned myself to a life sentence. I feel nothing for my Cousin—nothing but pity and, I must confess it, a mild repugnance. I have promised to wed her, & so I must. She is to be my Wife & companion as long as we both shall live. The commitment is made, & E banished—but she will not leave me.

June 9th

I have kept out of Anne's way all day, as far as possible. I would have enjoined her not to talk of our engagement to her Mother, had I not felt that it would make me seem reluctant—which, unfortunately, remains the truth. I know now that I have made the worst mistake of my life—that all expectation of happiness is lost forever. I can only hope that she will allow me to lead a largely separate life from hers. But I fear that even that hope is vain: she is delicate; her ill health will surely require me to remain in constant attendance. What have I done?

It is now incumbent on me to speak to my Aunt & ask her blessing on our union. I know full well that she will raise no objection: she has been promoting the match for as long as I can remember. Yet I cannot bring myself to speak to her today. Surely I may enjoy few days' freedom, before we lay the foundations of that monstrous edifice, a society wedding? And O, what will Georgie say?

June 10th

I cannot speak to my Aunt today, the anniversary of Sir Lewis de Bourgh's death; it would not be seemly. Neither did I accompany my Aunt & Cousin to church. Instead, I removed to the Library, to continue construing Virgil. This time, I resolved to avoid the account of Dido's wretched fate—but an evil destiny guided me instead to the tragic figure of Marcellus: '*Heu, miserande puer, si qua fata aspera rumpas, / Tu Marcellus eris.*' [Editor's note: Dryden translates this as: 'Ah couldst thou break thro' fate's severe decree / A new Marcellus shall arise in thee.'] I remember construing the passage in class, & old Norris telling us that when Virgil read these lines to the Empress Octavia, she, having recently lost her son Marcellus, fainted through sheer grief. I further recall turning to look at Byron, who was forever playing the fool in class, & observing with amazement that tears stood in his eyes.

June 11th

I dreamed of E all night. How can this happen, when I have forbidden myself to think of her?

Facing me across the breakfast table, the pinched features of my future bride. I left her abruptly, had Caesar saddled up & rode all morning alone.

Byron has called to remind me that Charles & myself are to visit him at Newstead. He proposes to repair thither immediately, & to stay all summer. I view his invitation with mixed feelings: though it would be an affront to abandon my betrothed so soon after she has accepted my offer, it would enable me to get away. I could not bring myself to mention my changed circumstances to Byron, but vaguely offered to write to him to confirm the date of our arrival.

I did not see fit to remind Charles of the invitation. I have not the leisure to visit him in Grosvenor Street.

At dinner my affianced bride wore a taffeta gown of a blue-green colour, which contrasted disagreeably with her sallow complexion.

June 12th

This morning, Anne & her Mother both came down to breakfast. This is so unusual for Anne that everyone commented on it. I suspect her of wishing to start a new life now that she is to be wed.

We breakfasted late, without G & Isabella, who were already abroad; we were still at table when Bolton brought in the post. My Aunt waved a letter at me. 'From Mr Collins. D'you recall him, Nephew?'

I bowed. Elizabeth's Cousin. Indeed I did recall him for a feeble-minded sycophant.

'He writes that he has just planted out his new orchard. Surely 'tis madness at this time of year! Trees should always be planted in November. What is he thinking of?' She continued perusing her letter. It appears that Collins has been spending the greater part of his time at Rosings, poking his nose into the minutiae of the household. Every little occurrence elicited a remark—even the chore of emptying out the earth-closets, which my Aunt has ordered to be done whilst she is away from home. My aunt persisted in reading aloud these details.

'O, & he had been on a short visit to Meryton to visit his Wife's family,' continued she. I had risen to help myself to coffee from the sideboard. At the mention of Meryton, I turned, coffee-can in hand.

'He has seen Miss Elizabeth Bennet!' she exclaimed. 'You recall Miss Bennet, Nephew?'

I bowed again.

'Why, he says she is much changed, quite low at present: seemingly, she is a moody young woman. I am somewhat surprized, as I had quite resolved that she was a loud, chearful female, given to unbecoming bursts of merriment. Surely Mr Collins must be mistaken.' She continued reading. 'Just listen to this: *"I guess at the cause of her grief: she now regrets her heartless rejection of the only eligible suitor likely to offer for her. Too late!"'*

I had forgot I was holding a cup. At Anne's exclamation, I realized that the coffee was spilling over. She was looking up into my face. I sat down.

On my plate, a half-eaten roll. So Elizabeth had told the whole world of my foolish proposal! I forced my attention back to what my Aunt was saying:

'Mr Collins goes on: *"Well may she regret her folly, since it deprives her of the pleasure of residing within hailing distance of your Ladyship & Rosings. But I am much better off with my dear Charlotte."* Ah yes, I remember now,' continued she. 'He offered for Miss Elizabeth before marrying his little Mrs Collins! Well, he did quite the right thing—tho' that brash young woman would have been much happier in our more lively society than she is now, tucked away in the obscurity of her Hertfordshire village. Why, I make the Collinses welcome at my own table, sometimes twice a week!'

We sat for an age. I was aware that my Cousin was observing me closely. At length, my Aunt rose. 'Come, Anne. I wish to drive to Wellby's to chuse the trimmings for our summer bonnets. You may accompany me. It is not often that you are up betimes in the morning.'

Anne rose to follow her Mother. I shewed them from the room, then returned to the table. I was determined to remain alone in the dining-parlour: Collins's letter was still there, left by my Aunt for her maid to take upstairs.

I suppressed my scruples, & picked up the letter. Collins writes an abominable hand, garnished with pretentious loops & curlicues, written on both sides of the paper, & in both directions. Ignoring propriety, I read this palimpsest, skimming over the descriptions of the chimney-sweep's effort to unblock the wash-house flue at Rosings, 'til I saw the word Meryton. I had to work my way through a paragraph of salutations & humble devotions from Sir William & all the Lucases, 'til, towards the end of the letter, I came on the name of Miss Elizabeth Bennet: *'These days she seems melancholy & sombre. Her customary merriment has quite deserted her,'* he wrote. And then the words my aunt quoted: *'I guess at the cause of her grief: she now regrets her heartless rejection of the only eligible suitor likely to offer for her. Too late!'*—Alas, he spoke a truer word than he knew. It *is* too late.

*   *   *

All day, I felt restless. I was obliged to remove to Jackson's a second time in one day for a bout of fisticuffs. Afterwards I felt exhausted, which was preferable.

June 13th
What has just happened? Am I sorry? Am I glad? I cannot tell. Writing it may help.

I did not see my Cousin again after dinner yesterday: the shopping expedition with my Aunt had left her worn out, & she removed to her chamber. Her supper was brought up to her on a tray. This morning she came down. From certain covert signs she gave me, I became aware that she wished for a private interview—but I had intended to take communion this morning instead of attending matins, & escaped to church instead. However, she was not to be put off, & came to me on my return.

'I must speak with you, Fitzwilliam.'

I rose, bowed & handed her to a chair. There

was a silence. She appeared to be labouring under some difficulty. At length, she said hesitantly: 'My dear Fitzwilliam, I fear you have not been honest with me.'

I bowed again. It was true: what could I say?

'I believe that your affections are already engaged. Do not answer me!' she put up her hand in a warning gesture. 'I saw it in your face,' she continued, 'when my Mother spoke yesterday of Miss Elizabeth Bennet.'

'Miss Bennet is quite out of the question for me,' I replied. I spoke only the truth.

'That may be so,' she answered coolly, 'But you love her just the same.'

There was a long silence. It was incumbent on me to deny it, but I could not. She continued to look into my face. I returned her gaze in increasing embarrassment. Finally I lowered my eyes, & muttered that I regarded myself as irrevocably bound to my Cousin, & would honour my pledge as she deserved.

'Indeed, Fitzwilliam, there is no need for such protestations. I am quite aware that this was to be a marriage of convenience for us both. I am persuaded that we felt much the same for each other—Cousinly regard, & dutiful affection; nothing more.'

I muttered some objection. She rose, & spoke loudly. I have never heard her raise her voice before: 'O, fudge, Fitz! You don't love me. I don't love you. Let's call it quits!'

I drew back, shocked at her words.

'We can be thankful,' continued she, 'that no child of ours is to see the light of day. It would undoubtedly have inherited the Fitzwilliam nose.'

Her remark made me blench, at once at the impropriety of this speech & at the thought of a child, hers & mine. I looked into her face then. How could not I have noticed that she sports the same aquiline nose as me? Indeed, it looks out of place in her small pale face. But she had not done: 'I have never been in love—nor am I likely to, with this to drag with me, everywhere I go.' With an angry movement, she actually raised her skirt a fraction. Above the ancle, I could see her leg in its white stocking, twisted & misshapen. That a lady should lift her skirt so crudely in my presence astounded me. Also, I was strangely preoccupied by a small detail: the ribbon of her shoe was undone. Might not she trip, walking thus, with her withered leg? Would it be indelicate in me to draw it to her attention? I could think only of this problem: her loveless state seemed of lesser significance.

'This must never be mentioned again, by either of us,' she commanded.

'Did not you speak of it to my Aunt?'

'I did not. You seemed unsure. I thought it more prudent to refrain for a day or two.'

I, unsure! When I had made such efforts to show myself willing!

She said, more quietly: 'I was aware that you did not love me. I was prepared to make the best of things with you: I hoped that, your affections being disengaged, you might eventually come to feel some regard for me. I never hoped for love. Not with this.' With her clenched fist she struck at her leg. 'But if you love another, that is quite a different matter.'

'You do not understand,' I replied. 'I cannot

205

propose marriage to Miss Elizabeth Bennet. She can never be mine.' I felt I owed it to her to continue: 'I own that in the past I was not indifferent to her; but in time it will pass.'

'No. That is not enough for me.' She stood up to leave the room. I rose too. She dashed the back of her hand across her eyes, & limped out.

I remained alone, listening to her departing footsteps, lest she trip over her shoe-lace in the hall.

I am writing this, a free man again.

June 14th

Determined not to share the house with Anne under the present circumstances, last evening I wrote by express to Byron to announce my arrival at Newstead in three or four days' time, and promised to bring Charles with me if possible. There are compensations to my sudden decision: Byron, for all his faults, is an entertaining companion—& both Charles & I would benefit from a change of scenery. I have mentioned it to Peebles, who is beside himself with joy at the prospect of visiting the country seat of his Lordship, whom he idolizes for the cut of his breeches & his general air of dishevelled elegance.

I called on Charles in Grosvenor Street, to urge him to come with me to Newstead. I found him alone with Miss Caroline, the Hursts having departed for a short visit to a Brother of Edward's in Sussex. Charles demurred at first: he finds this departure too hasty; & he is wary of Byron, whom he describes as *'rackety'*. However, he has finally agreed to come. Miss Caroline upbraided me for my neglect of her, & seemed downcast at our departure. She actually enquired *'if she could be of the party'*! One hesitates to blacken a friend's reputation, but Byron is not a suitable companion for an unmarried maiden of unimpeachable virtue. Miss Caroline received this information with barely contained disappointment, & lamented that it would be most improper for her to remain alone in the London house. Charles pointed out that Louisa & Edward are expected home tomorrow, but she did not seem grateful for this reminder. She seized the opportunity of Charles's leaving the room to tell me, somewhat indiscreetly, that the Hursts were expecting a happy event in the autumn. She feared that with a houseful of babies, she would be *'de trop'* living with her Sister. As she said this, she favoured me with a meaningful look. When I failed to offer a solution to her predicament, she sighed impatiently & turned her head away.

Charles & I have resolved to set forth in two days' time.

Georgie is to stay with the Fitzwilliams, which she is nothing loath to do. She will be accompanied by Isabella & Mrs Annesley. When I suggested that she remove instead to Pemberley, she pointed out that it would be unfair to Isabella, since they have a long list of activities arranged. I regret it: I could have joined her from Newstead. I would have preferred a quiet summer in my own home. I should have insisted, were it not for the memories of Elizabeth which bedevilled me on my last visit.

Mr Broadwood has sent word that the pianoforte I ordered months ago is now ready. I have arranged for it to be sent down to Pemberley, & for a tuner to be found to attend to it.

At dinner-time I discovered that there had been no need to run from Town—my Aunt & my Cousin are leaving this evening. I do not know how Anne has prevailed on her Mother to remove from my house—tho' I do know that despite her seeming passivity, she has a strong will of her own. Whatever the explanation, she is transferring both of them to their own Town house, where the redecoration work is nearing completion.

June 15th
To my dismay, my Aunt Catherine has sent word that after a night spent in her Town house, she finds it too lacking in comfort: she proposes to return here with Anne for a few more weeks. Can she be redoubling her efforts to make a match between us? I have written to inform her that, as I shall be absent, the house will be shut up, & she had best return to Rosings. I am now irrevocably committed to leaving London.

The day spent in packing & preparing for the journey—& we have had a disaster: poor silly Peebles, eager to impress Byron & his valet with the perfect state of my wardrobe, loaded himself up with all my top-boots & hessians, preparing to take them downstairs & polish them in the scullery. Unfortunately, he missed his footing on the stairs, & fell, scattering boots in all directions. The noise was such that we all came running out to see what was amiss. The servants picked him up & dusted him down, & he much shaken. I have sent for a doctor: I fear that he may have a broken ancle.

In the midst of all this, Mrs Annesley sought an interview with me, to express her unease at their removal to Fitzwilliam House. She is of my mind: my Aunt Fitzwilliam is somewhat too lax in her supervision of the young ladies. Mrs A is worried about G & Isabella. 'As her Ladyship's guest I shall have less authority over my charges,' she concluded. I have not had the leisure to give her anxieties much thought; somewhat against my better judgment, I have told her that her fears are probably groundless: my Aunt has brought up five girls already. Mrs Annesley has my direction at Newstead, & I have urged her to write without hesitation if she has any cause for concern. I hope that my departure is not imprudent.

The girls & their chaperone moved to my Uncle's this afternoon. We bade each other farewell, G kissing me & wishing me a brisk 'God-speed'; Isabella grew very red in the face when I shook her by the hand.

*   *   *

The doctor has attended Peebles, & says that it is a slight sprain, & that he will be right as rain in a couple of weeks. Meanwhile, he is not to put any weight on the injured ancle. 'At his age, he should take better care of himself,' he added. Poor Peebles cannot of course come with me to Newstead. I shall go & tell him so shortly.

*   *   *

Peebles had tears in his eyes when I told him that he must remain in London. He seems so distressed that I have hit upon another plan: he shall travel down with us as far as Hucknall. In the carriage, with his foot on the opposite squab, he should be quite comfortable. Charles & I can ride alongside—it will be more agreeable to travel on horseback, & we can go by easy stages. After Hucknall, Peebles will carry on in the carriage to Pemberley, while we turn off to Newstead. Peebles can stay with his Sister in the village, & recuperate there. When Miss Caroline heard that Peebles is to ride in the carriage alone, she found it most extraordinary that a mere valet should travel in such luxury. But I may need the carriage in Nottinghamshire, so it may as well go occupied as empty; besides, Peebles has been with me for as long as I can remember: he is much more than a valet. We set out at dawn tomorrow.

June 18th
After a three-days' journey, accompanying the carriage with its invalid occupant, arrived at Newstead on a drizzly, misty evening. The half-ruined gatehouse in the Gothick style seemed uninhabited, but, as the gates hung open, we pressed on. The drive is at least a mile long, & winding, with neglected trees dropping branches on either side. In one place the fallen trunk of a shattered oak almost blocks the carriage-way. The house is a long, low structure in grey stone. Attached to it at one end stands the ruin of an ancient Abbey, of which the façade only remains, its huge carven window open to the sky. Opposite is a lake, overlooked by a miniature fortress, almost like a child's playhouse.

It was now dusk, & no lights showed in any window. Not a soul was visible. Somewhere in the distance we could hear shooting. A great oak door stood at the top of a flight of stone steps, many of which were broken or missing. We tethered our horses to the shafts of an abandoned cart, & felt our way up these steps, which were slippery with the rain. I hammered on the ancient door. No body came—but the shots persisted, as if they were fighting a gun-battle inside. Charles seized the iron ring & twisted it. The door swung open. With a loud report, a bullet buried itself in the wall a few inches away from my left ear. I cried out. There was a confused impression of dark figures & flickering light, then came Byron's voice: 'What in the Devil's name . . . ?' Somebody thrust a taper under our noses, illuminating our faces. Then Byron's voice came again: 'Why, Fitz & Charles! Welcome to the Monks' Hall!' Our eyes becoming accustomed to the fitful light, we found ourselves in a huge vaulted chamber. A figure in a dark robe came forward. He lifted up his candle, & we recognized our host. He led the way through a small door at one end of this great hall, & into a dining-room of moderate size, elegantly furnished in the modern style. He threw aside his robe. Underneath—much to our relief—he was decently clad in normal attire. He made us welcome, poured us a glass of fine old wine, & stood leaning moodily on the chimney-piece, beneath a curious carven overmantel, bearing high-coloured portrait heads from the Elizabethan aera. He seemed to be deep in reverie, then roused himself, & insisted on taking us up to our bedchambers himself, along dark stone passages. My chamber gives a superficial impression of almost vulgar opulence, tho' the stone walls are riddled with cracks. It is splendidly furnished, with a vast bed upholstered

211

in red velvet, surmounted with *'A Napoleonic eagle'*, as our host has informed me. No sooner had he left me, than I hastened to fling open my casement to banish the smell of damp.

Dinner was copious, tho' far from excellent: a leg of fat mutton & coarse fish from the lake. Our host still persists in his curious habits, partaking of little else but potatoes & vinegar: I believe that he is terrified of growing fat. He drank no wine, but plied us with Port from his *'ancestral cellars'*. It seems the old Cousin or uncle from whom he inherited both title & house drank but little, so the wines of his forefathers have survived intact—or had done so until Byron began to make free with them. We were served by two handsome boys, clad in black velvet. His pages, as he calls them, & named them: Patroclus & Rushton.

After dinner, we begged to be excused from further intercourse, as we were fatigued after our long journey. 'Don't count on me during the day,' answered he. 'I spend most of my daylight hours alone in my chamber, recovering from the night's dissipations. I emerge, owl-like, at dusk. You must amuse yourselves as best you may.'

I remember Byron's idleness from school, but had thought that he had somewhat mended his ways—his writing, tho' at times offensive, is certainly *energetic*. However, it seems that I was mistaken. To prove that I am made of sterner stuff, I have made a point of writing this before retiring.

June 19th
I slept but little in my dank chamber. During the night I was persuaded that I could hear wolves howling outside my window. A sinister phantasy! I

212

must confess too that when day finally dawned I regretted the absence of poor Peebles, as no hot water was brought me, & my trunk had not even arrived. I was obliged to attire myself unassisted in yesterday's linen, & went down to breakfast somewhat discomposed.

As he had warned us, Byron did not come to breakfast today. He does not seem to keep a valet: we are attended by a miscellaneous pack of servants, all more or less uncouth. We requested that in future they remember to bring up our shaving water & lay out our small-clothes. We were served at breakfast by one of the two pages Byron keeps, the one he calls 'Patroclus'—a slender boy with tendrils of curling dark hair, & a somewhat effeminate appearance. Remembering Byron's taste for *ephebes* at school, we were not in the least surprized at this apparition. The boy answered our questions in a high-pitched, girlish voice, suggesting for our entertainment a row on the lake. Apart from that, & some fly-fishing, there seems little to amuse us here 'til our horses are rested from the journey: the billiard table is attacked by a growth of mould which throws off a white dust whenever we attempt to pot a ball; the stables are occupied by carthorses, except for Byron's own mounts, which we are not invited to ride; the woods seem well-stocked with game, if it were only the season. Several huge mastiffs, which Byron calls his *pets*, roam wild in the grounds. Rounding a corner of the house, we came face to face with—a wolf! There was no mistaking the animal's rough head, golden eyes & lurching gait. We stood stock still; luckily the creature seemed as alarmed as we were, & rapidly disappeared in the direction of the ruined chapel. Keeping a weather-eye out for further perils, we made the rounds of the park, with its many water-courses. We found a splendid Monument which, on closer inspection, proved to be the tomb of Boatswain, a dog, but recently dead. Byron had composed an indignant verse, contrasting the devotion of this animal with the falseness of Man, & had caused the words to be engraved on the side of this edifice. Overall, our expedition was agreeable on a first time, but these water-logged gardens will become monotonous if we extend our stay here. Charles says that we can visit the neighbouring great houses for entertainment. In a day or two I shall suggest an excursion to Pemberley, which is not much more than an hour's journey from here.

June 20th
Byron duly appeared at dusk last evening, & proceeded in his own way to entertain us. When we asked him about the wolf which roams the grounds, he replied carelessly, 'O, so you met Wolf, did you? He is a fine, loyal creature, but timid in company. I suppose you also ran into Bruin?' We assumed that he must be teazing us, but it turns out that he is quite serious: he has a pet bear, rescued from some mountebank, which likewise has the run of the estate. We can only be thankful that, on the evening we arrived, neither animal was abroad.

Today, it being Sunday, Charles & I have attended matins in the village. On the way back, Charles fell to wondering what we should be doing a year from hence. 'O, much the same as now,' I replied. He remarked in a melancholy undertone that at our time of life we should be looking to marry & settle down. 'It is a question of finding the right partner,' says I. He glanced at me sideways, but made no reply.

It rained for much of the way home. One of the pages, Rushton, offered us the choice between pistol practice in the Great Hall & a bout of boxing or a game of battledore in the Great Dining Room, followed by a cold plunge in the Slype. We deemed such exertions inappropriate for the Sabbath, & repaired instead to the Library, where I amused myself with a Petronius, copiously annotated in Byron's hand.

June 21st

At dinner last night, Byron, contrary to his custom, drank much wine. When I taxed him with being out of temper, he growled that he always felt uneasy with that Sabbath nonsense, then spoke of the virtues of the Muhammedan faith, which he witnessed on his travels. Of course, since he sleeps all day, he never attends church.

Later that evening, he waxed exceeding wroth against certain London literary figures, whom he accused of being *'lickspittle curs, gulping down their betters' excrement, & vomiting it up again.'* His language is strong indeed—but we could not help laughing at some of his more vivid expressions. His pages, Patroclus & Rushton, joined in the mirth with unseemly abandon. An old servant named Joe, who stood behind his Lordship's chair, was rewarded at intervals with the Port decanter. I actually observed the old fellow raise it to his lips, take a deep draught, wipe the bottle-neck with his hand, & pass it back over his master's shoulder.

Byron refilled his own glass from the selfsame decanter.

June 22nd
Today, in the absence of his Lordship, Charles & I amused ourselves by arranging an impromptu boxing match, with the page Patroclus as referee, then going for a swim in the lake. Charles insisted on ducking me, as a punishment for having defeated him in the fight. The water was brackish & unwholesome. I write this in my chamber, which, despite the warm weather, remains clammy & chill. Soon we will be summoned to dinner by an ancient cracked bell, which his Lordship claims once tolled the hours in the old ruined abbey.

*   *   *

This evening at dinner Byron was brilliant, witty & cruel at the expense of Mr Wordsworth, whom he accuses of being tedious & sentimental. I disagreed, having been much affected by Wordsworth during one long night on which I prefer not to dwell—but Byron would brook no dissent. Tho' he filled our glasses, he himself drank nothing; but his behaviour was no less unbridled for that: after dinner he invited his two pages to sit with us at table, & fondled both of them indiscriminately. His second page, Rushton, is a very young man whose beard is scarce beginning to sprout. During the course of the conversation, in which this latter youth was invited to participate, he revealed artlessly that he sleeps in a truckle bed in the antechamber to his master's bedroom. Byron, beware! Men have been hanged for less!

216

June 23rd

Our horses being now well rested, Charles & I out for a long ride today. The countryside around here is quite flat, & dotted with lakes, quite unlike the rolling hills around Pemberley. Too weary from the unaccustomed exercise to write much.

June 24th

Last evening, at dinner, while Byron was filled to bursting with energy & vitality, the two of us almost fell asleep over his great-uncle's Port Wine, he entertaining us the while with scabrous reminiscences of our Harrow days, which he claims were the happiest in his life: 'Do you remember when we were up to old Howlers, we used to play cards all night? And how I would cut classes to lie on the tombstones of Harrow Church writing poetry—abominable, turgid stuff?' &c., &c.

*   *   *

Rode out again today. From a distance, Newstead, with its vestigial monastery, resembles a haunted ruin.

June 25th

Byron was in a talkative mood last evening, describing his travels. He claims that Greece is the most beautiful & the most unfortunate country in the world, & told us that its finest treasures have been stolen by *'that abominable blaggard'* Lord Elgin, formerly His Majesty's Ambassador to Athens. I strongly disagreed with this intemperate judgment. Indeed, I have myself seen the fine marble sculptures, which but recently arrived in London.

This morning, returning from breakfast through the Great Hall, I almost collided with Patroclus, heavily burdened with several reams of white paper, which he was taking to his Lordship's chamber. Byron's rooms are isolated from the rest of the house, up a spiral staircase. We have not been invited to visit them. When I attempted to detain Patroclus with some enquiry, he objected that he must make haste, as his Lordship was running out of paper for his work. On my pressing him further, he explained that, far from idling in bed, Byron is engaged in a substantial composition, & writes all day, without ceasing, from dawn 'til dusk. He is, apparently, writing a kind of travel journal of his last year's voyage, in the form of '*a poem about a child*'. It sounds exceeding outlandish, but poor Patroclus is not the most lucid of informants. Doubtless the matter will be clarified when the work is finished. Patroclus begged me not to make enquiries of Byron, since he is under orders not to discuss his Lordship's literary activities with any body.

It rained again, so that we could not ride. We both being languid & unwilling to take exercise, Charles suggested a game of cribbage, but it seems that there is no such thing as a cribbage-board at Newstead. In the end we settled for piquet, a game which Charles does not like to play with me, as I generally win. Today was no exception.

June 26th
Byron appeared last evening in a gaudy native

218

costume, he says of Albanian workmanship. Decked out in a scarlet coat heavily embroidered in blue, with wide trousers & tasselled slippers, he resembled some mountebank, as we told him to his annoyance. He talked of his experiences in Albania, & of the Pasha who had made him a gift of the said costume. It must be remarked that, whatever his drawbacks as a host, he is endlessly diverting.

Today the weather has been sultry & heavy. We resolved to row on the Great Lake, but were so troubled by midges that we finally gave up, plunged into the water, & swam instead. Over breakfast, Charles & I have reviewed our situation, & resolved to visit Pemberley together for a few days. I have business to conduct there, & must see how Peebles fares; Charles would welcome an interlude in the more congenial surroundings of a well-appointed establishment. We leave tomorrow, & return in a few days' time. We will ride over—it is but a short journey. I write this on rising from table: at dinner, we spoke of our purpose to Byron. To our dismay, his large grey eyes filled with tears. 'So my friends desert me. It was always thus,' he said. He sat for a full five minutes in silence, fighting to control his emotion. Charles reminds me that at Harrow Byron was wont to blub like a girl, but I had assumed that he had outgrown the habit. Despite this show of grief, we held firm, but consented to stay away only a week.

Apart from this exchange, during this our last evening Byron was discussing the war. He believes that it is a matter of time before England is invaded. His admiration for Bonaparte (*'the Emperor'*) is unbounded. We pointed out that we are at war with the fellow, to which Byron retorted that one should be able to transcend such mundane considerations, & value genius at its true worth. I sincerely hope that he reins in his tongue when in Town, for he could incur the anger of all those who have fought in the war, or lost friends & family to his rapscallion of an '*Emperor*'.

I shall stop here, for we rise early to ride to Pemberley.

July 5th

Charles & I have now returned from our week at Pemberley. To my chagrin, I left this book behind, so have been unable to keep a daily Diary. I have noted the orders I gave to Pargeter in a separate ledger. The architect's drawings had arrived, & I looked through them with Pargeter. I find that the proposed new wing will destroy the harmony of the façade; worse, Cumberbatch is in favour of pulling down the Elizabethan parts of the structure, which he says are an anachronism. But I love them best! I cannot allow it. I have told Pargeter not to proceed until I have given the matter further thought.

Peebles is well, tho' still unable to put his full weight on his foot. He had himself conveyed to the house, & hobbled around pitifully, attending to my needs, & tut-tutting at the state of my coats: Byron's minions have, apparently, failed to brush them adequately. Furthermore, he was scathing about their efforts to shave me—he does not realize that I have been shaving myself, & I did not enlighten him. He insists that he is now fit to work, & longs to return with us to Newstead. I can scarce imagine how he would adapt to that raffish household, but, not wishing to upset him by telling him that I prefer to dispense with his services, I have ordered him back to London, to make sure all my appointments there are in apple-pie order. He is disappointed about Newstead, but delighted to be deemed indispensable. I overheard him informing Reynolds that he had essential business to conduct in Town. He will travel in the carriage, which can then return to Newstead in case it is needed.

Charles is delighted with Pemberley. He extolled the harmony of the buildings, the mellow stone, the ancient chapel, the view down to the lake & up the hillside opposite—even the Great Hall with its minstrels' gallery, the object of such contumely to Cumberbatch, who is resolutely modern in outlook. Charles is also taken with the countryside, & has been talking of looking for a suitable property to purchase nearby, 'If ever I do settle down,' he added.

We enjoyed a pleasant bachelor existence for a week, fishing or riding every day. I shewed Charles over the estate. Tho' inexperienced in land management, he is interested, & eager to learn. He would prove an excellent neighbour. I shall make shift to enquire in the district: I believe that Littleover House may soon be available. We rode over to view it from the outside—a comfortable modern abode set in a fine landscaped park. Charles also appreciated the Peaks, where we walked & climbed all day on Wednesday. He could become quite a Derbyshire gentleman.

Charles shewed reluctance when we decided that the time had come to return here to Newstead—but there is no call to be discourteous to Byron. However eccentric his Lordship may be as a host, he certainly provides for our entertainment—in his own way.

I have left 'til last the most memorable thing about our stay at Pemberley. It began as we rode up the drive, before we even reached the house: I felt *her* presence all around me—seated by the window at her sewing, laughing when Charles attempted a rendering of 'Greensleeves' on the pianoforte—I could scarce believe that he did not hear it. Often, particularly in the evenings, with Rufus's muzzle resting on my knee, I regretted the mistress that Pemberley might have had.

*　　　*　　　*

We left Pemberley for Newstead this morning. The weather, prophetically, turned, & once more we approached Byron's mansion in the mist, & I wished heartily that we had staid away. I believe that Charles feels much the same, but he is too civil to cast such a slur on his host. Byron has come downstairs to welcome us, tho' it is not yet dusk. He tells us that he has arranged a surprize for us this evening.

*　　　*　　　*

The other day I had observed that Byron's lame leg was now perfectly normal in size. As a schoolboy his right calf was monstrously thin. I had assumed that time had wrought a partial cure, but this afternoon I passed Old Joe hastening to his master's chambers, carrying a leather legging with a thickly-padded lining. He attempted to hide it behind his back. Poor Byron must wear this support to disguise his infirmity.

July 6th

Last evening, Byron bespoke a feast in honour of our return. For the first time we dined in an ancient vaulted chamber, part of the old Abbey. Our host calls it the 'Blue Dining Room'. It is situated near the former cellars where Byron keeps his menagerie of animals, & the evening's musical entertainment was provided by their roaring & bellowing—with accompanying wafts of a rich, putrid stench which made my gorge rise. A whole roast sheep was borne in; it reminded Byron of his travels in Anatolia or some such place. The appetising aroma clashed horribly with the feral odours from the menagerie. There were some twenty young men & women present, clad in monks' robes, the women with their hair down. From their speech I guess that they are local village people. Byron was drinking heavily, & proudly shewed off his drinking goblet—the top of a human skull mounted in silver & with a silver stem. He claims it is the head of an old monk, whose bones they dug up when hunting for treasure in the cloisters. It holds a whole bottle of clairet.

We were discomfited when, after dinner, the 'monks', by now well in their cups, began to throw off their habits, beneath which they were naked as Adam & Eve. It seemed that we were to experience a full-scale orgy. Charles objected that such an event was peculiarly unsuited to the Sabbath. 'That is precisely the point,' retorted Byron.

I believe that Charles left then. I shared his

223

scruples but not his self-discipline, & proceeded to take too much liquor. Later found myself under the dining-table. I have but little recollection of what happened next. I believe that a plump young maiden with brown curling hair attempted to fix my attentions—but I also dimly remember a pair of flaxen-haired wenches endeavouring to mount me together . . . I seem to recall Byron joining me under the table with Rushton—or could it have been Patroclus? I only know that, inebriated though I was, I could not bring myself to participate fully in these dissipations. I finally succeeded in extricating myself, & stumbled off to my chamber alone.

It is almost midday; my head throbs. When I go downstairs I shall have to face Charles, who, I am certain, is perfectly well & sober.

July 7th
Today it rained heavily all day. Charles & I balked at taking our customary stroll through the sodden grounds, & resolved instead to explore inside the house. It is a rambling ruin; whole corridors have been neglected for years. We went from room to room. They lack the Byronic golden eagles, scutcheons & scarlet hangings, & instead seem drab & old-fashioned. The hangings are tattered & dull in colour, the floor thick with dust. In one room a cloud of bats rose up as we entered.

Opening the door of the final chamber, we came upon Byron's two pages, Patroclus & Rushton, half-clad, embracing on the bed. We retired hastily & closed the door. I do not think that they observed us. I was shocked, & would have had it out with their master, but Charles dissuaded me.

224

'Remember how he was at Harrow—a rampant Horatian! He'll just laugh in your face! Try to pretend that it never happened. He must condone it.'

I objected that he might know nothing of the matter.

'In that case,' retorted Charles, 'it is as well to leave him in ignorance. Why interfere in matters which are not your concern?'

July 8th

I have been reflecting on Charles's words of yesterday. Am I habitually of an interfering disposition? Was Charles indirectly alluding to my efforts to save him from a disastrous marriage to Jane? Whatever her faults, was I wrong in presuming to come between Charles & the woman he loved?

July 9th

Last evening, after dinner, Byron enquired of Charles why he had refused to participate in the 'sport' at the end of last Sunday's banquet. I saw Charles hesitate, & glance nervously towards Patroclus & Rushton, who were, as usual, of the party. In the end, with some reluctance, he replied: 'I confess that I envy your ability to have concourse with any wench who takes your fancy, both in public & in private; but I simply cannot bring myself to do the same, I truly do not know why.'

'Darcy here is less delicate . . .'

They all turned to look at me. I refrained from observing that I too had abstained from joining in the 'orgy'. Byron said, with a cynical smile: 'Darcy is noted for his cool courtesy towards the fair sex.

How can he reconcile such polished social intercourse with his appetite for intercourse of quite another kind?'

'That is completely different,' said I. I could feel my complexion reddening.

'You are right indeed,' confirmed Byron. 'Why, wenching is an instinctual thing—an irresistible urge quickly dissipated in an explosion, which brings immediate relief. A little like—shall we say sneezing?'

I did not make the rejoinder that, however great the urge, satisfying it brings no relief whatsoever—at least in my case.

July 10th
Byron tells us that he has invited Fitchett, Andrewes & Tom Bullivant to be of our party. He must think us very dull, & so we are—Charles filled with melancholy recollections of Jane, I more taciturn than is my wont. Byron provides all the conversation for our evenings together.

July 11th
Byron has been furnishing what he describes as 'suitable entertainment for the Sabbath day' by reading aloud from letters to him by various women who fancy themselves in love with him. His prowess with the fair sex is extraordinary, but I find that he has scant respect for the ladies. He declaimed the pathetic, tear-stained missives with howls of laughter—and, indeed, some of the epistles were so exaggeratedly sentimental that we could not help joining in. Both Charles & I were ashamed of it afterwards, as we acknowledged to each other, walking in the shrubbery. Byron did

not chuse to walk, because of his foot, I suppose.

July 12th
Today Charles & I planned a boxing tournament, & asked Rushton to find us sparring partners. To our surprize, as we arrived at our impromptu 'boxing ring' in the formal gardens at the back, a figure awaited us in a hooded cloak. Rushton introduced him as a *'fine pugilist'*. We both recognized Byron at once, but goodnaturedly pretended not to know him. He stripped to his shirt & breeches, but insisted on fighting masked, to preseve his *'anonymity'*. He is a superb boxer, & duly vanquished us, one after the other. Thereupon, abandoning his perfunctory disguize, he challenged us both to a race across the lake. We all three plunged in, Charles & I knowing full well that Byron is a far stronger swimmer than we. Sure enough, he had reached the far end before we were scarce half-way over.

July 13th
At dinner last evening, Byron waxed eloquent about his noble ancestry. Throughout the evening he referred to himself constantly as *'Birron'*. When Charles enquired why he did so, he replied haughtily, 'Why, it is the ancient way, & my true name. Henceforward I shall answer to no other.' He went on to amuse himself at our expense by vaunting the superiority of his ancient lineage, 'til Charles pointed out that the Darcys too came over with the Conqueror.

'O, I daresay a Darcy served a noble Birron as his squire,' mocked Byron.

'You forget that on his Mother's side Darcy is a

direct descendant of the Conqueror himself,' objected Charles.

'O, on the wrong side of the blanket,' I demurred. My Aunt Fitzwilliam is never best pleased to be reminded of this—but it silenced Byron, who has no such scruples.

Today it rained. Charles was languid & melancholy. We sat together in the Library, I attempting to construe from a volume of Suetonius I took off the shelves. I saw Charles breathe on the rain-splashed window-pane, & trace letters on it with his finger. When he saw me watching him, he hastily rubbed them off.

July 14th

At dinner tonight, Rushton served us alone—for the first time, Patroclus was nowhere to be seen. When, over the Port, Charles enquired where he was, Byron took a long draught from his skull-cup, then amazed us by saying: 'O, 'tis too bad. The worst has happened.' 'Why, what is that?' I asked, assuming that Patroclus's shocking behaviour with his fellow-page had been discovered & he dismissed or even in prison.

'Why, the worst, I say. Patroclus'—here he gave a visible sneer—'*Patroclus* is great with child.'

We gaped at him in astonishment.

'Yes. I confess it: I have sired another brat.'

'But . . . Patroclus . . . is Patroclus a *woman*?'

'Yes, of course,' said Byron crossly. 'Her name is Lucy. I've sent her home to the village. 'Tis not the first time, neither—for me, I mean. These bastards cost me a fortune to maintain.'

We were both bereft of speech. How had we failed to realize, when we surprized her with

228

Rushton? The room had been in twilight, it is true, but on reflection it should have been obvious to both of us. We felt very foolish. We parted earlier than usual, Byron being much perturbed. To my relief, he has forgot all about 'Birron', & is Byron once more.

Charles came with me to my chamber, & we talked a while. 'How fortunate that we mentioned nothing about what we saw the other day,' said he. 'The child may just as well be Rushton's. Byron would be mortified if he knew.'

My instinct was to suggest informing him, but, mindful of Charles's strictures on my *interfering nature*, I made no remark. Charles has left me, & I write this in my chamber, by the open window, hearing a couple of the dogs baying outside in the dark, & waiting for Wolf to begin his nightly howling.

July 15th

Tonight Byron plans a second *orgy*, as he calls them. This time the preparations have been far more elaborate.

This morning, reading quietly in the Library, I heard terrified shrieks echoing through the house. Hastening forth, I came upon Fitchett, Andrewes & Tom Bullivant, newly arrived from Town, cowering in a corner of the Great Hall, hemmed in by Bruin. I chased him away, he shaking his great brown head at me the while, & told my friends to compose themselves, explaining that the bear is allowed an hour's daily exercise each morning, & is wont to approach the house guests, begging for treats. Tom quavered that, finding no body to receive them, they had ventured to enter the

Abbey. After such a fright, & following their long journey, our friends are like to prove heavy & slumberous during the evening's entertainment.

I write this in my chamber, listening for the bell to summon me to tonight's banquet. I am clad in a black velvet cloak of archaic cut, somewhat ill-made & improperly lined, provided by my host. I found it laid out on my bed. I both feel & look exceedingly foolish.

July 16th

Last evening's debauchery was carefully staged. We found the Blue Dining Room in the half-darkness, lit only by a couple of sconces holding black candles, which gave but little light. I wondered how they had been made: doubtless the melted wax was mixed with soot—there was a somewhat sooty smell in the room, which mingled disagreeably with the stench from the menagerie. Our host loomed out of the shadows, clad like all of us in a voluminous black cloak. The evening proved much the same as during the last orgy: Charles left immediately after the meal. I was of a mind to amuse myself in Byron's decadent manner. Why does he feel the need for such artifice? I selected for my entertainment a woman in a monk's habit—but at the last minute, could not bring myself to participate, & retired unobtrusively to bed.

*　　　*　　　*

Today, I rode out alone with Charles. None of the others had appeared after the night's activities.

I was unprepared for the conversation he had

with me, & have returned much moved.

It began with his remarking on my willingness to consort with unknown women, and, worse still, to participate in such a public debauchery, despite my correctness of manner. He continued: 'It is all very well for you, Fitz, fancy-free as you are. You can feel perfectly at liberty to indulge yourself.'

'Far from indulging, I retired soon after you,' I told him shortly. Why must my friends assert that it is *all very well* for me, when they know nothing? I wish I could unburden myself to him, but how would it be if he knew of my feelings for the Sister of his own lost love?

'Alas, for my part, I can never be free again,' continued he in a mournful tone. I replied as gently as I could that Time would soften the blow, & that he would one day find another soul-mate.

'You don't understand, Fitz. I no longer trust myself to pay court to any woman. I have shewn myself to be such an abominable judge of character, that I shall never get over it.' He went on to explain that he had truly believed his Jane to be a loving heart & the perfect companion for the rest of his life. The fact that he had failed to realize that she was a scheming minx, out for his money, has been haunting him ever since I told him of it.

He revealed this as we rode side by side. I could not help noticing how the freckles on his skin stood out against his white cheeks, & how his hands gripped the reins.

July 17th

I have made a resolution: I shall tell Charles the truth. He must know of Elizabeth's rejection of me, & of how she accused me of ruining not only

231

his own happiness, but also Jane's. It will be a relief to me to unburden myself at last.

I have dressed early. I shall go down to breakfast, & afterwards draw Charles aside for a quiet walk in the grounds. He will not wish to be near the others when he hears of this.

*   *   *

I have received such news as has driven everything else from my mind. I must to London immediately. Byron has attempted to detain me, protesting disingenuously that I must not travel on the Sabbath. But I paid him no heed. My carriage leaves within the hour.

Charles knows only that I have urgent family business to attend to. He will stay on, & return next week, as we had planned. I suspect that he would prefer to come with me, but he does have good company with Bullivant & Andrewes, & cannot in all decency cut his stay short. I have had to postpone my talk with him. I have sent word to Mrs Annesley & Georgie to be at home to receive me on Monday night.

July 19th
Finally reached home this evening. Georgie appeared delighted to see me, & chattered without ceasing about her stay at the Fitzwilliams'. After dinner I discreetly sought a private interview with Mrs Annesley. But it has not been possible tonight: G would suspect something. I shall speak to the lady first thing tomorrow.

Instead, I repaired alone to the Library, & once more unfolded Mrs Annesley's letter to me. She begins tactfully with polite enquiries after my health, but then come the words which have so alarmed me:

I am exceedingly concerned for the welfare of Miss Georgiana here in Fitzwilliam House. Miss Isabella having returned to Derbyshire, her Ladyship allows your Sister even more freedom than before; I strongly suspect that Miss Georgiana is conducting a secret intrigue with a young Officer, who has little to recommend him but his appearance. I do not feel able to deal with this matter unaided, & must beg you to return immediately to Town.

July 20th

There was time only for a brief meeting with Mrs Annesley before breakfast: Georgie was at her pianoforte. Mrs A suspects the young man of having serious designs on my Sister, but is unsure how far she has responded to his advances, if at all. I remarked that G had seemed merry enough last night. She replied that she does not think that G's affections are deeply engaged, but that she suspects that there is some sort of secret entanglement, & fears that the young man may trick my Sister into an unwanted commitment. I shuddered privately. Another elopement? It would be beyond enduring. I requested that Mrs Annesley be on her guard. It was impossible to be entirely frank with her, as she knows nothing of the Wickham episode. I refrained from expressing my outrage against my Aunt Fitzwilliam. What was she thinking of, allowing G to meet Officers, & she not yet out of the schoolroom?

I had thought my Sister unsettled & nervous at

breakfast. She kept jumping up & running to the window, looking to see if the weather was fine, for we were to ride that day in the Row, &c. Why did she seem so uneasy? It suddenly came to me that she might be expecting a visitor—someone she would prefer me not to meet. Could it be the Officer of whom Mrs Annesley had written? I instructed Bolton discreetly to tell me first if any visitor came for Miss Darcy, & succeeded in persuading my Sister to settle down at her pianoforte. I intimated to her that I was going out, but instead repaired to the Library to intercept any visitors. At midday, Mrs Annesley having been sent on some errand by G, Bolton came to me to announce a visitor for Miss Georgiana. I told him not to inform her yet, as I would receive the caller myself first.

I went down to the yellow Saloon, to find a likely-looking young pup in regimentals lolling on a sofa. If he blenched at my entrance, it was only for a second. He regained his self-control almost at once, & explained with tolerable composure that he had been asked by his Sister to leave a message with Miss Darcy. I raised my quizzing glass & eyed him at length. He continued unabashed to stare into my face. At first sight he appeared very young, with fair hair & large blue eyes. But there were faint lines around the mouth, & an air almost of dissipation about the eyes. Then I noticed his regimental buttons—the 9th Warwickshires: Wickham's regiment! The blackguard will have put him up to this! I pretended ignorance & enquired which his regiment was. I was not surprized when he made me a lying answer. So: a scoundrel, & up to every trick!

'Are you acquainted with George Wickham?' I enquired further.

'Wickham? The name seems vaguely familiar. Why do you ask?'

Nettled by his impudent smile, I gave no answer. 'I regret that my Sister is not at home,' I informed him, & rang for Bolton.

Undeterred, he said, 'Pray, when will it be convenient for me to call & deliver my message?'

'You may leave it with me.'

'O, it is a verbal message.'

'Very well. Tell it to me, & I will deliver it on my Sister's return.'

Instead he asked for pen & paper, & made a great show of writing his message. This kept him in my house for at least a quarter of an hour, & I was beginning to fear that G would come downstairs & discover him there. Finally, however, he put down his pen, asked for a wafer, sealed his note carefully, & took his leave. No sooner was he gone than I opened his letter.

My dear Miss Darcy,

I regret that I was unable to see you today to deliver my Sister's message. She ardently desires your company at Vauxhall Gardens tomorrow night. Pray send her word that you are able to come. She will be desolate if you fail her.

Your most obedient servant,
Lieut. Edmund Tully.

Sister, indeed! A Sister in regimentals. I rang for Bolton immediately, & instructed him henceforward to refuse the pup entry to the house. The impertinent youth, with his golden curls &

innocent blue eyes! Another diabolical manoeuvre by friend Wickham! Will I never be rid of him? Poor G is no match for these unprincipled individuals—& the *duègnes* are either complicit, or too simple-minded to outwit such cunning practitioners. Georgie desperately needs a true friend, a Sister, a woman both young enough to understand her & wise enough to protect her.

I cannot avoid speaking to G about all this—& to think that I believed her to be biddable & innocent!

*   *   *

All my expectations have been confounded as we rode in the Park. Just as we reached the Row, G remarked guilelessly: 'You know, Fitz, I was expecting one of the Officers to call this morning. I was quite disappointed when he failed to appear.'

'Do you mean Lieut. Tully?' I asked in surprize.

'O, I did not realize that you knew about him.'

'Why did not you seek my permission?'

She replied indignantly that she was grown-up enough now to have a modicum of independence, & preferred to chuse her own friends. I retorted that girls were one thing, gentlemen another, & upbraided her for striking up such an acquaintance while still in the schoolroom.

'But Fitz,' replied she, 'Lieut. Tully is a friend of Cousin James's, & my Aunt is quite easy about Augusta's & my being present when the Officers pay calls on her elder Sisters.'

'I am sure I do not know why she condones it,' I replied. 'It is not at all appropriate for a girl of your age.'

Georgie pouted a bit, & I felt sure she was about to indulge in one of her sulks. But no matter—I was greatly relieved to find that she was not embarking on a clandestine relationship.

She then alarmed me somewhat by revealing, with the utmost candour, that Augusta had fallen madly in love with another of the Officers. 'She swears that she will love him for ever, & that she cannot control her feelings,' continued she. 'And she refused to listen when I told her that she was too young.' A shadow came over her face as she spoke.

'There is no such thing as uncontrollable love,' I told her.

' 'Tis all very well for you, Fitz! You was never in love. You have no notion what it is like.'

All very well, yet again! To be informed that I have no heart, & by my own Sister! I could not restrain myself: 'Your conjectures are false,' said I. 'I have but lately suffered a wretched disappointment in love.'

Her surprize was so great that she was all curiosity. She begged me eagerly to tell her of my trouble.

I told her all: I held almost nothing back. I made no attempt to gloss over the graceless arrogance of my proposal of marriage. I acknowledged the wrong I had done Elizabeth, & accepted that she had been perfectly right to refuse me. I softened only the cutting words she had spoken in her indignation—I do not wish my Sister to think ill of her. 'I am very unhappy,' said I, 'And I do not think that I shall ever recover.'

'But perhaps, one day, Fitz . . .' she faltered.

'I shall never have the opportunity of seeing her

again. Never be able to explain or apologize.'

She made me tell her all about Elizabeth, about her family & why I had grown to love her. In the end, she said sadly, 'It sounds as if she could have been the perfect companion for you, Fitz. I think I should have loved her almost as well as you do.'

I was grateful to her for having made no attempt to denigrate Elizabeth for rejecting me. I was glad too that she seemed to have forgot all about that young spark Tully.

For the first time in weeks we spent the evening quietly together. She played to me, and, through sheer self-indulgence, I asked her to perform some of the arias by Herr Mozart I had heard Elizabeth sing. I feel happier now: at last there is someone who knows.

G is a bewildering mixture of wisdom & naivety. It is clearly unacceptable to leave her in London in the care of her Aunt. She is innocent, wilful, a quarry for unscrupulous fortune-hunters. I must find her a place of safety. And I shall have to speak to my Aunt Fitzwilliam about Augusta.

*   *   *

Before writing to my Aunt about Augusta, I have spoken to G. She says there is no need to '*bother my Aunt*', as Augusta's *sigisbeo* has left for the Peninsula with his Regiment, & is like to remain there for some time.

Meanwhile I am most uneasy in my mind about G. I have taken a sudden decision: I shall remove her to Pemberley for the summer. Time spent in our own home will do us both good. I have written by express to Reynolds to warn her of our imminent arrival. I shall attempt to get together a small party. I shall send to Charles—he can repair thither directly from Newstead. I may be fortunate enough to secure his Sisters also. I plan to visit them immediately.

July 21st
This night I awoke with the strongest feeling that I had learnt something important yesterday, but whose significance I had failed to perceive. I sat up in bed—& then it came to me: the name of Tully. I had quite forgot: it was to a Lieut. Tully that Jane wrote last November, making a clandestine assignation. If this is the same man, his behaviour with Georgie has shewn him to be palpably untrustworthy, malicious, &, worst of all, an associate of Wickham's. How could Jane have been taken in by such a creature? It seems impossible. I have concluded that he must have been lying, & that Jane cannot have been the author of the letter. And yet it was on the say-so of this scoundrel that I accused Jane of wantonness, & detached Charles from her!

But why should Tully invent such a lie? I realized at once that there are a thousand explanations. Most likely he made the allegation out of a pure spirit of mischief, for the pleasure of destroying the reputation of an innocent lady. Perhaps too he wished to appear glorious, the conqueror of an acknowledged beauty & a model of propriety.

But Captain Denny *saw* a letter, & asserted that it came from Longbourn. Who then wrote it? After much cogitation, I resolved to set aside this mystery. I may never know the author. For now it suffices that I am beginning to suspect that it was not Jane.

I shall have to speak to Charles about this, when he reaches Pemberley.

*   *   *

Charles's Sisters & Edward Hurst are to be of our party. Miss Caroline seems beside herself with delight. I have written to Charles at Newstead, & have no doubt but that he too will honour us with his presence. To my immeasurable relief G is happy & excited at travelling down to Derbyshire, particularly as the new pianoforte will be installed & tuned by now.

I write this in the Golden Hart at Bedford. I ride alone to Pemberley, & shall arrive a day early, to make ready the house for my guests. They follow almost immediately in the carriage, & should be in residence on the following day.

END OF PART IV

Part V

PEMBERLEY

July 23rd

How strange is life: how does happiness surprize us when our spirits are at their lowest! During my long, solitary ride to Pemberley, I was recollecting with much unease how, when I am there, my thoughts unfailingly turn to Elizabeth. At every visit, her ghost seems to haunt the house. This time I was hoping to dispel my strange fancy by filling the place with friends; but I was not confident of success.

This morning, as I neared the house, my thoughts of E were stronger than ever. The illusion was even more powerful than last Christmas. This time, as I rode down the long drive, admiring the woodland with its majestic beeches, I truly felt that she was by my side. With every bend, I could sense her mounting excitement. We rounded the last curve, & at last I could shew her the whole park spread out, leading down to the lake, & above it the noble façade of the house, bathed in sunshine . . . I upbraided myself for my phantasy.

I rode down to the stables, & left my horse with Young Joe, astonished to see me a day early. Then I walked alone round the side of the house. Again E came into my mind, & I found myself thinking so earnestly of her that I convinced myself that when I turned the corner she would be there.

And then—had my obsession finally lost me my reason? It was so. She stood on the terrace, surveying the landscape, a gentle smile illuminating her countenance. I stood still & contemplated my dream, marvelling at the skill with which my imagination had worked on every detail. My phantasy had accounted for the lapse of time: she wore a straw bonnet which I had never before seen, but which became her exceedingly; beneath the brim her hair appeared to curl more luxuriantly about her brow. My fertile brain had even dressed her in a light summer gown. A parasol shaded her face, an unexpected detail which, after all, was appropriate for the season. Her expression was milder than I was accustomed to see in her: surely this my wishful dream had transformed her into a sweeter version of her real self!

I came forward, filled with a longing to speak to the apparition, even touch it: such was my madness. At the sound of my footsteps, she turned, & fixed her eyes on me. Her expression changed to one of horror & amazement, & then I knew: it was no phantasm. This was the real, flesh-and-blood Elizabeth!

I stood still in astonishment. I did not even have the wit to formulate the question: what was she doing in this place? She appeared equally confused. We stood there—stared at each other— it seemed for an eternity. Then I murmured something—her name perhaps, I really do not know—& she too said some words. She was blushing deeply now. I became aware that people were standing nearby, her companions, I supposed. I muttered an excuse, turned & almost ran from her.

I entered the house through the stables. No body was about. I caught sight of myself in a looking-glass: how must I have appeared to her, in my travel-stained & dishevelled state! I hastened upstairs to my chamber, & made myself presentable. Then I was struck by a fearful notion: surely she would not stay to suffer another such encounter with me! I moved to the window, & looked out. She was nowhere to be seen.

I leant against the window-frame. She had departed: once more, I had lost her. I gazed blankly out at the empty grounds, the sunlit lake, the woods beyond—& no human being in sight, save for old Crabbe, scratching away at a rose-bed. Crabbe! He might, just might, know where she & her companions had gone. Was there still a chance for me to overtake them? I raced downstairs, & out through the front door.

The first thing I saw was their carriage, discreetly waiting at the entrance to the stable wing. From despair I passed to elation, but was sufficiently in command of myself to interrogate Crabbe with a semblance of equanimity. He informed me that the visitors were even now walking in Limetree Coppice. I made my way thither.

I soon caught up with them, and, schooling my emotion, accompanied them along the path. This time I believe I acquitted myself slightly better. She is travelling with an Uncle & Aunt from London, who seem to be agreeable, well-bred persons. Once I even walked with her alone, &, miraculously, felt the weight of her hand on my arm. How many times had I remembered that touch, only to recollect that I would never feel it again! For the first time since I came upon her, I felt happy at finding her again. I knew that she was never to be mine, but with her hand on my arm the pain of it melted away.

She explained in trembling tones that she had

245

believed me to be from home, else she had never consented to visit my house, 'For your housekeeper informed us that you would certainly not be here 'til tomorrow; and, indeed, before we left Bakewell, we understood that you were not immediately expected in the country.' Then they departed, but not before I had extracted a promise that I might call on them at their hotel, & bring Georgie.

Fate has given me an unmerited, unbelievable opportunity. I must take advantage of it this time! I must shew her, come what may, how earnestly I have taken to heart her censure at our last meeting, almost three months ago. When I think back to the arrogance of my demeanour on that occasion, I am filled with shame. My repentance is sincere indeed!

July 24th

I am supposed to be changing out of my riding clothes before breakfast, but my thoughts will fly off to the inn at Lambton. What is Elizabeth doing at this moment? Did she walk out this morning? G, with Charles's Sisters, has arrived from London, without Edward Hurst, who has unexpectedly removed to Netherfield on the pretext of casting an eye over the property. He will be required in London in a month or two, for Mrs Louisa's confinement. Charles himself is arriving alone from Newstead some time this morning. Fitchett and Andrewes are staying on there; nor can Tom Bullivant be of our party, as he has business in Town.

I rode out early, before breakfast, Rufus running along behind, & went as near Lambton as

I dared, hoping to discover Elizabeth walking in the countryside nearby, & to repeat the extraordinary coincidence of my meeting with her—but there was no sign of her, & I was obliged to turn back to receive my guests. I have resolved to remedy this omission by calling on her as early as seems decent.

I scarcely listened to my guests' accounts of their various journeys over breakfast. As soon as the repast was over, I invited G to attend me in the Library. But when the door opened, it was not she, but Miss Caroline, who entered. She ceremoniously presented me with a green parcel tyed up with red ribbon. I was surprized: she has no cause to offer me a gift. I opened it—& found inside, duly completed, the slippers she was working for me last autumn at Netherfield. I contrived to smile & thank her, tho' in truth I have rarely seen anything so ugly. They are large & untidy, the embroidery clumsy. On the left shoe, in addition to the lover's knot, is a crude representation of my family crest; on the right one, which I had not seen in the making, two crossed sticks. Before I could venture to enquire what they might represent, she proudly informed me that she had chosen the fishing-rod & the gun as representing my leisure pursuits. She added: 'I would have included a book, since you are such an assiduous scholar, but I did not think it would look well.'

For this I can only be thankful. But I fear that I shall be obliged to come down to breakfast tomorrow wearing these red-and-green objects on my feet. What will Peebles say?

Why have I written at such length about a paltry

pair of slippers? It must be an attempt to distract my thoughts from my forthcoming visit to Lambton. I confess that I dread my next meeting with Elizabeth. True, she did agree to my attending her, & bringing G with me; but when we arrive, will she have thought better of it? Will she chuse not to be at home? It will be a clear message to me to importune her no further.

I am as nervous as on the day I made my disastrous proposal to her—& far less confident of the outcome.

*   *   *

I waited for an hour before G came to me: she had been in the stables with Snowball. Tho' far too old & too small for her to ride he remains a dear friend, & visiting him is always her first care on arrival. I persuaded her to accompany me in the phaeton to Lambton. It was not an easy task: when I revealed that Elizabeth was even now staying in the inn there, G would not believe me. I was forced to enumerate all the circumstances of E's arrival, & the wonderful, terrible coincidence which led to our meeting. When G was finally convinced, she at first refused to make the visit with me. I could not understand why, 'til she explained that she would be intimidated at meeting with the woman who has fixed my affections. I was obliged to plead with her, & eventually, with great reluctance, she consented.

The inn parlour is panelled in wood, and, with the shutters up against the heat, it was dark & cool. I tried in vain not to gaze at E, who wore a light-coloured muslin gown, her arms bare. I have never before beheld her so thinly clad; I was utterly ravished, & in no condition to help G, who had become completely tongue-tied. E's uncle & aunt, Mr & Mrs Gardiner, were the only talkers. Elizabeth herself seemed discomposed, but exerted herself to draw G out, & partly succeeded. I can recall nothing of the conversation: I was aware only of her, & of the hammering of my own heart. I had forgot the low, pleasing sound of her voice, & the small dark mole on the inside of her left wrist. Luckily, Charles, arriving shortly afterwards, created a diversion. I became a little calmer, & was able to observe E's manner, & to witness her pleasure at meeting him. She is truly of a forgiving disposition.

We have invited E & her party to dine with us the day after tomorrow. I visited the hothouses & selected fruits for the occasion, informing Cucklett that I have friends at Lambton whom I particularly wish to impress, & that the best of our produce is to be served to them.

Later, Wolstenholme & Carruthers having arrived from Town, we made an interminable dinner. Fortunately, G was prevailed upon to play & sing afterwards, so that I was spared the necessity of conversation. I could not endure the prospect of making small talk to Miss Caroline & the gentlemen. I imitated Mrs Louisa, who is listless & fatigued, & retired early. Neither did I go down to supper, but have remained here in my chamber, writing all this down. Nothing I put on paper can do justice to the turbulence of my feelings.

July 25th

I entertained no hope of seeing E today, but had arranged to meet her uncle, Mr Gardiner, for a fishing expedition at noon. Accordingly, I repaired to the river with Charles, Wolstenholme & Carruthers, where Mr Gardiner awaited us, & we enjoyed an hour's trout-tickling. I was just wondering how to persuade him to allow me to accompany him back to the inn, when he remarked in passing that his Wife & Niece were presently in my house, paying a morning call on G. Pleading urgent business, & abandoning them without ceremony, I ran back to the house. I arrived there breathless & discomposed, to find E & her Aunt Gardiner in the saloon with G, Miss Caroline, Mrs Louisa & Mrs Annesley. Rufus had joined the party uninvited, & E was stroking his head—he seems to have taken an immediate liking to her. The ladies were partaking of fruit from the hothouses. I was relieved to observe that Cucklett, inferring that these must be my important guests, had sent up the finest of the summer peaches.

Following our visitors' departure, Miss Caroline exclaimed: 'How very ill Eliza Bennet looks this morning, Mr Darcy! I never in my life saw anyone so much altered as she is since the winter. She is grown so brown & coarse! Louisa & I were agreeing that we should not have known her again.'

I endeavoured to stem this ill-natured tide by remarking that E was quite simply tanned from her summer travels.

This produced a diatribe against poor E's appearance: 'Her face is too thin; her complexion has no brilliancy; & her features are not at all

250

handsome. Her nose wants character; there is nothing marked in its lines. Her teeth are tolerable, but not out of the common way; & as for her eyes, which have sometimes been called so fine, I never could perceive anything extraordinary about them. They have a sharp, shrewish look, which I do not like at all.'

I was quite disgusted at her outburst, & left the room, remarking coldly that, for my part, I considered E to be very handsome.

END OF PART V

Part VI

THE SEARCH

July 26th [Editor's note: This entry and the first part of the following day's are dashed off at speed. Unlike the rest of the text, they have proved difficult to decipher.]
Tomorrow at dawn I leave for Town. My love in distress, & through my fault!

July 27th
Bedford. A day's hard riding—Why cannot one ride on through the night? Instead, I must cool my heels in this confounded inn—All, all my fault— Absurd, stiff-necked arrogance! To see her weep, when I could have prevented it! I ride on at first light.

          *   *   *

I have now supped—must keep my strength up. Calm myself, & take notes of what to do:

Where to Find Them
1. At Mrs Younge's—I am convinced that she is my best hope. She & Wickham are confederates of long standing; she assisted him in abducting G.
2. At a regimental friend's house
—*Pro:* Wickham knows all the raffish ne'er-do-wells in the regiment.
—*Con:* Too many of his friends know Lydia—the Bennets a respectable family—would they aid & abet such a disastrous elopement? Lydia just sixteen—the whole regiment must know that.
    Query: What has possessed Wickham to run away with her? Frivolous, empty-headed child of

barely sixteen, virtually penniless? & he on the look-out for a rich bride!

Everything points in one direction: he can have no intention of marrying her. He will abandon her in London, return to his old pursuits as tho' nothing had occurred, & resume his attempts to marry money.

Result: ruin of poor little Lydia, misery for her family.

3. Shielded by London friends? Try Inns of Court: he was a student of Law, & must have associated with shady individuals among the Legal profession.

4. Byron? Nonsense. Byron at Newstead—& he would have scant sympathy for such an elopement. But remember poor Patroclus?

5. Making his own arrangements unaided? Unlikely—W an exploiter & completely without funds.

<u>Some body somewhere must know where he is.</u>
I am not like to sleep tonight. Instead, I shall write it all down, as lucidly as I can: an account of what happened when I arrived at the inn at Lambton. It seems like months ago—can it only have been yesterday?

I walked into the parlour, where Elizabeth was alone. My joy at beholding her turned swiftly to dismay. She stood up as I entered, swaying on her feet. I have never seen her thus pale. In her left hand she held a letter, gripping it so tightly that her hand trembled. I exclaimed stupidly. I believe I offered to fetch her wine.

She whispered something like: 'I thank you, I am quite well. I am only distressed by some dreadful news which I have just received from

Longbourn.' I durst not press her further. She finally murmured that there was no point in concealing the truth, which would presently become public knowledge. She sank back onto her chair, & began to weep. I stood before her, not daring to comfort her.

It would have been more discreet in me to have left her then, but to do so was beyond me. I waited in dumb silence. After begging me to keep it secret, she whispered, between her sobs, 'I have just had a letter from Jane, with such dreadful news. It cannot be concealed from any one. My youngest Sister has left all her friends—has eloped.' Then followed the blow: Lydia's seducer none other than Wickham!

In my perturbation I scarce grasped what had happened. As soon as I understood it, I knew that I must act. The fugitives were travelling towards London from Brighton. I must find them. The scandal cannot be entirely averted, but if I can force that monster to wed Lydia, the family may ride it out. I determined to leave for Town immediately. I longed to comfort her. As it was, I could only promise not to reveal her secret, & take my leave.

As I was in the stables, giving orders for the carriage to be made ready, Charles appeared. We walked up to the house together. My mind was too full for me to attend to him. I told him shortly that, greatly to my regret, I had been called away on urgent business, & would be obliged to leave them at first light.

'How can this be, when the shooting season is just about to start?' he objected. 'You said nothing about it when the post came this morning.' Then, restraining himself, he added: 'Pray excuse my indiscretion. I have no wish to pry into your affairs.'

For the life of me I could think of no way of explaining, so I merely bowed. There was an embarrassed silence, then he said, in a somewhat faltering tone: 'I should have wished to discuss a personal matter with you, Fitz.'

'What is it?' I could not refuse to hear him out.

'Seeing Miss Elizabeth here has brought it all back, as painfully as before.' He paused, perhaps to give me time to reply, but I could not.

'Last November—when you discovered that Miss Bennet—Jane—is a fortune-hunter . . .' His voice trembled, & once more he stopped—& once more I could find no reply.

'Miss Elizabeth is so charming, so innocent. It makes me wonder . . . How can the Sister of such a one be the monster you describe?'

I owed the poor fellow an honest answer—but now is not the time: I have no choice but to defer the explanation 'til such time as Lydia's misdemeanours have become public knowledge. I took him by the arm, & squeezed it. 'I hope one day to see you happy,' was all that I could trust myself to say. He left me abruptly, & strode away across the lawn towards the wilderness. It was some time before he returned, I believe—tho' I had not the leisure to observe his movements, occupied as I was with my own preparations for departure.

It has proved difficult explaining to my other friends that I was abandoning them. I found the ladies sitting under the big cedar tree, Mrs Louisa half-dozing, Miss Caroline fanning herself: 'Do

258

you like this heat, Mr Darcy?'

I replied that I was too preoccupied to pay it much attention.

'You strong men are fortunate indeed. For my part, weak woman that I am, I can think of nothing else.' And Miss Caroline plied her fan more enthusiastically than ever. When I revealed that I was shortly to leave them, however, she droppt the fan, & lifted her two hands to her cheeks, saying, 'O!'

I was more concerned by G, who stared at me in puzzlement & alarm. I bowed to them & was hastening away when she murmured something to her guests, rose, & walked with me.

'I am sorry that you are to leave us so hastily, Fitz—but at least you will be present when Miss Elizabeth Bennet & Mr & Mrs Gardiner dine with us tonight.'

'On the contrary, our guests send their apologies: they have been obliged to leave today on urgent family business.'

G stood still. I stopped too. She was looking at me in astonishment. I began to walk again, & she ran to catch up with me. Then she said, 'O, Fitz, both leaving so suddenly? I do . . . I do hope that this does not mean trouble between you!'

I stopped again & looked down at her anxious face. 'O no, indeed, their departure is nothing to do with me,' said I, & took her hand. She gave a small sigh, but said no more. I would fain have told her all: but I have promised Elizabeth. Not a word shall pass my lips.

*   *   *

It occurs to me that when I reveal the truth about Lydia to Charles, I am like to make his dilemma more painful than ever. He may feel reluctant to ally himself to a family thus tainted by the scandal of a disgraced Sister. I begin to feel sorry for Jane—first, her prospects seem ruined by what I now take to be ill-founded gossip; then no sooner does she appear to be exonerated than a catastrophe befalls her family which makes her an impossible match.

*   *   *

I must now try to sleep a little. I set off at sunrise, & should be in Town in good time.

July 28th
I arrived home and hastily partook of some cold meats, knowing that my first task must be to visit Mrs Younge. I had not seen her since Margate, & had devoutly hoped never to set eyes on her again. But it had to be. I changed out of my travelling clothes, & made my way directly to her house.

    Two years ago, when I made my first visit to Mrs Younge's Academy in Edward Street, I felt pleasure & anticipation at meeting the lady who seemed likely to prove the ideal *duègne* for my Sister. How different were my feelings this morning! *Then*, she had been warmly recommended—I learned afterwards that it was indirectly through Wickham. *Now* I noted that the paint was peeling, & the whole establishment seemed outwardly less prosperous than before. Evidently I have not been the only one to find the lady wanting.

I mounted the front steps, & pulled the bell. It was answered by a manservant. On an impulse, before leaving home, I had picked up a stray visiting card from the hall table, & thrust it in my pocket. I now presented it to the manservant. The house is a sizeable one, as befits an educational establishment for young gentlewomen; but inside, as outside, there was an air of shabbiness which had not been evident when G was a parlour pupil here—& a strong smell of boiled bones. I was staring at a row of galoshes, caked with dried mud, under the hall stand, when the servant returned, & ushered me into a small parlour.

Mrs Younge stood up as I entered, then, seeing me, recoiled. However, she swiftly gained control of herself: she is brazen indeed. She offered me her hand, which I could not bring myself to take. 'O, Mr Darcy! What a surprize! I am not sure however that it is a pleasant one.' She glanced at the visiting card she held in her hand: 'Since when has your name been Sir Thomas Bullivant?'

I made no answer: I had not set eyes on her since her betrayal of Georgie.

'You find me here in straitened circumstances,' continued she. 'After Miss Darcy's so-abrupt removal from my care, many of the other young ladies were withdrawn by their Mammas. I have been obliged to change direction, & have lately been taking in lodgers.'

I bit back the indignant retort that rose to my lips. She seemed almost to be reproaching me for removing my Sister from her tender care!

'How is dear Miss Darcy?' she continued. The impertinence!

'That is nothing to the purpose. I am come to

261

ask you for Mr Wickham's direction,' said I.

'Why? Is dear Mr Wickham in Town?'

'You must know he is.'

'That I do not, & if I did, you would be the last person I would tell it to.' So saying, she rose, pulled the bell-rope, & directed the manservant to shew me out.

Before I knew where I was, I found myself in the street. There was nothing more I could do—Mrs Younge has proved useless. Yet I am convinced that she knows where he is. Why have I been so woefully incompetent in extracting the information? I think it must have been because I had not seen her since her betrayal of G. I was quite simply in turmoil. The moment I was outside, I knew that I should have offered her money. Tomorrow I shall return to the charge, & bring my purse with me.

Not wishing to spend the rest of the day in idleness, I tried various inns & coffee shops at random—a very unsatisfactory process. In the evening, I made the rounds of all the clubs & gambling dens I know of, thinking that once in London Wickham would have been unable to resist the lure of the tables. I enquired after him everywhere, but no body has seen him. At Brooks's I ran into one of the Officers from his regiment, whom I had met at Meryton, but the fellow has been on furlough for three weeks, & knows nothing of Wickham & his doings. This activity took me all day, & much of the evening. I returned home at midnight.

July 29th

This morning I awoke full of anxiety about Georgie. It had not struck me before, but how she hears about Wickham's elopement is of paramount importance. I would not have her informed of it by any malicious, unsympathetic gossip-monger. I must tell her myself before it is too late.

After breakfast I sought out Mrs Younge again. She greeted me with the utmost *sang-froid*, motioned me to a chair, & sat down opposite me, saying thoughtfully, 'I was expecting you to call again.'

'Which means, I take it, that you have some information for me,' said I.

She shrugged. Yesterday I was too perturbed to observe her dispassionately. Now I noted that she seemed aged & somewhat haggard. She wore an unbecoming cap pulled low over her brow. 'I have already told you that I know nothing of Mr Wickham's whereabouts,' said she.

I indicated that I could make it worth her while to tell me.

'Always so generous,' said she. I did not like her smile.

I had a purse with me, which I shewed her.

'What? You expect me to betray a friend for thirty pieces of silver?' she exclaimed, in mock outrage. Once more she rang for the man to shew me out. I hesitated whether to insist on having it out with her, but realized that I did not have enough money with me to make the endeavour worthwhile.

*   *   *

I am now convinced that Mrs Younge is playing cat & mouse with me. I shall have to try again tomorrow. Meanwhile, wishing to leave no stone unturned, I went to the London Headquarters of the 9th Warwickshires, in Artillery Row. I asked to speak to someone in authority, & was shown into the Adjutant's office. He is a Major Mainwaring. I explained about Wickham's escapade. Mainwaring was reluctant to discuss it, but I inferred from his manner that he is already acquainted with the details. He wished to know what had prompted my interest in the affair. I felt myself justified in asserting that I was representing the Bennet family. The Major then unbent so far as to inform me that he has no clue as to Wickham's whereabouts in London. However, he undertook to let me know if he hears anything, which was more than I was entitled to expect.

It occurred to me that W might well have resorted to pawnbrokers or moneylenders for funding—assuming that he & Lydia have anything worth pawning. I therefore visited some ten establishments of doubtful respectability. Faugh! I have returned home none the wiser. Although I paid for information, all denied knowing George Wickham. Indeed, one of my interlocutors, more honest-seeming than the rest, suggested that it would be most unlikely of him to have given his real name. And, indeed, why should he? I have been wasting my time.

Tomorrow, if I have no success with Mrs Younge, I shall try such of Wickham's friends as I am acquainted with myself. I have also written to Pemberley. I believe that he has severed all ties with the place, but there is just a possibility that

Reynolds or perhaps Dovedale might have some notion of his whereabouts. This evening I plan to visit some of the *bordellos* frequented by Officers. It would be outrageous for him to visit them when he is with Lydia, but Wickham is capable of every outrage.

Meanwhile, I feel more hopeful. Today, Mrs Younge surely implied that she does know where the scoundrel has concealed himself. Tomorrow I shall offer a more serious reward.

July 30th
No success in the bawdy-houses last night. Before that I sought out any body who might have known him. I ran into Snow, Brackenbury & Leigh in the Cocoa-Tree. None of them has seen him. Brackenbury remarked that after that episode with the fishmonger's daughter in Cambridge, he has no desire ever to set eyes on him again. They were curious to know why I was so anxious to find him, but I told them nothing.

Meanwhile, it occurred to me that I should make the rounds of places of entertainment, in view of Lydia's fondness for amusements of every kind.

Tonight I shall go to the Theatre Royale. I must arrive early, & watch the crowds as they stream in.

Other possible attractions for Lydia:

1. *Theatres:* Pantheon, Sans Souci, Sadlers Wells, Covent Garden, Royal Circus, Sanspareil.
2. *Pleasure Gardens:* Marylebone Gardens, Vauxhall Gardens, Green Park, St James's, Hyde Park.

If I have no luck with Mrs Younge, I shall visit lawyers. I have remembered that Wickham was articled at Coven & Conway, solicitors; will they have any information for me? He left under a cloud some four years since. I seem to recall that he was then in lodgings off the Gray's Inn Road.

*　　　*　　　*

I have realized that it will be useless to visit theatres, since they will almost all be closed for the summer. There remain the various pleasure gardens. But no—it is ridiculous in me to attempt to visit them: I might go on a Wednesday, they on a Thursday, or visit Hyde Park on the day that they chuse Vauxhall Gardens.

Instead, this morning I return to Edward Street, resolved to brook no further concealment from Mrs Younge.

*　　　*　　　*

I am supping alone off a tray in the Library. I have resolved to spend the evening committing today's doings to paper.

*　　　*　　　*

I reached Edward Street at about eleven o'clock. Mrs Younge received me with her customary insolence. I again requested Wickham's direction.

'May I ask why you desire it?'

'I have private business to conduct with him,' said I shortly.

Her hand, resting on her knee, pleated &

upleated the stuff of her gown. There was a long pause. Then she said, 'If I did know where he was, I should be under no obligation to reveal it to you, of all people.'

'That is true; but it would certainly be worth your while.'

'How, worth my while?' She was nothing if not to the point.

I offered her 50*l*.

'What is this business you have with George Wickham that is worth 50*l*.?' she asked. From her expression, I had the strong feeling that she knew it full well.

'My business is, as I told you, private,' I replied. 'However, I can assure you that it will be to his pecuniary advantage. He will not thank you for keeping us apart.'

'You must be nearly affected to be offering so much money,' said she shrewdly.

I should not have shewn myself to be so eager. Would she keep me dangling for the sheer pleasure of tormenting me?

That error on my part cost me dear. I was forced to plead with her for a half-hour together, & finally left her having paid out not 50 but 100*l*. Still, I had Wickham's direction in my pocket. I should never have found it out without her help: he is lodging in a private house in Long Acre, off the Strand. I had them at last!

The house is small, & somewhat run-down. A serving-wench in a soiled apron answered the door. When I asked for Mr Wickham, she gave me a blank stare. Of course: they must be travelling under an assumed name! I hastily revized my approach, & asked to be shewn up to the young couple who lodged there. Again she looked blank, & I began to fear that Mrs Younge had tricked me. But finally she nodded, & stepping aside to allow me to enter, preceded me up the stairs, past the reception rooms, to an exiguous apartment on the second floor. She knocked, & Wickham's voice bade us enter.

The room smelt stuffy & airless. There was no sign of Lydia. Wickham lay on the uncurtained bed, smoking a pipe & staring at the ceiling. When I entered he glanced in my direction, then raised himself on one elbow & bowed with the upper part of his body. He did not attempt to rise. I felt an overwhelming urge to stride over & haul him off the bed. I said, 'Where is Miss Lydia Bennet?'

He shrugged, took the pipe out of his mouth, & said: 'O, so you've finally come. You took your time.'

'What on earth do you mean?' I asked in surprize.

Wickham sat up on the bed. 'Lydia is, I think, downstairs, sitting in the dining-parlour. She likes to look out at the street, I believe.' He paused, & pulled at his pipe. 'At any rate, you must take some of the blame for what has happened. I only eloped with her because of you!'

I was so astonished I simply stared at him.

He resumed gazing at the ceiling. We remained thus for what seemed an age, 'til I finally requested an explanation of his last remark.

He took the pipe from his mouth: 'Well, I knew you was mooning after her Sister Elizabeth— didn't see why you should enjoy your little romance in unalloyed bliss. Lydia has brought discredit to the whole Bennet family. Your young lady is no longer marriageable, you will find. What a pity!'

'I assure you, there is no understanding of any kind between Miss Elizabeth Bennet & me. You are sadly mistaken.'

He gave a scornful laugh: 'Pooh, Fizzibuzz! Tell me another! I have it from an eyewitness that you are head over heels in love.'

I could not resist asking who this 'eyewitness' was.

'Why, Lydia's little friend, Miss Maria Lucas. She was with you & the fair Eliza at Rosings, & could not but observe how you dangled after her. It smelt of May, she said. Lydia laughed about it with the Officers in Brighton!'

So I had been making a spectacle of myself, exhibiting my unhappy love for all to see! I bit my lips & remained silent. This would be something to occupy the wakeful hours of the night.

After a long silence, I was master enough of myself to say: 'You will apprehend that this latest escapade of yours puts paid to the allowance you have been receiving from me.'

'O, why?' Wickham had risen now, & was lounging against the door-jamb. 'I still have a secret to reveal that would destroy your Sister's reputation for ever.'

'Who would believe a blackguard like you? You have forfeited any credibility now. Besides, it is a year since it happened: why should you have kept quiet for so long?'

He had the grace to look somewhat crestfallen, but he continued to hold out against me. I have to give him credit for the most blatant impertinence. 'I can prove that you have been paying me to keep quiet,' he said, with a contemptuous smile.

'Not so,' said I. 'I paid you out of a sense of duty to my late Father's *protégé*. All will agree that your present conduct has released me from any obligations towards you. No. If you want money from me, you can have it, but only on one condition.'

'What is that?' asked he, trying to keep the eagerness from his voice, but I could tell by the way he drew himself up that this was a question that meant everything to him.

'Why, by marrying Miss Lydia Bennet.'

He replied angrily: 'Marry *her*? Why, she's just a child!'

I was so shocked that I sat down heavily on the nearest chair. After a long silence, I said: 'If you want so much as a penny from me, you'll have to marry her.'

There was another silence. Wickham appeared to be thinking deeply. 'What's it worth to me?' he asked at length.

The question took me aback. I had been so desperate to find the two of them out that I had not considered what my terms should be. 'I shall have to think about that. I cannot give you an immediate answer,' said I.

'You can come back tomorrow, then.'

I have insisted on speaking to Lydia alone tomorrow. Wickham would fain have prevented me, but he knows he cannot push me too far if he wants his money.

*   *   *

I went immediately to Gracechurch Street to see

Elizabeth's Uncle & Aunt. It is imperative that the Bennet family be informed as soon as possible that Lydia is found. The servant informed me that Mr Bennet himself is with them, but leaves tomorrow. I did not ask to be received—I do not chuse to present myself as the saviour of the family to Elizabeth's Father. I shall return tomorrow.

I have spent the whole evening pondering on Wickham's calculating mind. What a risk he took, in destroying his prospects on the offchance that he would hit a raw nerve in me! What folly, if it had transpired that I was indifferent towards Elizabeth! On what long odds has he gambled! But then he was always a gambler . . .

Tomorrow, then, I see Lydia. I shall make the best possible provision for her future—and, I hope, rescue Elizabeth from the misery of a prolonged disgrace.

July 31st
Frantic days. No time to describe them.

August 3rd
At last I have sufficient leisure to describe the flurry of activity of the last few days. I am staying at the Golden Hart for the night, with nothing to occupy me but my Diary. Tomorrow I purpose to reach Pemberley in time for dinner.

*   *   *

On Saturday morning, as agreed, I went to the lodging-house off the Strand & saw Lydia alone. She had been sitting in the window. When I entered, she sprang to her feet, & turned to me, laughing, a bonnet in one hand, a bunch of red ribbons in the other. 'Mr Darcy!' cried she, 'Wickham said you was coming to see me. Here I am, in Town. Is not it exciting?'

I said nothing, but I must have looked disapproving, for she said, 'O, do not put on such a long face! I'm a grown woman. I know how to run my life.'

I said, 'Nevertheless, I think that you would be better at home with your family. They are most concerned about you.'

'O, pooh! What do they care? They always treat me like a child. La! I tell you, I'm grown up now.' And she sat down composedly, smoothing her skirts.

I attempted to reason with her, & to persuade her that her future in London would be bleak indeed if Wickham deserted her. She would not hear of returning home. Then I asked her how she would like to be married to Wickham.

There was a silence. Then: 'O, married? Yes! I should like it of all things! What a joke, to be the first one to marry! I should take precedence over all my Sisters, even Jane!' She laughed, & tossed her head. Then she said more quietly: 'Has Wickham really agreed to marry me?' I told her that arrangements were being made, & that there was every prospect of their marrying. I made no mention of the way he bargained with me the day before. She jumped up again: 'O, good! I must arrange my wedding-clothes at once! I shall send to Papa for money.' She gave a little skip of delight.

I was hard put to it to persuade her that she would have to be married from her Uncle's house.

I verily believe that she is afraid to leave Wickham's side, lest he disappear the moment her back is turned. I could not persuade her to come away with me.

*   *   *

Afterwards, I had a further interview with Wickham. His one concern was with the extent of the sums to be settled on him.

I began: 'I am willing to pay your debts—provided of course that they are within reason. Then you may be able to resume your place in your regiment, & no harm done.'

'Not enough,' he replied immediately.

The discussion took a good hour, with him bargaining over every point, & me attempting to ascertain the extent of his debts. He agreed to give me a comprehensive list on the morrow.

Thinking over the above, I am even more astounded at Wickham's conviction that I would find them, & strike a bargain with him. Why then did not he chuse a place of concealment easier for me to discover? Of course! He did not wish to be found by anyone but me. Lydia's Father & Uncle could not have afforded the exorbitant sums that he proposes to exact from me. He & Mrs Younge have hatched a pretty plot between them!

Before I left him, Lydia came in. He received her embrace with scant enthusiasm. She is the same age as Georgie was when . . . Shameless as she seems, I am beginning to feel almost sorry for her.

I then repaired to Gracechurch Street. Mr Gardiner was there alone; his Wife was due back from Hertfordshire later that day. He was astonished at my calling, & even more surprized when I revealed that I had found Lydia with Wickham. He insisted at first on taking the matter into his own hands. I was hard put to it to convince him that I alone must take the responsibility for the arrangements, since it was my foolish reserve, & reluctance to denounce Wickham for what he was, that had done all the harm in the first place. He has undertaken not to tell the Bennets of my part in the proceedings.

*   *   *

On the Sunday, I was obliged to hold further discussions with Wickham about the settlement. In the end, I agreed to pay some 700*l.* worth of debts (an outrageous sum!), to buy him a commission in a new regiment billeted in the North of England, & to settle the sum of one thousand pounds on the couple.

Afterwards I went to Gracechurch Street to inform Mr Gardiner what had transpired. Mrs Gardiner was present, & thanked me with tears in her eyes for finding the runaways. They invited me to dinner, but they appeared so shaken by the events of the weekend that I preferred to leave them in peace, & dine alone at home. I undertook to bring Lydia to them the following day.

*   *   *

On the Monday I saw Batchelor, who has persuaded me to be circumspect about how I pay moneys to Wickham. Accordingly, to Wickham's disgust, I have refused to advance the money I promised him directly into his hands. On Batchelor's advice, I have not made my intentions quite plain to Messire W: I propose to hold the money in trust for Lydia alone. Wickham will have access to the interest only as long as he remains with her. If he abandons her, she keeps the money. I devoutly hope that such a device will maintain this ramshackle marriage in some semblance of order.

Wickham, realizing that he will get no more moneys out of me for the present, has finally, & with an ill grace, agreed to the marriage. He attempted to make me pay his debts before the wedding, & told me that it was the least that I could do; but I have refused: I do not trust him to keep to his part of the bargain otherwise. I have been obliged to sign a promise to pay him what we have agreed the minute he is married.

Lydia was very reluctant to leave him & move to Gracechurch Street. I can understand it: Mrs Gardiner is indignant, & purposes to scold her roundly. Furthermore, I suspect that even now Lydia can scarcely believe that she is truly to be married. She is in a state of febrile excitement. Mostly, she greets every new development with shouts of raucous laughter; but once, I noticed her surreptitiously wiping her eyes. During our journey from the Strand to Gracechurch Street she was hanging out of the carriage window like a small child, exclaiming at the London streets. Her habitual defence against censure is impertinence & a determined levity which deceives most people into thinking her abominably pert. Amidst the general atmosphere of disapproval, I believe I am the only one to feel a touch of pity for her: her Aunt & Uncle will, I fear, be less compassionate.

Now that things are finally settled, the Gardiners purpose to write at once to Longbourn, & relieve the poor Bennets' anxiety. They are sending a letter by express delivery—but my name will not be mentioned.

I am eager to be back at Pemberley, to attend to my neglected house guests.

August 4th
Reached Pemberley in good time for dinner. There I found my Cousin James Fitzwilliam, arrived yesterday with his Sister Augusta. Georgie had asked them to stay. She has taken to issuing invitations without consulting me. G in the highest of spirits at having Augusta here with her, & Augusta is chearful & not at all mindful of her erstwhile *Romance*. They both amused themselves commiserating with me for '*mouldering in stuffy old Town*' in this hot weather. Augusta's playful manner reminds me a little of Lydia's. How can such an ebullient young person be daughter to my redoubtable Aunt Fitzwilliam?

Among the correspondence awaiting my return I have found a shocking letter from my Aunt de Bourgh:

Mr Collins has given me some scandalous news from Hertfordshire, she writes. *The youngest Sister of Miss Elizabeth Bennet has cast all propriety to the winds, & eloped like some common trollop with an Officer of the 9th Warwickshires. I understand he is none other than the son of your dear Father's late agent, Mr Wickham. How fortunate that neither your Papa,*

276

nor Mr Wickham père, who was, I understand, a very decent sort of man, should be alive to see this day! And as for the Bennet family—well! I was of the opinion that they were very poorly brought up—all five Sisters out at once! And Miss Elizabeth Bennet herself, so pert & immodest! I am not in the least surprized at the news. This escapade puts a stop to this raffish family's aspirations to gentility.

I put by the letter for fear someone should see it. I had not been aware that my Aunt enjoyed spreading malicious tittle-tattle. How shall it be for Elizabeth if mine own Aunt is capable of such voluble malevolence! I am tempted to write & upbraid her for her reprehensible gossip-mongering—but then I remember my episode with her daughter. Is my own behaviour so irreproachable that I can take a high tone with my Aunt?

*　　　*　　　*

Thinking over my indignation with Aunt Catherine, I find I can no longer despise the Bennet family, whatever their situation. I am indeed a different person from the proud popinjay who presumed to make Elizabeth that excruciating offer of marriage!

With these thoughts in mind, I went off to the river to tickle a few trout. In the midst of landing a fine fish, I suddenly thought that I should tell G of the elopement immediately, before she hears of it from the likes of my Aunt. Unfortunately, she & Augusta are spending the day with Isabella at the Parsonage. It will have to wait 'til tomorrow.

August 5th

I have told Georgie what has happened up 'til now, urging her to keep it secret for the present. To my amazement, she shewed not the slightest distress at Wickham's involvement in the tale. All her thoughts were of Elizabeth, to whom she has taken a strong liking. 'Have not you written to her, or seen her?' she asked. 'The poor lady must be beside herself with anxiety.'

I explained that I had left Elizabeth at the inn without revealing my plans. As far as she knows, the business with Lydia has been managed by the Gardiners alone. Georgie expressed some surprize at this; I explained that I told Elizabeth nothing because I feared to raise her hopes only to dash them. I would not have had her disappointed in me.

'But now that it is all over, she must learn the part you played!'

'No. I do not wish her to feel any obligation towards me,' said I. G attempted to remonstrate with me, but I refused to discuss the matter further.

'But what is to happen to Miss Elizabeth's Sister & to Wickham, now that they are found?' then asked G, pronouncing his name without the slightest consciousness.

'I may give you no details at present, but shall have to travel back to Town presently in connexion with this matter. If only I were not obliged to have any further dealings with him! In truth, I never wish to set eyes on him again.'

'Neither do I,' said she, & actually smiled! So she is entirely recovered! I find this almost

278

incredible, & can only attribute it to her extreme youth—and, despite her horrible experience, to her innocence.

The wheat is ripe, & ready for cutting. We start tomorrow.

August 6th
Seeing Charles as melancholy as ever reminds me of something that much concerns me: when he learns of the scandal, will he still cleave to a woman whose Sister has been so dishonoured? In his place, I would prove steadfast . . .

Despite Mrs Louisa's reminding them that it is most unseemly behaviour in gentlewomen, the younger ladies have wished to take part in the harvesting. They accordingly donned sunbonnets like common farm girls, & joined in with the labourers, uttering screams of alarm at the small creatures which run from the scythes. The weather continues fine. The harvest is excellent this year. The cold Spring & hot Summer have proved ideal. We had a picnic by the side of the cornfield. The girls picked bunches of cornflowers & poppies, & decorated the table with them. We drank my Aunt's Kentish cider, which was deceptively strong. Our labour was punctuated by much merriment.

Rufus hurt his paw chasing a rabbit through the stubble. Young Joe has bandaged it up.

August 7th
Pargeter came early to discuss draining Hanks Pond when the harvest is finished. I am of the opinion that we should wait—this is a very busy time of year, & the labourers cannot easily be spared for such work.

Miss Caroline has set up a pall mall tournament today, in which we must all participate. The ladies drew names out of a hat to find gentlemen partners. Mrs Louisa drew me, & announced that, as she was feeling languid & wished to have her Husband by her side, she would change places with Miss Caroline, who had drawn the said Edward.

*   *   *

The post has arrived, & Charles has learned of the elopement from one of the Officers. He was just beginning to tell me this when Miss Caroline positively ran into the saloon:

'Reynolds told me you was here,' she gasped. 'What do you say to your Miss Eliza now, Mr Darcy? A fine family, eh? You have had a lucky escape. Just think—you could have been obliged to address that little hussy Lydia as "Sister"!'

I bowed coldly. 'Miss Elizabeth Bennet & I are not in any way attached, as you well know.'

'As I said—you have had a lucky escape!' & she actually tapped me playfully with the fan which she has taken to carrying everywhere, & ran off to organize her pall mall tournament.

'I must confess that the news gives me pause,' said Charles later. 'I cannot view the Bennet family in the same light as I did before. I blame the parents. Why did not they attempt to educate, or at least to control that young hoyden?'

'Miss Jane Bennet is scarcely responsible,' said I.

'No, indeed!' answered he warmly. 'I am far from reproaching her for another's misconduct. I only wish that I might have helped the family.'

Then he turned to me anxiously, & asked: 'Do you think that this misfortune will have dampened down Jane's tendency to flirt? I realize that it is too late to venture to try again with her, & have accepted your view that she would make but a poor partner; but for all my best efforts, I cannot forget her.'

So he will not let the family's disgrace interfere with his love for Jane! I think the better of him for that. However, I was unable to reassure him. The Gardiners insist that Lydia's marriage must not be mentioned to any body 'til it has actually taken place.

Miss Caroline & I emerged victorious from our tournament. G took me on one side to complain that we had an unfair advantage: '*You* are always tops at all sports, & *she* has been practising in secret these past ten days.'

August 8th
I have been thinking about how to raise the money to pay off Wickham. I had intended to build the new milking shed *this* year—the old one is most inefficient. I had planned a fine brick-built structure with the automatic sluice recommended by Anne, & had set aside 300*l*. for its construction. Also, I was just about to order myself an extravagant new curricle, in the latest style, costing upwards of 150*l*. I confess it is this latter piece of excessive frivolity which I shall regret giving up—tho' I daresay I should not have used it above ten times this season. The new ballroom wing at Pemberley cannot at present be built. Georgie will be very disappointed.

The ladies have continued helping with the

harvest—we are now binding the sheaves—all except Miss Caroline, who has remained indoors, tho' everyone begged her to join the party. Georgie whispered to me that Miss Caroline is bitten all over by harvest mites, & dare not venture out for fear of a further assault. I suggested that G discreetly approach Reynolds, who has a remarkable pharmacopoeia by her for such eventualities.

August 9th

Walked with James down to the kennels to view the Pemberley hounds. On the way he told me that he has heard of the Bennets' disaster from Miss Caroline, who has turned into an inveterate gossip. He took me to one side to tell me that he had seriously contemplated making Elizabeth an offer, last Spring, at Rosings. 'The poor girl is not to blame for anything,' said he, 'but it would indeed be difficult to be associated with such a family as this. I daresay I am well out of it.'

I knew better than to give my opinion of this judgment.

The harriers look to be fit, & well prepared for the season. Lockworth says they are eager, & ready to mark the quarry with voice. I had feared an outbreak of distemper, but it seems we have 'scaped it. Afterwards we all repaired in carriages to Georgie's favourite spot on the Peaks, where she had organized a substantial picnic.

Today I received a letter from Mrs Gardiner in London. The wedding is arranged, the licence purchased, the rings too. She writes that Lydia is insufferable, paying no attention whatever to criticisms of her behaviour: *'The girl has the gall to want a festive wedding, & is annoyed that no friends are invited, & that she may not purchase new wedding clothes,'* &c., &c.

Mrs Gardiner, for all her merits, forgets that the poor child is only just sixteen!

August 10th

I broke it to G today that she would not have her new ballroom in the immediate future. To my surprize, she flung her arms around me & broke into merry laughter. 'Why, Fitz, I am delighted!'

'What do you mean?' I asked.

'Why, that I never liked the notion. I love the Great Hall with the old minstrels' gallery. It seemed a shame to pull it all down!'

'But . . . I thought you wanted a change,' I stammered. I was truly astonished.

'O no,' replied she. 'It was only an idle suggestion. Then you became so involved in the project that I durst raise no objection for fear of dampening your enthusiasm.'

She danced away to pick late roses for the table.

August 11th

Charles is most anxious to leave for Town with me the day after tomorrow. He has come up with a new plan: to travel on to Hertfordshire to assist Jane's family. He is irked at my persuading him that now is not the time to do so: their continuing distress must preclude their receiving visitors. After much argument, I have prevailed on him to stay behind at Pemberley to look after my guests 'til I return. I am beginning to suspect that nothing will keep him from renewing his addresses to Jane. This afternoon, he sought me out, & walked with me in the garden. He talked much of Jane. As soon as Lydia is safely wed, I shall take him into my confidence.

August 12th

The Glorious Twelfth—& the grouse are plentiful this year. All the gentlemen went shooting this morning. Rufus shut up in the house, howling the place down. Beaters & dogs did good work, & we came home with an excellent bag. Regret that this is to be my last day at Pemberley. Spent the afternoon making myself ready for my departure.

I wonder what tricks Wickham has in store for me in Town? I shall not rest 'til he is safely wed. Last night I dreamt about him, & woke recalling an episode in our childhood. We were about 13 years old. Wickham dragged me off into the woods—doubtless on some poaching enterprize. I followed him with some reluctance, & when I caught up with him, found him surrounded by a trio of hostile village louts. He was on his knees, whimpering with terror, & begging them to spare him. I was obliged to come to his rescue. Taller & stronger than they, I sparred with them, & chased them off in short order. To my amazement, at dinner that day, Wickham drew attention to my black eye, & recounted the whole episode, shamelessly reversing our roles. My Father was impressed & grateful to Wickham for his courage. I opened my mouth to explain the true course of events, but realized that to defend myself would make them think me absurdly pompous, or, worse still, a liar. Wickham favoured me with a quizzical, mischievous look. When I caught him alone, I asked him indignantly why he had told such a gratuitous falsehood. He shrugged, laughed & replied, 'O, it was a simple joke, Fizzibuzz. Cannot you take a joke?'

August 15th
Arrived in Town in time for a late breakfast. I have been on the road for the last two days: an uneventful journey.

Later, I hastened to Gracechurch Street to make sure that the wedding preparations were all proceeding according to plan. Mr Gardiner assures me that Wickham is quite secure, & a regular visitor to the house. The Gardiners have been hard put to it to remain civil towards him. The ceremony will be performed two days hence in St Clement's in the Strand, & afterwards the Gardiners have, somewhat reluctantly, offered their Niece a small wedding breakfast. No body will be present but the Gardiners, the newly-weds & myself. I wish that I did not have to be of the party. It will scarcely be a joyful occasion.

Lydia is behaving like her old self: she will not be lectured by her Aunt, & tosses her head petulantly at each meaningful reproach.

August 16th
After matins, Batchelor attended me in Grosvenor Square to put the finishing touches to the settlement. I have not yet been given the grand total, but the scoundrel's debts will amount to a tidy sum. In addition, there is the settlement on Lydia of 1000*l*., & the purchase of Wickham's new commission—which will run to several hundreds. Batchelor is scandalized at my profligacy, & not best pleased at having to attend to these matters

285

on the Sabbath—tho' he is too good a man of business to let it show.

Tomorrow, on the wedding day, I have resolved to be at Wickham's lodgings betimes.

August 17th
I got to Long Acre early. Wickham was still a-bed, & the room filled with the stench of liquor. When I finally succeeded in rousing him, he told me sulkily that he had drunk himself into a stupor the night before.

' 'Tis as well you came up with me before I was awake, Fizzibuzz,' he added, 'Even now I have half a mind to escape.'

'You will do no such thing,' said I indignantly. 'It is your bounden duty to wed the poor girl. Besides, if you go back on your word you will get nothing from me.'

'I know, I know,' he grumbled, sitting up in bed. 'I am caught in a trap, that's for sure.'

He continued in this vein as he staggered out of bed & pulled on his clothes. 'Why must I bind myself to this child?' asked he. 'She is scarce more than half my age; she has nothing to recommend her apart from being a healthy wench—& her looks, & all the rest of her, have long since lost their charms for me. What will my life be like when she is forty?' &c., &c.

I did not trouble myself to make the obvious retorts. Indeed, I could see that he was genuinely distressed.

He shrugged himself into a blue coat with brass buttons, far too showy for a trumped-up occasion such as this, splashed himself with some perfumed essence to disguise his unwashed & inebriated state, & took his place beside me in the carriage. 'Til the last minute, I feared that he might jump out & take to his heels. His being the worse for liquor was doubtless providential.

We reached the church before the bride—then I saw her little face, peering anxiously out of the carriage window. She too must have been wondering if he would keep his promise. When she saw him, she broke into a happy smile.

Watching this ill-assorted pair make their vows at the altar, I found myself picturing their future— her gradual awakening to his vicious propensities, the slow erosion of her optimism, their disillusionment with each other, the long years of bickering & misery . . . The poor child has a look of Elizabeth about the eyes.

The wedding breakfast was a lugubrious occasion. Mr & Mrs Gardiner were tight-lipped, Lydia more foolishly exuberant than I have ever seen her. She boasted that it was she who had wooed her Husband, by writing him what she called *'one of my anonymous enticing notes'*—which gave me food for thought.

In the midst of the 'celebrations', Wickham took me on one side & in confidence presented me with a long list of his creditors—everything from a hatter in Town to a certain Madam Magenta, who runs I know not what sort of establishment in Brighton (& to whom he owed 17 guineas). He had not bothered to add up the total. I find it is for 847*l*. 17s—even more than I was expecting. He then demanded that I hand over Lydia's 1000*l*. When I informed him that it is already settled on her, & that the interest will be paid to her in person in three-monthly instalments, he pushed his

287

face close to mine, & hissed that I had cheated him of his due. Returning to the dining room he embraced his new Wife with the utmost charm. He seems to have no trouble in acting the hypocrite, which, I suppose, is all to the good.

The happy couple then departed for Longbourn, & the Gardiners & I were left alone. They tell me that Mr Bennet has been most reluctant to receive the newly-weds, but has been persuaded to do so for the sake of keeping up appearances. Mrs Gardiner added that Mrs Bennet is much more sanguine about the whole affair than her Husband. They did not mention the other daughters, & I did not venture to ask.

After leaving them, I felt inclined to visit one of Byron's dubious establishments—but instead repaired home. I am sitting alone in the Library. Their carriage has by now arrived at Longbourn. They will all be sitting in the dining-parlour. Lydia will doubtless be holding forth. I found myself picturing the lively amusement in Elizabeth's dark eyes. Or no—she would rather be solemn & a little sad at the display of ebullience in one who, but lately, was a source of such anxiety.

August 18th
Felt very flat & dull today—it must be the Anti-Climax, following the feverish activity of the last few days. After a strenuous bout at Jackson's, spent the day in preparations for my tomorrow's journey, & in plotting my next course of action. On reaching Pemberley, I shall have to break the news of Wickham's marriage to Georgie—& to Charles.

Dined with the Gardiners at Gracechurch Street. They are most agreeable people, & the evening was enlivened by an unscheduled visit from the two eldest children, a boy & a girl, whose arrival coincided mysteriously with the sweetmeats'. Seeing how affectionately her Aunt scolded the little ones for escaping from their Nurse I had a vision of Elizabeth thus bending towards a child, gently chiding it. I banished it as quickly as I could. I must stop thinking about her. Since I can find no pretext for importuning her at present, I have resolved henceforward to cease repining for the time being. At least we parted on friendly terms.

August 20th
Have been travelling since dawn yesterday, two long days' riding. During my journey, pondered on Lydia's remark that she has been in the habit of sending anonymous notes to young men whom she admires. Surely this must be the explanation of the flirtatious letter from Longbourn, which the Officers attributed to Jane! That giddy young minx Lydia has been responsible for more disruption than anyone imagines.

Arrived at Pemberley at nightfall, to find Charles & his Sister alone in the Saloon. G was in the stables feeding carrots to Snowball, the gentlemen out riding. Charles received me warmly; Miss Caroline had engaged herself to play at draughts with my Cousin Augusta, & left us together. Mrs Louisa was upstairs, resting. I observe that Miss Caroline is always eager to be of our party. She follows us gentlemen everywhere: rarely do I find the opportunity to speak to Charles alone.

The moment we were out of earshot, Charles

confided that during my absence he has been greatly preoccupied. After much soul-searching, he has tentatively expressed a desire to renew his addresses to Jane. As he put it with a rueful smile, he wishes to *'seek my approbation'*. I demurred at the suggestion that he was thus subservient to me. He laughed, & retorted that, as I could see, he was feeling almost emboldened to strike out on his own. 'If possible, her misfortune makes her dearer to me,' continued he. 'Why need her youngest Sister be faultless? After a few years the whole affair will be forgot.' He blushed, & murmured: 'If she changed her name, few people would remember that she is Sister to the unfortunate Lydia Bennet.'

I was thankful to be able to reassure him on that score at least, with the news of Lydia's marriage. He was so overwhelmed that he did not think to ask me how I knew. Instead, he continued: 'And as for the other, stronger objection, despite your assertions I am still unconvinced Jane is a gazetted flirt.'

I know not if I am being foolish: I resolved there & then to refrain from telling him the truth 'til he has paid his court to her. How much more will he value her, if his love is strong enough to transcend what he believes to be her flawed nature! I therefore said nothing, & left him pacing in the shrubbery, deep in thought, & went to speak to Georgie. As I hoped, she received the news of Wickham's marriage with perfect equanimity.

August 21st
I sought out Charles in the Library this morning, to walk with him, James, & the other gentlemen to

church. I failed to find him, but instead ran into Miss Caroline in the red Saloon. She jumped up when I entered, waving a letter: 'See here, Mr Darcy! Charles is being so ill-natured about this: he refuses to listen. I have the most amusing news from Meryton!'

I was forced to enquire what it was, tho' I knew full well.

'Why, that little Miss, Lydia Bennet, has got herself married after all! It makes not a whit of difference: her reputation is ruined, & the whole family disgraced. If they have any decency, they will never hold their heads up again—but I suppose that they are all as brazen & shameless . . .'

I interrupted her, saying in a rush: 'Pray say no more. I count the people of whom you speak among my friends.' Rufus, at my heels, began unaccountably to growl. I murmured some vague farewell, & left the room immediately.

I am truly shocked at her. I knew that she disliked the Bennets, & she has been increasingly impolite about them. But the vindictive glee with which she has revelled in their discomfiture shews her in a thoroughly disagreeable light. My outburst will have created a rift between us—but I have no intention of apologizing.

*   *   *

Charles had been intending to hasten to Jane's side, hoping to win her since she had become an outcast from society. Instead, he finds the whole family reinstated.

'Should I nevertheless go down to Netherfield?' mused he. 'The shooting is excellent, it will soon be the First of September, & I have too long neglected the house . . .'

I represented to him that Lydia & her new Husband were even now residing with the Bennets at Longbourn. 'You will not wish to intrude on the family at such a moment, I believe.'

'For how long?' enquired he impatiently.

'They were proposing to stay for two & a half weeks.'

'On what day were they married?'

'It was last Monday.' I continue to be surprized & relieved at his lack of interest in my part in this affair. I would have expected him to enquire how I knew so much, but he does not. His whole attention is entirely fixed on Jane. Instead, he said quickly, 'Then they will be at leisure to receive me in two weeks at the most.'

'Why such unseemly haste? At least give them a few days to compose themselves.'

'I daresay you are right,' he conceded. 'Must I then wait 'til the following Monday? But not a day longer.' He made to leave the room, then, stopping at the door, said 'I must return to Town at once. I need new linen, & a visit to the barber's.'

I have with difficulty prevailed upon him to wait a few days, & come up to Town with me next week. I purpose to return thither, to ensure that Mr & Mrs Wickham have been safely packed off to Northumberland, & to set in motion the preparations for Georgie's Coming Out. Neither she nor Augusta will come out *this* year, but we shall have to start making preparations for *next*. I shall write accordingly to my Aunt Fitzwilliam.

August 22nd

Charles is determined that I should accompany him to Hertfordshire, & visit the Bennets with him. He wishes me to view Jane with a dispassionate eye, & decide whether she really is as bad as she is painted. I am undecided. It is too soon . . .

Meanwhile, Miss Caroline has declared her intention to leave Pemberley as soon as possible, & to repair with her Sister to Scarborough. She is certainly acting out of pique against me—but I have made no attempt to dissuade her. The house-party seems to be breaking up. James's furlough is almost over; Wolstenholme travels to Scotland next week for the shooting; the others too have engagements. Georgie will be left with only Augusta & Isabella for company, but all three seem content with this arrangement.

August 23rd

Mrs Louisa does not wish to accompany her Sister to Scarborough, disliking the thought of the journey. In view of her condition, her reluctance is understandable enough. Miss Caroline, however, will not let the matter drop. I left them arguing together in the morning-parlour. I must confess that I shall be glad to see the back of Miss Caroline.

Spent the morning fishing with the gentlemen. Georgie, Augusta & Isabella are amusing themselves helping Reynolds make preserves from a magnificent harvest of plums. At breakfast we were made to compare three different pots of plum jam made by each of the three girls. G was overjoyed when I preferred hers.

Today we again went grouse-shooting. Charles

engineered the situation so as to be out of earshot of the others, & put further pressure on me to come with him to see Jane.

I have decided to humour him in this. I shall observe her, & attempt to determine whether she still cares for Charles.

During my visit I must not importune Elizabeth in any way: as far as she is concerned it will be a courtesy call—nothing more.

August 24th
The Bingley Sisters leave for Scarborough in two days. They will have to return to Town in a few weeks, in time for Mrs Louisa's confinement.

G seems not in the least put out at their departure, & has refused to accompany them, tho' they pressed her to do so (in any case, I should have put a stop to any such scheme). She seems happy to remain at Pemberley 'til Christmas, when I shall return for the festive season, then escort her to Town.

*　　　*　　　*

A most unexpected talk with my Cousin James. He took me on one side, in confidence, to discuss his marital prospects. The situation grows more acute, since he is soon to sell out of the militia. 'How shall I fare, as a half-pay Officer? I do not wish to bring disgrace on my family & friends by being lowly circumstanced,' said he despairingly.

I had a sudden inspiration. 'Have you ever thought of approaching our Cousin Anne?' I enquired. 'She is well-born, rich, and, as far as I know, unattached.'

'But it has always been understood that you & she . . .'

I assured him that there was no chance of my Cousin & me pairing off, & swore that I would never make her an offer in future. If one day Anne herself chuses to tell him what passed between her & me, so be it.

James was set against the idea. 'Though I do not love Anne in the least, I do respect her, & have a deal of Cousinly affection for her. I could not envisage exploiting her in this way.'

I persisted, & averred that he would be doing our Cousin a favour: 'Poor Anne is unlikely ever to receive any other offers.'

'Why do you say so? Apart from her magnificent fortune, Anne is a pretty girl, with those violet eyes.'

Try as I might, I could not recollect the colour of her eyes. I merely said: 'She is shy & diffident. I feel sure that she would liefer live with a Cousin whom she has known & liked all her life, than with some stranger, whom she would doubtless suspect of being a mere fortune-hunter.'

'And am I not just such a fortune-hunter?' asked he ruefully.

'My Aunt would welcome your suit,' I continued. 'You know that family connexions matter greatly to her.'

'My Aunt is hoping for quite a *different* family connexion, however,' he retorted.

'But as that can never be, she will doubtless be content.'

I spoke at some length about his own advantages of rank & character, & of the desirability of the match, 'til I finally prevailed upon him to give the matter some further thought.

'But I assure you that nothing will come of it,' he concluded.

August 25th
Rode out all day on Caesar. Card-games & music this evening. Miss Caroline addressed several remarks to me in a rather shrill tone. I merely bowed.

August 26th
After matins we saw off Miss Caroline & Mrs Louisa, who have departed for Scarborough. Miss C wrapped up, her bonnet securely tied on with a thick scarf for fear of the sea breezes. She bad me a cool farewell, barely touching the end of my fingers with hers. I wish both Sisters well, but the house feels the calmer for their absence.

A busy day, with constant visitors to me in the Library: Pargeter is anxious for my instructions on the leases coming up for renewal. James has considered my suggestion & sees its wisdom: he is, albeit with reluctance, prepared to make a trip to Rosings before rejoining his regiment. 'If, on seeing Anne, it appears to me that she might entertain my suit, I may be emboldened to proceed. I daresay we could both come off worse. I respect her & am fond of her. But it is not what I could have wished.' He sighed. 'To think that I had previously found a woman who seemed perfect in every respect—but that her want of fortune precluded any serious consideration. In any case, since her Sister's fall from grace, she is out of the question.' There was no need to ask to whom he alluded.

Reflecting on James's words about E, I realize that he was within a hair's breadth of offering for her & carrying her off, while we were at Rosings! Even now . . . Let him but see her once again, & he may be unable to resist the temptation.

We leave tomorrow for Town.

August 28th

All in all, it has been a pleasant enough journey. We rode most of the way. Charles was prevented by James's presence from constantly speaking of Jane. He appears more in love than ever—I earnestly hope that the lady's affections prove equally constant.

Not 'til we reached Town this evening, & James left us, was Charles free to unburden himself. I must confess that I was incapable of listening without respite to his panegyrics on his lady-love, & allowed my attention to wander. I found myself thinking about James & his possible attachment to Anne. I cannot tell how she will view his proposal. I am sure that she will see it for what it is: an opportunity for them to forge a businesslike alliance. He gets a fortune, she an agreeable & well-born Husband. I do not see why they should not deal pleasantly together.

*   *   *

I had much to do in Town. Charles, however, has other plans. Immediately before retiring, he has informed me that he has been unable to control his longing to be with Jane, & is determined to leave immediately for Hertfordshire.

We set off tomorrow.

END OF PART VI

Part VII

LONGBOURN

August 29th

Netherfield. We have arrived. The house opened up. Nicholls delighted to see her master once more. Peebles tells me she complained about Edward Hurst, who staid here for part of the summer, but told them not to bother to remove the Holland covers, and, when not fishing, spent much of his time below stairs. I did not enquire what he was doing there.

Charles has lost all confidence, & exclaims again & again: 'O, what's the use? She'll have forgot me long since. I had much better keep away. It would be mad to court further disappointment.' As for me, for all my efforts to remain calm, I have several times been on the point of saddling up & returning to Town. Only the embarrassment of explaining myself to an incredulous Charles holds me back from an immediate departure.

At dinner, we ate but little, but drank too deeply, & separated early. I write this in my chamber. Unfortunately, I have been unable to banish the memory of last Autumn, when we staid together in this house. I particularly recall encountering her on the stairs one morning. She wore a low-cut gown in some pale stuff, & her hair loosely gathered up. She descended first, & I afterwards, admiring her from above . . .

August 30th

I have received a brief letter from Scarborough. Miss Caroline excuses herself for shewing insufficient compassion for my *friends' misfortunes*. However, she adds that she is merely echoing the sentiments of every body. *'This affair will not so soon be forgot, nor brushed under the carpet,'* she concludes. If this letter is meant as an apology, it is a grudging one indeed! To think that I once thought her a good-natured, agreeable girl!

Prompted by the same need for distraction (his avowed, mine secret), Charles & I went out for a long day's walking.

September 1st
Start of the shooting season, & a welcome diversion. Charles unwilling to seek any such solace, & refused to accompany me out. He could not endure the suspense of not knowing whether the Bennets are free to be visited. He resorted to the basest of subterfuges, and, inventing some pretext for his enquiries, ascertained from Mrs Nicholls, via the Meryton butcher, that Lydia & her new Husband left Longbourn several days since. He seems to have forgot his former reluctance, & proposes to call on the Bennets at Longbourn tomorrow. I am to accompany him. He has asked me to observe Miss Bennet closely.

I shall concentrate on Jane, & view E as a friend.

September 2nd
I was supposed to be observing Jane; but I must confess that I was aware only of Elizabeth. She was sitting very upright on an ottoman, her head bent over her sewing—some scarf or wrap in an ugly dusty pink. During the whole of our visit, the needle never ceased to stab through the pink cloth, & she never raised her eyes.

On the ride home, Charles questioned me

closely: 'How did Jane seem to you? Was not she disappointingly calm, & unaffected by the sight of me? Surely I can hope no longer!' &c., &c. I said very little in reply: I had dimly perceived that Miss Bennet seemed quieter & more uncertain than before. Certainly not a flirt, & possibly like someone who has been disappointed in love. I shall have a chance to observe her more closely in a few days, when we return to Longbourn for dinner.

September 3rd
Charles refuses to be discouraged: he is more in love than ever with Miss Bennet, & proposes to press his suit. I cannot help it—my own hopes have arisen once more. If Charles gains his objective, I will in future see Elizabeth from time to time. Even she must acknowledge that I may attend my friend's wedding; & then there can be frequent visits to Netherfield. But what if, once he is safely married, Charles decides to purchase his own estate? He may withdraw with his new Wife to— who knows? Cornwall, Scotland, anywhere! Well, I can follow him there, & hope that the new Mrs Bingley will invite her Sister also. We may spend weeks, months together under the same roof. Unless Elizabeth has informed her Sister of my most unwelcome proposal, in which case Mrs Bingley will ensure that our visits never overlap. Nay more, she may find reasons for persuading her Husband to forego our friendship. Charles is so obliging & easy-going; besides, he must feel a grudge against me for having interfered with his happiness for so long. He will allow his Wife to detach him from his old friend.

I could confide in Charles myself, & seek his

help. But what is the use, if the lady cares not a rap for me? I had much better return to London.

September 5th
Tomorrow evening, at Longbourn, I have undertaken to observe Jane, & pronounce once & for all on her feelings for Charles. This task I shall conscientiously perform.

I have a second preoccupation. After a long struggle, I have reached a decision about Elizabeth: tomorrow will tell me all. If she gives me any signs of encouragement, I shall take the matter further. If not, I shall have enough self respect to retire with dignity.

September 6th
Of Elizabeth, & of my observation of her during this evening's dinner-party at Longbourn, I shall not write first. I fought to keep my attention from her, & instead observed her Sister. I now have no doubts left about Miss Bennet's affections: as Charles entered the room I noted how her colour changed; despite her apparent composure there was a consciousness about her every gesture. She surely does not view him with indifference. I wonder now that I ever believed so. I can only assume, to my shame, that I was set against her in my mind from the first, and, unbeknownst to myself, eager to believe the worst of her.

I am less happy for myself than for Charles. All evening, Elizabeth steadfastly kept apart from me. I managed occasionally to catch a glimpse of her. Her hair was tied back more severely than is her wont. We were seated at opposite ends of the dining-table; after we gentlemen joined the ladies, when I approached her as she poured the coffee, she surrounded herself with young women, giving me no opportunity of addressing her. I finally succeeded in exchanging a few words: she asked me if G was still at Pemberley, then, almost impolitely, turned her head aside.

She wishes me to infer that she has no interest in me.

*　　　*　　　*

On the way home, I attended to Charles, & left it 'til later to assess the import of my observations of Elizabeth. I now saw no reason to hold back the truth about Jane. I told him straight what I had suspected for some months: I had been mistaken. Jane was no flirt, but as virtuous as she seemed.

'A single evening's observation was enough to tell you this?'

'O no, I have suspected it for weeks,' said I rashly.

There was a silence. 'Why then did not you inform me of it at once?' he enquired in an angry tone.

I told him that I had wished first to see her with mine own eyes to be sure, adding mendaciously that, as he mentioned Jane but rarely, I had mistakenly believed that he had ceased to miss her, & had thought it best not to remind him of her.

'I, not miss her? Why, man, I have thought of her every day, every hour since . . .' He broke off, & covered his face with his hands.

'If that be so, I am truly sorry. It compounds the wrong I have done you in separating you from her.'

'If what you tell me is true, & she be blameless,

how were you so grossly deceived as misjudge her so abominably? And how durst you malign her to *me*?'

I was obliged now to explain my mistake about the clandestine letter, & my present belief that she was entirely blameless in that matter.

By the carriage-lamps I saw that Charles's face was set & angry. We sat in silence for some time as our conveyance bumped over the rough track, I racking my brains to find some words of comfort. Then he said, with an effort: 'I can see that you believed you were acting for the best, Fitz. It is just that I cannot bear what you have done. By attending to tittle-tattle, & by failing to trust my judgment, you have deprived me for ever of all prospect of happiness with Jane.'

'It may not be too late,' I replied.

'Say you so? Well, I tell you that with her beauty & sweetness of temper, she will not stay single for long. Without a doubt she has formed some other attachment. I cannot offer for her now.'

I began to tell him that I was convinced that she still loved him—but, with almost an imperious gesture, he held up his hand to silence me.

When we reached Netherfield, the lamps were all extinguished, the hall lit only by a few candles. He picked one up, & turned from me to mount the stairs, honouring me with the most perfunctory of salutations. I am not accustomed to seeing him thus, with a white, set face.

'Wait!' says I.

He stood silently, holding aloft his candle.

'Might it perhaps be better for me to leave for London tomorrow?'

He bowed again, turned & left me.

This day I have lost them both—him & her.

September 7th

I have avoided inflicting my presence on Charles at breakfast. I have no option but to withdraw, & cool my heels in Town, hoping that he will eventually see that I meant well. I have resolved however to write to him before departing. Let this be the nub of my argument:

DRAFT LETTER

I am most anxious to make redress as far as possible, & accordingly wish you to know that, from mine own observation last evening, I am now convinced that Miss Bennet still cares for you alone, & asks for nothing better than that you should renew your addresses. She had eyes for no body but you. I am positive that what I say is the truth.

I shall begin with the politest of salutations, & conclude with a handsome apology.

*   *   *

I gave my letter to a servant to deliver, & went out for a walk, while Peebles packed my bags. After about half an hour, during which I paraded up & down in the shrubbery, I heard Charles call my name. I turned. He was running eagerly towards me, waving his hat in his left hand, & a paper in his right. As he drew near, I saw that it was my letter.

'Is it really so, Darcy? All is not lost?'

'I am sure of it.'

He clutched at my arm, staring eagerly into my face. 'You are absolutely positive?'

'Absolutely.'

There was a pause while he took this in. Then he exclaimed: 'I have been thinking it over all night. Perhaps I have been too ready to despair. If so, I have everything to play for!'

He clappt me on the back, laughing, then grew more serious. 'I was angry & uncivil with you last night, Darcy. For that I seek your forgiveness.'

'The fault is all mine: your anger was entirely justified. I allowed myself to be hoodwinked by a consummate liar.'

He smiled, & held out his hand. We shook hands gravely, & walked on together.

Later, he asked me to tell him all I could of Jane. I told him everything I knew.

'Jane was in Town this winter, you say?'

I nodded.

'My Sisters must have known of it.'

I vouchsafed no reply. It is not for me to tell tales on ladies.

'They must have known! Jane is their friend. She will certainly have written to them. She may even have called on them.'

'That is not for me to say.'

He then entreated me to stay at Netherfield. I remain here for a day or two longer.

September 8th

Charles is unable to forget the part played by his two Sisters in separating him from Jane. He tells me that he has thought of little else since I told him. I felt obliged to remind him that I too have been guilty of concealing the truth—but he

308

retorted: 'You, I know, thought you were acting for the best. They have been prompted purely by malice.' I have never seen him so angry.

I believe that I do understand his rage: it has been evident for some time that Miss Caroline at least harbours an ill-natured, unjust resentment of the Bennet family. On the other hand, if she particularly dislikes *one* of the Misses Bennet, it is certainly not the one chosen by her Brother!

I have advised him to forget his anger, & instead look forward to his next meeting with Jane. The thought has put him in a flutter. He is even now walking alone in the grounds.

September 9th

I returned to Town today. Charles begged me to remain, but in truth I believe that he was relieved to see the back of me—it leaves him free to concentrate all his attention on his pursuit of Jane. He made me promise to return soon. I am truly happy for him, & hopeful of his success.

London is a melancholy place at this time of year. I went to several clubs this evening, but saw no body. All the fellows away shooting. Home early; I am sitting in the chilly parlour, wishing myself anywhere but here.

September 10th

To Jackson's. No body I knew was present. Afterwards rode in the park. Decided to recommence cataloguing. Accordingly did about 35 books this afternoon & evening.

September 11th

To church in the morning; spent the rest of the day

cataloguing books. The dullest pursuit in the world.

September 12th
To Angelo's. Afterwards, Peebles persuaded me to visit my tailor & order more breeches, which I did with little enthusiasm. I never wish to wear dress-clothes again. What is the use of seeking company in the evening? Instead remained alone at home.

I cannot help but feel that I would be better off at Pemberley—but if I return so soon, everyone will wonder at it, & suspect that I have quarrelled with Charles.

September 13th
Today, received a letter from Charles:

You were right, Darcy! I had allowed myself to be too easily discouraged. She still cares for me, & we are engaged. I have spoken with her father, who gives his consent. I am the luckiest man in the world. She is the sweetest, gentlest creature. I cannot begin to list her qualities.

I cannot bear to copy out more of this encomium. He concludes his letter:

I have informed Jane that you have promised to return in a few days' time. I am eager for you to become better acquainted with the future Mrs Bingley, since from now on you will be seeing much of each other. I am the happiest of men!

I shall have to find some pretext for turning him down. I am truly overjoyed for him—but I must confess that when I first read his letter, I felt a pang of jealousy. He is right: he is the happiest of men.

September 14th
Catalogued 48 books today. Would have ridden in the Park, but that Caesar has cast a shoe.

September 15th
Whiled away the morning chusing a landaulette, suitable for a lady to drive. Dark green, with the crest on the panels & green plush upholstery. It is Georgie who will be taking the reins. No body else.

Peebles greatly irritated me by insisting that it was time the barber was called, & refusing to be gainsaid. What is the use of all this primping & preening?

September 16th
Today, I feel more hopeful. Will not her Sister Jane's engagement influence her mind? But has any woman ever accepted a man whom she has once rejected? *'You were the last man in the world I could ever marry . . .'* I must not forget those words.

Tomorrow I shall go back to Harrison's, & cancel the order for the carriage. Tonight I shall go to the Cocoa-Tree: Carruthers has sent word that he is back in Town, & will meet me there.

*   *   *

I have had a most extraordinary visit this evening. I was just leaving to meet Carruthers, when my Aunt de Bourgh was announced.

My Aunt! She who considers it vulgar to set foot

311

in Town before the start of the Season, in my house, weeks before her time! I had no desire to see her, having not forgot her recent insulting letter about the Bennets. I hesitated: should I pretend to be from home? No, it would not do. I went to the Saloon, where she awaited me.

She rose when I entered, & held out both hands to me; but her smile denoted little ease of mind—indeed, she seemed pale & agitated. I helped her to a chair, observing how heavily she leant on me. I wondered if she were suffering from some secret ailment, & had come up to Town to consult a physician. Her whole person gave off an old, dusty, sickly odour—possibly of vetiver, I am not sure. I found it distasteful. My conscience smote me for my uncharitable thoughts.

'What's the matter, Ma'am?' I asked with some concern.

'Matter? Why, nothing! Nothing at all.' She continued staring at me, with the same fixed smile. She seemed almost deranged. Might she have obtained some knowledge of my brief & disastrous engagement to her daughter? Dismayed, I rose and, turning my back, leant on the chimney-piece, gazing into the empty grate.

Behind me, I heard her shift in her chair. Then she said: 'I am glad to see you well, Nephew.' I could not but turn & face her to make my bow.

She was still fixing me with the same intensity. 'I have heard the strangest rumours, dear Fitz.'

Surely I had guessed aright! I waited in some trepidation for her to continue.

' . . . They tell me that you are engaged. Is not that curious?' She gave a little false laugh, then waited for my reply. She was evidently in a high

312

state of nerves.

'You do me too much honour, Aunt,' said I. 'I am not engaged to any young lady.'

'I *knew* it!' cried she. 'The impudent gossip-mongers! How dare they spread abroad that you have thrown in your lot with that shameless little upstart?'

'Upstart . . . ?' I repeated. Cousin Anne, an upstart?

'A gentleman's daughter, indeed!'

'Of whom do you speak?'

'Why, of that impudent minx, Miss Elizabeth Bennet,' she exclaimed loudly. As for me, I was too astonished to utter a word.

Taking my silence for approval, she gave another laugh. 'Is not it absurd, that folk should have invented such a demeaning falsehood? Of course I put them all right. I do not think that anyone in the county of Kent will venture to make such assertions again. So, come to us! You will be quite safe, at least at Rosings.' And, leaning forward, she patted my hand. The rough feel of her black lace mitten on my skin made me shiver. I withdrew my hand.

'You do not seem as grieved as I could wish at this false rumour,' said she.

I looked into her eyes then, & what she read in mine seemed to alarm her. She rose, took three tottering steps towards me, & sat down heavily again. She opened & shut her mouth a few times, 'til I began to fear that she had been struck down by an Apoplexy. Then she found her words, spluttering: 'So—*that* is your *affianced bride*?' She almost spat the words out, no longer perplexed but furious.

313

'I repeat that I am not engaged, Ma'am,' I replied indignantly.

'What? Lying to my face? Impudent boy! How dare you confront your own Aunt thus? Your nearest living relative!'

From whom had she acquired this unalterable conviction? I cast around for an answer, unable to attend to her hectoring voice: ' . . . And you expected by the whole family to honour your commitment to your Cousin Anne. Do not interrupt me, Sirrah!' (for I had raised my hand) 'I know what I know. Cease to prevaricate, & tell me the truth, once & for all. Are you engaged to Miss Elizabeth Bennet?'

'I am not.'

She was breathing so fast I feared lest she fall into a swoon. She started fanning herself with the gloves she held. Her next question came out in a gasp: 'Do you undertake never to enter into an engagement with her?'

For an instant I was tempted to give her my word; but I pressed my lips together, & kept my peace.

'At least you have the grace to remain silent, unlike Miss.'

Then it dawned on me: she was talking as if she had discussed these matters with Elizabeth herself. Had she really sought her out? How could this be? What had Elizabeth said to her? I durst not ask— but there was no need, for my Aunt continued at once: 'I have come directly from Hertfordshire. I hastened thither the moment I heard of this most ill-judged engagement. And do you know what the hussy had the gall to say? She claimed that there was no reason for you not to chuse her—& no reason for her not to accept you! That she is your equal in rank! That if you do not mind them, all her inferiorities of position & reputation will matter not a whit! That your understanding with Anne need not deter you from offering for *her*! She declares herself willing to enter into an engagement with you! Why, you are as good as married. But learn this: once you are wed to that upstart, you will never again darken my door!' She leant back in her chair, & closed her eyes. Her nostrils were pinched & white.

I stood there in silence, amazed at her words: Elizabeth, willing to marry me? I longed for my Aunt to gain command of herself, so that I might question her further. Finally she opened her eyes, & said angrily: 'It is the talk of Hertfordshire. My rector Collins told me—he had it from the Lucases.' She paused for breath, & absentmindedly sipped at the ratafia which Bolton had placed by her elbow. 'It has been a most inconvenient journey—eight hours in a coach, & the most appalling inns on the way. When we reached Bromley The Bell was closed—for family reasons or some such nonsense. I always stop at The Bell—& then, when I arrived in Hertfordshire, to be faced out by a mere chit, who refuses to renounce you, & insults me into the bargain!' She took several deep breaths, then said, in a quieter tone: 'Come, Nephew, give me your word. Then we can be comfortable again.'

'How can you assert that Miss Elizabeth Bennet is willing to marry me, when there is no understanding between us?' asked I, attempting to keep the eagerness from my voice.

I was forced to repeat the question twice, before

my Aunt took note of it. Then she said, grudgingly, 'She did not precisely say that she was willing, but that she refused to rule it out as a possibility— which amounts to the same thing. But you will not be so unreasonable. You will pledge yourself never to wed her, will not you?' She spoke in a coaxing tone I had never heard her use before.

So Elizabeth has not rejected all thought of me! Do I no longer disgust her? I scarcely took in my Aunt's question; I was aware only of a sudden surge of hope, so strong that my legs almost gave way beneath me. Then at last I found words: 'I should never dream of making such a promise— not even to you, Aunt.'

'Then my journey has been entirely in vain.' My Aunt rose, staggered slightly, summoned up her strength & swept past me, & out of the room. I heard the front door slam. I sank onto a chair, & buried my head in my hands.

Elizabeth refused to reject me! She refused! What can it mean? I dare not speculate. I long to see her, at once. I long to look into her face, & try what I can read there . . .

September 17th

If only, if only it were true! Aunt Catherine, you might insult me as much as you chose, & I the happier for it. I can scarcely believe what my Aunt has told me. Did she really travel all the way to Hertfordshire to confront my so-called betrothed? I feel hot with shame at it. What can Elizabeth think? No doubt she attributes to me the source of all this frenzy? What does it mean? Am I to be cast down by it? Am I to be exalted? She who told me I was the last man in the world she would ever marry!

*   *   *

I took my hat, & wandered out. I had no fixed purpose. Should I go to Jackson's & attempt to find oblivion in some hard hitting? I let my steps lead me in the direction of Bond Street. But instead of Jackson's, I stopped at Stedman & Vardon's. I found myself inside—& asking to see some parures.

I have bought an exquisite set of rubies in yellow gold. As I write, I have the case open in front of me. I have always thought that rubies would suit her . . .

September 18th
Can she really hate me still? Steadfast & true, she will lie to no body—not to herself nor to others. Why did she refuse to give her promise to my Aunt? Could it be because she has some feeling for me? I have been dwelling on our last days together in Derbyshire. I remember the affectionate regard she shewed for Georgie. Surely this was no longer the Elizabeth who rejected me with such contempt!

September 19th
The anniversary of dear Mamma's death. To church in the morning; but I confess that during the sermon my mind wandered. To lose a Mother at the age of twelve is misfortune enough; but what of poor Georgie, who has been motherless since her birth? Fortunately, she can scarcely regret what she has never known—& yet I feel I can

317

never do enough to make good her loss. And what of me? Surely Mamma would have understood my feelings, & encouraged my hopes—surely she would not have shewn as much prejudice & disapproval as her sister, my Aunt Catherine!

*   *   *

I have been recollecting E's cold reception of me at Longbourn twelve days ago. Her manner revealed nothing but indifference. But then, surrounded by her family, & with the meeting between Jane & Charles at the forefront of her mind, how could she have shewn her true feelings?

I must put all these fruitless speculations to one side. I shall reach a decision in due course. Meanwhile, I shall visit Carruthers at the House. If I fail at Longbourn, I may find an outlet for my energies in taking my seat in Parliament.

*   *   *

Spent three hours in the Public Gallery. The interminable speeches provided no distraction. I wish that I could confide in somebody—but there is no-one. At any rate, I know at least that I cannot in my present frame of mind contemplate becoming a Member of Parliament.

September 20th
I forced myself to go to bed, & slept heavily & dreamlessly all night. This morning, when I woke, my mind was made up. I believe there is a chance that Elizabeth's feelings for me may be changed. I cannot be sure, & may well be mistaken. But as I

see it now, I have nothing to lose. If she is still set against me, she will reject me once more. If she has changed, who knows?

In three days time I shall return to Hertfordshire, and, for a second & last time, ask her to be my Wife.

September 21st

Must I really wait for two more days, when my happiness is at stake? Why should not I leave at once?

Spent the whole morning sparring violently at Jackson's—ran through three opponents. Stopped only when I was in danger of damaging my face.

On return, found a letter from my Aunt Fitzwilliam. Aunt Catherine has sent her some 'disturbing news', which leads her to express her sincere hope that I will think carefully before performing an impulsive action which I may later regret. To my surprize, her letter is relatively cordial—I have reached the cynical conclusion that she is anxious not to alienate me, as she hopes for material assistance in the matter of Augusta's joint Coming Out with Georgie . . .

Rode alone in the Park.

Tried reading in the evening—Walter Scott's new romance—but could not concentrate. Drank far too much Port Wine.

September 24th

Let me set it down as it occurred.

I arrived at Netherfield yesterday at noon, having screwed up my courage to behold her that very day. But I had reckoned without the assiduity of a successful lover: Charles spends every day at

Longbourn, & had been there since before breakfast. I did not feel I could shew my face there unescorted, & therefore was obliged to roam aimlessly about, awaiting his return—which did not happen 'til after supper.

For the remainder of that evening, I was regaled with a fulsome account of Jane's perfections, the charms of successful courtship, &c., &c. Fortunately for me, Charles was so preoccupied with his own narrative that he failed to observe that I was on edge. He kept me up 'til well after midnight, & then insisted that we rise early, as we would be riding over to Longbourn betimes. I lay down & forced myself to rest, but sleep came there none.

*   *   *

This morning—it seems like months ago—we rode out early as arranged. On arrival at Longbourn, Charles suggested that we all walk out, as he wished to separate himself from the company, & have time alone with Jane. I was to walk with Elizabeth & her Sister Kitty. I was mortified when Kitty proposed that we call on Miss Maria Lucas, since Maria had seen me with Elizabeth at Rosings, & had bruited it about that I loved her. She must have told Kitty, who was giving me sidelong glances & smirking behind her gloved hand. Only Elizabeth was oblivious. I offered her my arm, but she refused. I scarcely looked at her: I could not have told whether she was wearing a pelisse, nor the colour of her bonnet. When we reached Lucas Lodge, Kitty, with a barely suppressed giggle, suggested that she leave us to walk on alone.

It happened almost immediately: to my surprize, Elizabeth thanked me for what I had done for Lydia. I felt at once dismayed & glad that she had discovered it; moreover, it gave me the opportunity to unburden myself to her. I sensed that if I did not act at once, my courage would fail me. Without pausing to reflect, I spoke. I do not know what I said: something about how I still loved her, & had not changed since I made my first proposal. I offered her my hand & heart, once more & for the last time.

There was a long silence. I concluded that I had spoken too soon, & that it was all over. I started to take off my hat to her: I must leave her now, turn & leave forever. For the first time that day, I looked down at her face, so sweet & lovely beneath her blue bonnet. Her eyes were lowered. The long eyelashes, the curve of her mouth, the brown curls I longed to touch, all gave me pain. This then was to be my last sight of her.

Then she spoke, so quietly that I had to bend towards her to catch her words. I shall never forget them: 'My sentiments have . . . have undergone so material a change since you first spoke, that . . . I now welcome your assurances with gratitude & pleasure.'

I listened to this tortuous little speech without registering its import, & had to repeat it to myself internally before I finally understood: she accepts me! She accepts me! I blurted out my joy, my pride, my delight. I took her gloved hand & drew it through my arm. We walked on together— together. She did not once look into my face, & hers was mantled with a deep blush—more

321

beautiful than ever. What did we say? We talked of my Aunt Catherine, & how her ill-judged interference had had the opposite effect from what she intended: it had tempted me to renew my suit. 'I knew enough of your disposition to be certain that had you been irrevocably decided against me, you would have acknowledged it to Lady Catherine frankly & openly,' said I.

She laughed, & replied: 'Yes, you know enough of my *frankness* to believe me capable of *that*. After abusing you so abominably to your face, I could have no scruple in abusing you to all your relations.'

I then spoke of my first, disastrous proposal, & of my shame on recollecting it. She exclaimed at that, & at last raised her eyes to my face, & we exchanged our first look as lovers. I raised her hand to my lips. I longed to put my arms around her. We dimly perceived that we were late, & that our absence would be remarked upon. We wandered back to Longbourn, where we both sat quietly for the rest of the day. Fortunately, the family's attention was directed towards Charles & Jane, so our mood of dreamy contentment passed unnoticed.

In the carriage home, Charles began to question me eagerly on my opinion of Jane. But I knew that if I did not wish to mortify him, I should let him run on no longer before imparting my news. I then found myself tongue-tied. I had kept my feelings to myself for so long, I was well-nigh incapable of letting them out. Finally I managed to croak out that I too was engaged.

There followed a long silence. Then Charles said, in a faltering tone, 'What do you mean, engaged?'

Further solicitation elicited the fact that Elizabeth was to be my partner in life.

'Elizabeth? You? But you are scarcely acquainted! Are you jesting with me?'

I was forced to explain about our time together at Rosings & at Pemberley. I explained how my love for her had slowly blossomed, omitting only my first, ill-judged proposal of marriage. It occurred to me to wonder if Jane had been told of it. I must ask my dearest Elizabeth. If Jane does know, she has been discretion itself!

'By why, why did you say nothing of it to me? Such reticence cannot be viewed as an act of friendship,' said Charles in a hurt tone.

I explained that his unhappy love for Jane prevented me from speaking of her Sister, & furnished him with further details.

After much eager questioning, he finally clappt me on the back, & said, 'So it is really true! I am overjoyed. I had long cherished the hope of our being Brothers. So it will come to pass after all, tho' not in the way I first intended.'

I was puzzled by this remark, 'til I concluded that he must be referring to—Miss Caroline! I did not offend him by retorting that I could never have entertained such an idea, but merely said, 'Yes, we shall be Brothers.'

As I write this, I confess that I have always known in my heart that Miss Caroline singled me out, shewing almost excessive partiality. Furthermore, I could not fail to observe how consistently she has denigrated my dearest Elizabeth. If I had allowed myself to dwell on her behaviour, I could not have failed to attribute it to jealousy. I chose not to recognize any of this & not to admit it to myself: too great an awareness of Miss Caroline's interest in me would have interfered with the pleasant, friendly intercourse between our two families. Indeed, at one time, I in turn hoped that Charles would become attached to my Sister . . . I trust that I can continue to pretend that nothing has been said on this matter, otherwise I shall henceforward be obliged to keep my distance from Miss Caroline.

*   *   *

Charles & I talked late into the night. We have agreed on a joint wedding; then after our several honeymoons Charles suggested that we should meet at Pemberley for Christmas. I demurred: 'We must refrain from making all our arrangements without reference to our brides. Elizabeth at any rate will have decided views on what must be done.'

'O, I am sure that Jane will be happy to accommodate herself to the wishes of all,' replied he, smiling.

Then I said, 'I am so happy!' I think it is the first time I have ever spoken those words.

September 25th
Last night I dreamt that I was a child again . . . I was playing alone on the terrace, riding my hobby-horse. I have not thought of him for years: he was black & white with scarlet reins, & bells. I named him Bellerophon. I looked up, & saw Mamma smiling & waving her hand in a gesture of farewell. Then she drew the curtains shut. The last thing I

saw was her hand, with its pearl bracelet, holding the curtain. Then she was gone. I woke in a mood of calm contentment.

We rode over to Longbourn after church. Mrs Bennet looked surprized to see me again. The sooner I speak to her Husband the better. Every time I set eyes on Elizabeth, she appears different. Today there was a gentle languor about her eyes, as though she had slept but little. I dare not think of her nights . . . We walked out again, & when Charles teazingly suggested that my love & I should walk alone, Kitty agreed with alacrity to stay behind. I know not where we roamed. Elizabeth has begun to mock me, very affectionately, & I find for the first time no inclination to stand on my dignity. We returned for dinner. I know not what we ate, nor what I said to my neighbours—I believe I was seated between Mrs Bennet & Jane, who pressed my hand softly: she knows now.

After dinner, I went to Mr Bennet in the Library, & formally requested the hand of his daughter in marriage. He drew back in astonishment. So the parents have had no inkling of our understanding—tho' presumably all the daughters know of it by now. He was unexpectedly punctilious in his response, concerned that his daughter should lead an independent life, & offering only a provisional consent 'til he should have spoken to her alone. She went in to him after I left him, & on her return some time later, her radiant smile confirmed that all was well. We scarcely spoke together after that.

*   *   *

I write this in my chamber. I have just told Peebles my news: 'How would you feel if I told you I was getting married?'

He hung my coat up & began brushing it assiduously. His back was turned to me. 'I would wish you the very best, Sir.'

'Should you like serving a married man?'

'Oh, as to that, Sir,' he turned to face me. 'I was intending soon to broach the subject of my retirement.'

'You, retiring?' I was astonished.

'Why, yes, Sir. I am nigh on seventy, & feel that I am no longer spry enough to serve as a personal valet. Besides, I have my Sister to consider, now that she has been widowed . . .'

I looked at him then, standing there with the clothes-brush in his hand, which was trembling a little. He is so familiar to me that I scarcely ever notice how he is gradually ageing. His head is bald, fringed with white; his shoulders bowed, his face wrinkled. 'But I could never manage without you!' I exclaimed.

'Nonsense, Master Fitz. You & your lady will require more modish servants. I daresay a married couple would suit you. I understand that there are excellent French servants to be had now in London—people who have fled from Paris for one reason or another.'

'I do not wish for any fancy French servants!' I cried.

'Come now, Master Fitz, nothing goes on for ever. I shall always be at Pemberley. I thought, if you would permit it, I might keep your clothing in order while you was absent from home.'

326

'And when I am home too,' I told him warmly. 'I shall want to see you every day.' He smiled all over his wrinkled old face. I shook hands with him, & ended up promising him one of the free cottages on the estate & an annuity for the rest of his days. But how I shall miss him!

September 26th
I have begged Elizabeth to destroy the letter I sent her, the day after she rejected me. I told her that it was full of pique & of unworthy sentiments, to which she sweetly said: 'The letter, perhaps, began in bitterness, but it did not end so. The adieu is charity itself. You must learn some of my philosophy. Think only of the past as its remembrance gives you pleasure.' But she did agree to burn the letter.

I have another, secret reason for wanting it burnt: I would not have Georgie discover it, & learn that I have told my future Wife a garbled version of her experience with Wickham. Thank Heaven, my Sister is now serene, seemingly recovered from her ordeal, & looking forward to her Coming Out next winter, for which she will now have my dear Wife as chaperone. We are immeasurably fortunate—all our lives could have been ruined in so many ways by Wickham's villainy. As it is, poor little Lydia suffers for us all.

Perhaps one day, when we have been married some time, I may persuade Elizabeth to soften her heart towards her youngest Sister. Poor child! I could almost be willing to receive her under my roof—always providing, of course, that she refrains from bringing her vile Husband with her.

September 27th

Today I made a quick trip to London. I wish my Wife to wear the family jewels, which are at present kept in Coutts's vault. I took advantage of being in Bond Street to have a mill at Jackson's, & ran into Byron, just back from Newstead. We fought, he won (as always), & afterwards we repaired to Boodle's for refreshment, I taking care to slow my pace because of his leg. There I told him the news of my forthcoming marriage. To my surprize, he remained silent, shading his eyes with his hand. After a long pause, he said, in a faltering tone: '& thus again I am to be bereft . . .'

I did not understand his meaning, & I must have drawn back, because he reached out & held onto my arm. There was another long silence; by now I was feeling somewhat discomfited. Then he said: '. . . bereft of yet another sparring partner!' He took his hand away from his face, & I saw that he was laughing. Was he making a fool of me?

'O, you are best matched with Jackson himself. You get the better of *me* every time,' said I.

He laughed, shrugged, & replied sarcastically: 'I wish you joy of the married state.' He went on to threaten to take my new Wife off my hands if she were pretty enough.

I made no answer, thinking his remarks in the worst of taste. Soon afterwards, I rose to leave. 'That's it—leave us poor bachelors to our life of wretched dissipation,' he called after me. As I left the room, I saw him move towards the card-tables, where a group of hard-drinking fellows were at play. Walking home, I thought over what had occurred. Despite his cynical & insulting manner,

& his mirth at my expense, I had observed that, when he heard my news, Byron's eyes had been wet.

I think that, once we are married, I shall introduce him to E. Despite his hard-hearted manner, I find him a touching, almost pathetic figure.

September 28th
Among the jewels I have taken from the vaults, I found Mamma's pearl bracelet, which I thought was lost years since. Nothing has given me greater pleasure than to clasp it about my future Wife's wrist. She loves it, & says she will wear it always. It now remains to complete the preparations for our joint weddings: we have agreed we will all four be married on the same day, at Longbourn church. It is to be soon, on October 30th. That will give us time for a brief spell of travel before we meet again at Pemberley for Christmas. I should have wished to take my bride abroad, perhaps to Italy, but we have agreed that springtime is the best season for such a trip, providing that Boney has ceased his rampaging over Europe. Georgie is arriving soon from Pemberley. She will stay with us at Netherfield. She has bespoke a new gown for the wedding. Augusta & her family have also been invited. We have written to all interested parties to give them the news, & to invite them to share our joy.

Today I have received the most insulting letter from my Aunt Catherine. From now on, all relations between us are severed. The same post brought a civil letter of congratulation from my Uncle Fitzwilliam—with a scribbled note from

James at the bottom, teazing me for being a *'dark horse'*, & threatening to spend much time at Pemberley *'paying court to your charming Wife'*. I shewed it to my dearest E, who laughed, & said that a little *jealousy* would keep me on my toes, so she would encourage James in every possible way. Tho' I sometimes find it puzzling, I enjoy the way she teazes me, & look forward to more. On arrival at Longbourn, Jane shewed us a letter from Miss Caroline in Scarborough, addressed to *Her dearest Sister Jane*. She & Mrs Louisa are shortly to return to Town, as Mrs Louisa's confinement grows imminent. Miss Caroline was fulsome in her congratulations, & writes: *'One is scarcely surprized to learn, dear, that not one, but two of the Bennet Sisters have found fulfilment in wedlock. I have been expecting the announcement of dear Mr Darcy's engagement for at least a month—but doubtless other family matters distracted the Interested Parties from the matter at hand.'* She concludes, *'Pray offer my sincerest congratulations to Mr Darcy—& to the future Mrs Darcy. I look forward with pleasure to playing a central part in the celebrations.'* I glanced at Elizabeth, & saw the sparkle of merriment in her eyes. However, out of consideration for Charles, our deportment remained irreproachable.

The weather continues perfect—a real Indian Summer. For me, every day now is like a festival day. Elizabeth devises new excitements for us—an excursion to picturesque ruins, a picnic by a lake— & many opportunities for the two of us to ramble off alone. These solitary conversations are the best part of our courtship: but I cannot, cannot wait for October 30th! Before then, I may hold her hand, or occasionally touch her hair with my finger-tips:

it is not enough. I long to be completely alone with her, completely married. Soon!

My dream of the other night has been working on my mind. This book, my Diary! It was my sacred task, the task assigned to me by you, Mamma, before you died. It has been like a thread linking me to you when there was no living soul in whom I could confide. Now that I am to marry, I shall have my Wife always at my side—& I have no need to keep this Diary. From now on, my innermost thoughts are for Elizabeth. I cannot shew this book to her, though: some of the pages are not for a lady's eyes.

Shall I destroy it? No: I cannot at present bring myself to do so. But I shall put it where no other eye can see it . . . If this is the last entry, I shall have lived & died happy.

THE END

EDITOR'S NOTE

Last year, the contents of one of England's great houses came up for sale at Christie's. One of the items was a fine regency rosewood bureau with tapered legs and marquetry ornamentation, which sold for £36,000. On examining this piece, a Christie's Expert discovered a secret drawer, hitherto unknown to the family. Inside were five moleskin-covered notebooks—a diary dating from the reign of George III, which was duly handed over to an Expert in the Books and Manuscripts Department.

The Diary covers the writer's adolescence and early manhood, and contains many fascinating details about the daily life of a wealthy landowner. But then, in the fifth volume, the Expert made an astounding discovery: the final pages of the Diary echo in every respect the story of Elizabeth Bennet and Fitzwilliam Darcy, as told by Jane Austen in her novel *Pride and Prejudice*. How could this be a genuine document? Further research confirmed that in all other respects the Diary was authentic. The inescapable conclusion was that Jane Austen had based her novel on real events. It was decided to prepare the relevant pages of the Diary for publication.

The family's permission had first to be obtained before Mr Darcy's version of the story could be set before the public. Jane Austen had changed the names of the people and places involved; the fictitious names she chose have been used throughout. As the Diary is very frank, the family are extremely anxious that their true identity should never come to light. It is not known how Jane Austen heard of these events, and in such detail too—can she have known the real-life model for Elizabeth Bennet?

The extracts printed here begin on the day that Mr Darcy and Elizabeth Bennet met. He appears to have discontinued his Diary shortly before their marriage, but must have been reluctant to destroy it, and must himself have hidden it in the desk.

The handwriting is elegant throughout, save for the occasional more hastily-written entry, when the content is painful or disturbing. Mr Darcy used a quill pen. He favoured a walnut-based ink, which gives a pleasant brown colour. [We are indebted to Technograph GL Laboratories for analysing the composition of the ink.]

ACKNOWLEDGEMENTS

I would like to thank Terence Allott, Noël Annesley, Hilary Bradshaw, Sally Bradshaw, Tusi Butterfield, Charlie Campbell, Barbara Karsky, Mary Anne O'Donovan, Ann Pasternak Slater, Barbara Pendlebury, Isaac Raine, Nina Raine, Anne Rook, Lydia Slater, Michael Slater, Nicolas Slater, Sasha Slater and everyone at Orion.